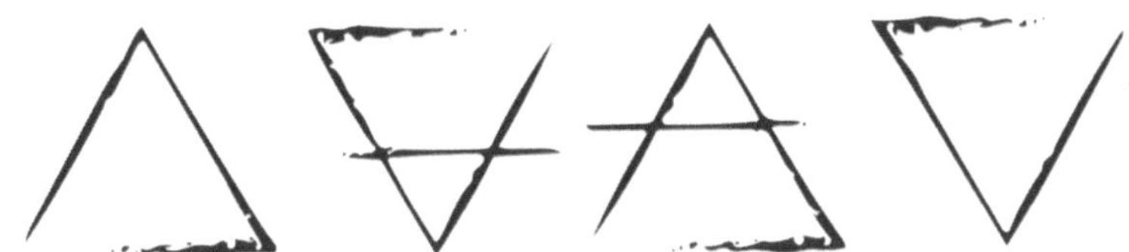

To Ilaris, In Desperation

Amanda Ross

CONTENTS

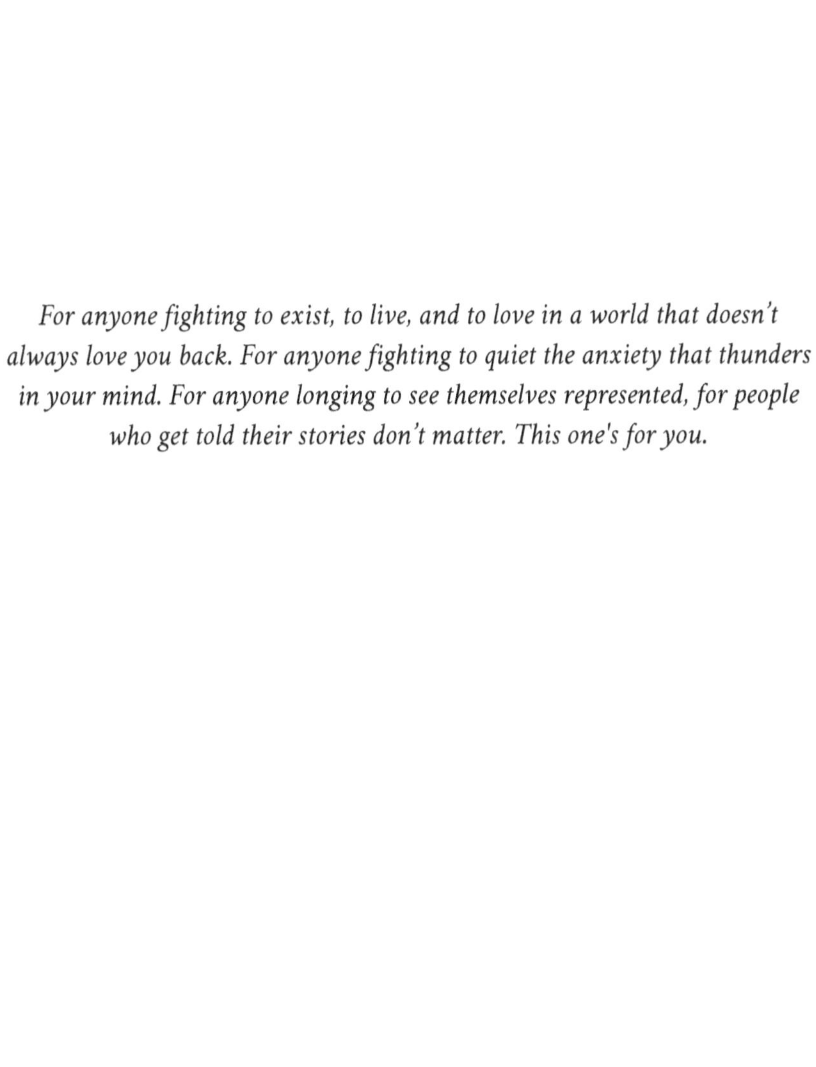

For anyone fighting to exist, to live, and to love in a world that doesn't always love you back. For anyone fighting to quiet the anxiety that thunders in your mind. For anyone longing to see themselves represented, for people who get told their stories don't matter. This one's for you.

By Valeria LeFebre
Senior Editor, *Jonquil*

Now that we've all come down from our collective Astera hangovers, it's time to talk about the elephant in the room: how Witchkind's most important event went from a boozy brunch to a witch versus vampire brawl in a matter of minutes.

Like many of you, I've seen the fight clips everywhere from TikTok to The Shade Room. I saw 21-year-old Mercury Amell, the relative of two prominent Council members, throw down in a battle against vampires. Amell even went so far as to use powers that aren't inherently his (being an Air Hand, Amell draws his powers from the element of Air, but in the video he can be seen using fire). Also, like many of you, I was unsure about the cause of the brawl. After some digging, I've got the full tea on the whole shebang—the five w's if you will.

First, Amell was a college student at UCLA. He attended a frat party hosted by the notorious Upsilon Gamma Nu (UGN) fraternity (widely known to be *the* vampire fraternity), and shortly thereafter got into a fight with one of the senior members of the fraternity, a 23-year-old vampire by the name of Conner McGrady. McGrady's girlfriend, 21-year-old Delanie French, was somehow killed during the fight, prompting Conner and his band of fraternity brothers to chase Amell and his friends—Sloane Salvanera, 21, Ellis Hall, 22, Joelle Whittaker, 21, and Griffin Whittaker, 21—across the country.

By the time the vampires arrived at Astera, they already had a few tussles with the group and had amassed dozens of rando vampire acolytes eager to venture into Witchkind's most sacred space and wreck some shit. The fight ensued; Amell, his friends, and several other witches, including three Council members, fought and won. O'Brian and several other vampires were killed, as was Councilwoman Effie Hyunh, 41. No criminal charges were brought against the witches, and local police ruled the slaying as self-defense.

Though this battle royale was the talk of the town, it wasn't the only thing to happen at Astera. Head of Council Oliana Murtaza signed a peace treaty with vampire President Harvey Vael, known as The Corvius Accord. The treaty ensures a plot of developable land called Kinheld for witches to use as they see fit. In exchange, The Witches' Council has agreed to back some of Vael's current initiatives including the Identity Act, a law that requires witches to wear dog tags to identify themselves as such.

Some see Kinheld as a chance for American witches to escape the disenfranchisement suffered under Vael's presidency and start anew. Some see it as the equivalent of "separate but [sort of] equal". The most prominent opponent of Kinheld is none other than Amell himself. He has already led one protest against Kinheld, perching outside of the Council Building with his merry band of Made witches and any other witch who would join them for the better part of an afternoon. According to my sources, he has more protests planned over the coming months in an attempt to drum up support for the anti-Kinheld movement. Though it's not totally clear what Amell will do with that support, you know you'll get the true tea here.

Now I would be remiss if I didn't take a moment to discuss our fallen colleague, Freddie Karr, on the two-month anniversary of his death. Karr was my mentor, and losing him felt like losing a brother. We here at *Jonquil* have been keeping up with the police investigation into his death, though we fear that the Oakland PD have let the case go cold. You can access the GoFundMe set up for Karr's husband, Marquis, and their children here. To keep up with the case, follow us here and on Twitter.

Finally, I'd like to take a moment to introduce our newest writer—Sloane Salvanera. A close friend of Amell's, Salvanera was intimately involved in protecting Astera from the vampire invasion. She's a talented writer with a lot to say, so follow her on Twitter at @SalvaSlo and say hello. As always, take care of yourself and blessed be.

BY VALERIA LEFEBRE
SENIOR EDITOR, *JONQUIL*

A chain by any other name would doubtfully feel as oppressive as those recently foisted upon witchkind. The Identity Act passed by Congress has taken effect, in what has to be the shortest legal turnaround time in modern history. Now, those who have even a smidge of magical abilities must wear a dog tag with the word "Hexe" emblazoned beneath a pentagram, color-coded according to each element. This co-opting of ancient symbols is nothing new—haven't we been taught that God's son requires devotion in the form of a pine tree and eggs? Haven't Christians decided to reinforce the "hallow" in "Halloween" with tired, milquetoast trunk-or-treats?

We are used to our sacred symbols being used against us, but this time it feels different. More sinister. Perhaps it's the fact that the cultural zeitgeist has lauded witches for years. Shows like *Bewitched, Charmed* (both iterations), *Sabrina the Teenage Witch*, and movies like *The Craft, Practical Magic*, and the beloved *Hocus Pocus* had made witchcraft cool. We were Halloween costumes; we were slang for ballsy women; hell, we were even portrayed by American sweetheart Sandra fucking Bullock.

But truth is stranger than fiction, and our truth is that people like the idea of witches but not the reality of witches. We're only fun if we're casting spells to get a man or to fight the ultimate villain, but the second you see us teaching your children or cooking your food or sitting next to you in the boardroom, you balk. You decided we are not worthy of protection, and you passed a law that will strip away our livelihood, our dignity, our worth.

Dhampir pundits insist that the Identity Act is necessary. They parrot vague statistics about witches being involved in nearly every major violent crime in 2022 so far, but they don't bother to mention that their involvement could be and most likely is on the other side of that violence. Like DJ AMA Deus, who still languishes in a backwoods Southern jail for standing up for himself. Like Rita Nash, the school-teacher who was murdered by one of her students' fathers in the name of heresy. Like Freddie Karr, who was blamed for his own death by political pundits and Cordelia Edwards, the vampire wanna-be and writer for the Dhampiric rag, *The Vanguard*.

They say the Identity Act is to protect each citizen, witches included. In reality, it's just the target on our back for regular citizens to exact their one pound of magical flesh with which to blame us for our own demise.

CHAPTER 1

"Ready to get tagged?" Sloane asked.

Mercury groaned, both at his best friend's bad joke and his longing for a good, strong cup of coffee. It was seven in the morning and the brightness of the sun did little to erase the sleepiness from his eyes. He sat in the middle of a corner booth at Pothead, the new-aged diner a block away from the Iron Bird tattoo parlor, wondering how his friend even had the energy to make such a bad joke. The rest of the group was late, as usual.

When the Identity Act passed, Mercury had known it was only a matter of time before he'd have to get his tags. Just the thought of wearing something that forced him to identify himself on someone else's terms angered him. He was a proud witch, but that didn't mean he wanted to be at the mercy of other people's biases.

Weeks ago, he received a notice in the mail from the Witch Acculturation Services, or the "W.A.S." as it had been dubbed, letting him know he had one month to get his tags or he'd face a fine, jail time, or both. Having watched video footage of witches camped out in front of buildings as if they were waiting for discounted TVs and laptops on Black Friday, Mercury mentally prepared himself to stand in line for hours on his own. His father's tags already had been procured for him, just like the rest of the Witches' Council.

He'd been chatting with Sloane, Griffin, Joelle, and Ellis in their group text thread when Griffin mentioned he'd received a letter from the W.A.S, too.

"Word?" Mercury responded.

"Yeah, came in a day or so ago. What do I do?"

One by one, his friends chimed in, letting him know they'd all received the same letter. Letting him know the Identity Act meant to cast a wide net over anyone with any magical abilities and screw them over.

Mercury's heart had dropped. He could deal with being tagged for being a witch—he was born this way and proud. But he couldn't help the guilt that snaked its way into his heart. Learning that his friends were now being called to broadcast their abilities to the world? Abilities that they wouldn't even have if he would've skipped out on the party that night? Mercury struggled to shake the thoughts that pervaded his mind. He coordinated a date and time for them to meet, all the while typing and deleting his profuse apologies for the continued disruption of their lives.

"So, I guess that's a no," Sloane muttered. She slid into the booth beside Mercury and wrapped an arm around him. Her high ponytail brushed against his face as she pulled away.

"I'm not talking to you until there's coffee on the table," Mercury grumbled.

It had been Sloane's idea to meet at Pothead beforehand so that they could have breakfast and enjoy themselves before spending hours in line baking in the hot, Southern California sun. Sloane clutched her imaginary pearls then chuckled and waved over a waitress. She ordered their drinks—an iced mocha for her and a latte for him—and swiftly began studying the menu.

Mercury shook his head. "Don't you order like the same thing each time you're here?"

She scoffed.

"I could say the same thing about you, Mr. Eggs Benedict," she teased. "Besides, maybe I might branch out today."

"Uh huh," he replied.

He folded his arms and gazed out the window. Ellis jaywalked across the street, hands stuffed into the pockets of an oversized hoodie, a neon pink beanie pulled down almost past his eyebrows. Luckily, he crossed before a red Ford Mustang zoomed by, ignoring the yellow light up ahead. A bell above the door rang as Ellis entered the diner, this time with one hand in his pocket.

"'Sup, Gloria," Ellis said, waving a hand at the manager of the cafe who'd hired him on as a busboy a month ago. At first, he'd tried to be discreet about getting a job; he'd spent most of his life having enough money to buy anything he wanted that he never thought he'd ever have to worry about it. When he returned from Astera, however, his parents cut him off. No longer was he driving a BMW. He now either walked or called an Uber, refusing to take the bus.

"It's too early for this shit," Ellis groaned. He slid into the booth next to Sloane just as Gloria set their coffees down on the table.

Mercury smiled at her and took a long sip of coffee. Already he could feel himself waking up.

"You're late," Mercury said, his fingers still wrapped around his cup.

Ellis scoffed.

"Don't you have to get up early as fuck to start working here?" Mercury questioned.

"Yes, but today's my day off. And on those days, I don't like to get out of bed before noon."

"That's probably why you're so tired all the time, son," Gloria said. "If you kept your sleep schedule tight, your body would adjust."

Ellis groaned again. "I know, I know. Gloria, could you hook me up with one of your world-famous hazelnut cappuccinos?"

Gloria nodded and walked away.

Sloane blinked repeatedly. "Wait, how come you didn't tell me she makes hazelnut cappuccinos?"

"Because you didn't ask, Slo." Ellis smirked and Sloane flipped him off. Mercury rolled his eyes at his friends' flirtation.

Minutes later, Gloria set Ellis' drink down and asked if they were ready to order. Sloane let her know they were waiting on two other people to join them.

Mercury looked at his phone.

7:15.

He wondered what was keeping them, deciding to give them a few extra minutes after unlocking his phone then locking it again.

"Did you sleep okay?" Sloane asked Ellis.

He shrugged before cupping his coffee in his hands. He moaned as he gripped the cup and slurped the warm liquid.

"What about you, Merc?" Sloane asked.

Mercury shrugged. He downed another sip of his latte, avoiding his friend's gaze.

"Still having those nightmares?" Sloane asked, just above a whisper.

He paused while licking the foam residue from his lips. He'd been having nightmares about Delanie since they came back from Astera. Each night he woke up with his sheets soaked, barely being able to return to sleep for fear of what would play out behind his eyes.

I killed somebody, he thought. The thought made him shiver. Sloane reached out and grabbed his hand.

"I think I'm going to be dealing with them for a very long time," he replied.

Both Sloane and Ellis nodded.

"I'm here for you whenever you need to talk," Sloane said.

"Me too, Merc," Ellis added.

Mercury nodded, suddenly feeling self-conscious. He didn't want to focus on his trauma, at least not over breakfast.

"So, what're you going to order?" he asked, pulling away from Sloane's grasp.

They looked up as the bell above the door jangled.

Griffin and Joelle stepped inside the restaurant, both wearing workout clothes and sunglasses. They walked at a snail's pace with their heads tilted down. To Mercury, they both looked hungover.

"Hey," Mercury uttered as the twins slid into the booth. Joelle grumbled and pulled the hood of her bright blue hoodie over her head. Griffin nodded, crossing his arms over himself.

"You two alright over there?" Sloane asked.

"Hungover," Griffin said.

Joelle groaned again.

"Ah. That's why you look like death," Ellis teased.

Joelle flipped him off.

"That's two in one morning. Seems like I'm on a roll." Ellis winked at Sloane.

Mercury shook his head then focused on the twins. "Hungover? Did you two solo-cup it in your dorm or something?"

"Nah. We went to a dorm party," Griffin explained. He pulled his glasses off and rubbed his eyes.

There was a pang in Mercury's stomach. He missed dorm parties; hell, he missed parties in general. The last party he'd been to was the one at Astera. They'd returned to Los Angeles the Monday after Astera concluded with so much to process in such little time.

He tried to go back to school and conduct himself as though he hadn't gone on a two-thousand-mile road trip from hell with a group of friends to whom he'd given illegal magic tattoos. After a few weeks, however, Mercury realized none of it mattered to him. He didn't care about studying Dostoyevsky or learning music theory. He already read much better authors on his own, ones whose stories he could relate to more than some 180-year-old white man. And he didn't need some former-'90s-grunge band member with a thinning ponytail, a striped bowling shirt, and a soul patch to teach him about music theory. He'd been playing the drums, piano, and guitar for years.

More importantly, Mercury couldn't stand by and watch as his father struggled with the Iron Bird. Construction began a few weeks after they'd returned. Though his father had the opportunity to move, he chose to stay and use his renter's insurance and a little help from the Witches' Council to rebuild the only home he'd ever owned, to rebuild the last place he lived with his brother, Troian, before his murder. They opted for hotel living in the meantime even though Mercury had already had his fair share of it on the road.

Though the tattoo parlor and their apartment above it were now completely restored and they had a place to live again, his father needed another tattoo artist. Mercury dropped out of school with a clear conscience, knowing that helping his father was the right move and knowing that whatever he wanted to do in life he could do without the help of a college degree.

Yet still, he found himself wishing he'd been invited to a dorm party.

"Oh, was it cool?" Mercury asked, trying not to sound too interested. He picked up his cup and realized he had finished his latte already. He sighed.

"It was fun," Joelle said.

"As fun as any party full of straights could be," Griffin quipped.

Mercury chuckled, glad to hear that it wasn't the best time they'd had.

"Whatever." Joelle snapped. "I had a good time."

"Who threw the party?" Ellis asked.

"You probably don't know them," Joelle remarked.

Ellis leaned forward. "Honey, I was at UCLA a lot longer than you. I'm sure I've at least *heard* of them."

Joelle rolled her eyes. "Kelsey Chambers."

"Ha. She's still throwing ragers I see," Ellis said, leaning back against the booth. "Merc, remember that time we went to her party and her roommate almost rode their bike through the sliding glass door?"

Mercury chuckled. "Yeah. That was fun," he recalled. "I miss those types of parties."

"Well, if you hadn't dropped out, you'd still be able to go," Joelle retorted.

The group quieted and looked at her. Mercury's heartbeat quickened.

"Damn, the shade," Sloane said.

Griffin side-eyed his sister.

"What? I mean, it's true."

"I'm gonna flag down the waitress to get us some coffee and food. Maybe then you won't be such a Petty LaBelle."

Joelle grunted and pulled out her phone.

"I've got to hit the restroom. Order for me?" Joelle asked, turning toward Griffin and placing her phone on the table. When he nodded, she darted toward the back of the restaurant.

"Just forget about her," Griffin said to Mercury when Joelle was out of earshot.

Mercury looked over at him. His gold-rimmed glasses glistened in the morning light. His dreads, which were now dyed blue at the ends, were coiled on top of his head in a bun. Without thinking, Mercury put his arm around his friend in a hug. Griffin's long arm reached around him and squeezed him briefly.

"Was it that obvious that it got to me?" Mercury asked.

Griffin shrugged. "She's been on one lately. When we came back, she dove right into schoolwork and tried to find a sense of normal. I think she was kind of projecting. She was bummed that you dropped out, a little sad that Ellis did, and now—"

"Wait, she was sad that I dropped out of college? *Me?*" Ellis asked.

"Well, you were one of the only people she knew on campus," Griffin shrugged.

"Damn, I didn't think I'd be missed. It feels, kinda, sorta, right," Ellis said.

Sloane glowered at him and pushed him.

"Goofy," she said.

Mercury shook his head then shifted his attention to Griffin. "What were you saying?"

"Well, she's tense about drop out shit because I told her last night I was thinking of dropping out, too."

Mercury scowled then gawked at Griffin. "Really? Why?"

Griffin tilted his head to the side, his dreaded bun slightly lopsided. "I just don't know if I'm feeling it. I started with engineering because that's what I thought would make my dad happy. And I liked it because I liked solving problems. But after the shit that went down at Astera, it just didn't feel like me. So, I'm either going to change my major or drop out."

Shock covered Mercury's face as his body tensed. He hadn't realized that their journey at Astera would have this much of a ripple effect on his friends' lives. *No wonder Joelle's petty this morning*, he thought.

"So, when're you going to make a decision?" he asked.

"I told Joelle I'd stick it out for another two weeks. That gets me to the end of the semester and after finals, if I still feel this way, I'll drop over summer so it's a clean break."

"Well, I support you whatever you decide," Mercury offered.

"Thank you," Griffin uttered, choking back the emotions seeping into his throat.

Gloria returned and took their orders, a mixture of savory and sweet breakfast entrees. Once they handed her the menus, Sloane turned the conversation back to the tags.

"How long do you think it'll take to get them?" Sloane inquired.

Mercury shrugged. Joelle returned to the booth and slid in, her dark coils now in a large bun atop her head.

"You two really are twins, huh," Ellis asked.

Ignoring Ellis' comment, Joelle picked up her phone.

"You okay, girl?" Sloane asked.

Joelle nodded and gestured at them to keep talking.

"Did your dad already go and get his tags?" Griffin asked.

"Nah. He was lucky. The whole Council got theirs at their last council meeting, since they also have a tag that signifies they are on the Council."

"Sweet treatment," Joelle added.

"Yeah. Even Faegan was spared the fate of having to go to the W.A.S." As Mercury fixed his gaze on Joelle, she turned toward the group.

"I was surprised that we had to go get them. I mean, I didn't think we qualified as witches," she said.

"It was a special little loophole Vael added into the bill," Sloane explained. "He wanted anyone who even thought about adding a little magic to their tank to know there'd be consequences."

"Come on, *60 Minutes*," Griffin said, hyping up his friend.

Sloane smiled bashfully.

"What is this Witch Acculturation Services place, anyway? Have you ever been there?" Ellis asked.

Mercury shook his head. "It's a whole new division that Vael put in place. We'll all be finding out what fresh hell is in store for us together."

They all traded looks in silence until Gloria returned with their food.

"Alright, guys. I've got your orders here. Who ordered the Eggs Benedict?"

CHAPTER 2

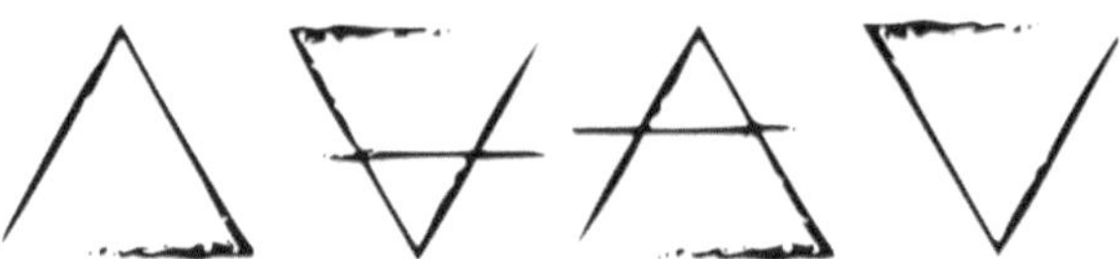

AN HOUR LATER, THE GROUP PULLED UP TO A SQUAT, WHITE BUILDING.
Black signage with the name "Witch Acculturation Services" plastered
the front. The white paint was so crisp and the landscaping around
the building so expertly manicured that it made Mercury's stomach
clench. This place felt so sterile, and he wondered once again what
awaited them inside. It was only eight thirty but already a line snaked
along the side of the building.

As they walked to the end of the line, Mercury waved at a few
witches he recognized. They each returned his gesture with a wave
and a smile.

"How long do you think this'll take?" Ellis asked, looking at his
phone.

"Why, you got someplace else to be today?" Sloane questioned.

Ellis tipped his head and pursed his lips. "I feel like I'm at the
goddamn DMV already."

"Yeah, same. Why does bureaucracy always take for fucking ever?"
Joelle added.

Annoyance bubbled in Mercury's belly. If they'd been on time, they
might have gotten to the W.A.S. before every other witch in town.
They wouldn't be standing at the end of a line at least 100 people

deep. He especially would've been able to savor his breakfast without the fear of being late disrupting his thoughts.

Once they reached the back of the line, he pulled out his phone and began scrolling on Twitter, ignoring the group's complaints.

He was reading an article about a waitress who reported the boutique blood bar she worked at for being drained without her consent when he heard the roaring of a super truck pulling into the parking lot. They had moved several paces and were no longer last in line, but they weren't anywhere near the front door. The truck seemed to be headed right for them. Mercury slipped his phone into his pocket and stared at the truck, a spell for stopping an object already in his mind when the truck suddenly veered off course and stopped just short of a small concrete divider lined with bushes that separated the parking lot from the building.

The truck's owner slid out of the car wearing tight jeans, cowboy boots, and a button up shirt. Atop his head rested a baseball cap with President Vael's slogan, Restore, written on the bill.

"Who the fuck wears cowboy boots in Los Angeles?" Ellis asked.

Sloane scoffed. "People who came to town from Bakersfield or Oildale."

The man pulled a large sign from the bed of his truck. As he did, two other men stepped out of the car, looking just as California country as their friend. They grabbed signs as well then stood in front of the divider and held their signs up high.

"Thou shalt not suffer a witch to live, Exodus 22:18," read the first sign.

"Witches are evil—end them all!" read the second.

"How many vampires have to die before witches are stopped?" read the third and final sign.

A spike of guilt slithered up Mercury's spine, but he refused to give in to his thoughts. He shook his head and turned back to his phone.

"Hey, isn't he that witch that killed those vampires up in Maine?" one of the men inquired.

"Well, I'll be damned," said one of the other men.

Mercury suppressed a groan as he heard the men talking about him, saying he didn't look so tough, that they could probably take him easily, and asking why he was still a free man after killing those vampires.

"What was his name?" one of the men asked.

"Something weird, like Jupiter, Uranus—"

"Mercury," one of the men said. "Hey, Mercury!"

Mercury ignored him and stepped forward in the line, keeping his gaze on his phone.

"Why is that guy calling you?" Sloane whispered.

"I'm talking to you, *witch*," the protestor spat. As he did, Mercury heard the truck's other doors open.

"Why are they trying to talk to you?" Griffin asked.

Mercury shrugged. He tried to keep his face calm. His cheeks grew warm and his heartbeat quickened. *It's not going to happen again. It's not going to happen again.*

"Just ignore them. They're trying to start a scene."

One of the men inched closer, standing halfway between the building and his friends. Mercury could smell the Drakkar Noir wafting off him.

"Hey, Mercury! Don't you hear me talking to you?"

By now, other people in the crowd were murmuring. The witches that hadn't recognized his face had recognized his name. Many of them turned to observe the scene unfolding before them, their eyes wide with curiosity.

"Just because you're talking to me doesn't mean I want to talk to you," Mercury replied. His voice remained neutral. Though every bone in his body wanted to lash out at the men with his magic, he knew he had to keep his cool. For one thing, he didn't want any trouble from a W.A.S. security guard—he could tell they carried Thurguards, and Mercury didn't doubt that the cuffs' magic sapping ability would be strong. But Mercury was also hesitant for a different reason. The last few times he'd gotten into a fight, someone ended up dead. He couldn't go through that again.

Just stay calm, he thought.

One of the men laughed. "Is that because you're too afraid of that guard over there?"

Mercury scoffed. Once again, he had to fight to keep his gaze and attention on his phone. He heard murmurs from other people in line.

"Why is he just standing there?"

Calm, he thought. *Stay calm.*

The line moved ahead several paces. Now, he could see the door into the building, but there were still so many people ahead of him, and many more were behind.

Within seconds, another car pulled up next to the truck, and a group of people jumped out of the car with signs similar to the men's —one even said that witches were the devil's spawn. Mercury scoffed at the stupidity of it all.

Almost there, he thought. They were only thirty-five people away from the entrance. *C'mon.*

As more people pulled up next to the Witch Acculturation Services building brandishing signs, he could feel his friends and the people in the crowd getting antsy.

"Why the hell would they come here to protest?" Joelle questioned.

"Why not? They know that a bunch of witches will be all in one place," Griffin said.

The protestors shouted in the background. Some chanted things like "stop them all" and "restore humanity".

It wasn't a particularly warm morning, but Mercury found himself sweating. He could feel it on the back of his neck, could feel it in his armpits and on the palms of his hands. He prayed the wet spots weren't visible on his shirt. He wanted nothing more than for this day to be over. He wanted these people to go the hell away. Mercury wasn't looking for a fight, but it seemed as if some of his friends were.

While Griffin and Joelle stood with their heads huddled together and staring at something on Griffin's phone, Ellis and Sloane shouted back at the protestors.

"Yeah, fuck you!" Ellis yelled, his middle fingers in the air.

"You can't get rid of us!" shouted Sloane. "We're here to stay, assholes!"

Behind the shouting and the protestors' chants, Mercury could hear another sound, something more controlled. He looked behind him to see two men standing nearly toe to toe with two of the protestors who yelled in their faces that they should burn because they are witches.

Mercury could see the tension bubbling between them, which sent his brain into overdrive.

"Man, get the fuck out of my face before I drop you," warned one of the men.

"Go ahead, hit me, witch. I'll make sure they fry your ass extra crispy for it," the man taunted.

"Man, teach this fool a lesson," said the other witch.

Mercury immediately stepped out of line, not wondering whether he should try to diffuse the situation.

"Save my spot," Mercury called out.

Griffin looked up from his phone and nodded briefly before turning back to it.

Mercury barreled toward the group, his heartbeat reverberating in his ears with each step.

The taller witch scowled down at the protestor, his hands clenched. The protestor glared at the witch behind a set of thick glasses.

"Yo, cut this shit out," Mercury said.

Both men looked at Mercury, surprised he'd try to intervene.

"Why don't you mind your business?" said the shorter witch. He didn't even look in Mercury's direction.

Mercury shook his head. "You see all these fucking people here? They are here for one reason—to try to get witches to assault them, magic or not. They want to show the world that *we're* the violent ones. Look at how many of these Beckys have their phones out."

The witches looked over toward the mass of protestors. Several people stood with their phones out and pointed in their direction. Two women made eye contact with Mercury and one leaned over to whisper to the other. The taller witch looked from the crowd to Mercury. He glanced at his friend then stepped back.

"I'm not trying to go viral on some 'witches are evil' shit," the tall witch stated.

His friend scoffed.

"I'm not gonna let some dhampir disrespect me." The shorter witch closed the gap between his friend and the protestor.

The man brought his fists up. "You're the dangerous one here; you all should be locked up."

Before Mercury could do anything, the witch pushed the protestor. Other members in the line gasped and shouted "ohhhh" as the protestor returned the gesture.

"Yo, stop this shit," the friend shouted. He tried to grab his friend, but the bespectacled man knocked him back into the crowd of people. Sloane, Ellis, and Griffin rushed over.

The witch gestured for the glasses to slip from his face then immediately smashed them beneath his tennis shoe. Mercury winced at the sound of the glasses being ground into the concrete.

"Intefadu," Mercury uttered, hoping the small spell could give him a subtle enough boost of strength that the guard wouldn't notice.

"Break this shit up," Mercury shouted, pulling the witch back just as the protestor nearly landed a blow to the witch's jaw. "You're just giving them what they want."

"Fuck them. I won't be disrespected," the witch bellowed. He faced Mercury head-on, who stood blocking his way to the protestor who was still on the ground.

"Why are you protecting him?" the other witch questioned.

Mercury could see the security guard running toward them. He clutched a small, black bag attached to his belt.

"I'm not protecting this piece of shit," Mercury explained. "I just know that giving in to them trying to insight a fight while we're here trying to get tags that we know we don't need but they say we need will only feed into their idea that we're violent and can't be trusted."

For a minute, the other witch was silent. He stared at Mercury with angry, narrowed eyes before sneering.

"Fuck it," he said. He turned back toward his friend and the pair walked to their place in line.

Mercury turned toward the protestor.

"Get out of here," he demanded, the depth of his voice surprising him.

"I'm an American. I have every right to be here," he argued.

"If you don't leave, you'll see what we can really do," threatened Griffin.

"Yeah, get the fuck out of here!" roared another voice.

Soon the whole line shouted at the man to leave. For several minutes, Mercury wondered if he was going to step even closer. Finally, he turned back toward the wall of protestors and quickly became lost in the crowd.

Relieved, Mercury and his friends walked back to their place in line, which Joelle had dutifully kept. The guard eyed them warily as he eased back to his place in front of the door. Though quiet at first, the chatter resumed once everyone noticed the coast was clear.

The group finally stepped inside the building forty minutes later. It smelled like Pine-Sol. Everything was gray, from the floors to the seats to the countertops. The workers sat behind a glass panel, their separate desks divided by the same glass paneling. There were twenty-five open windows, seventeen with a worker sitting behind it, and no one looked happy to be there.

They each pulled a number and took a seat. Joelle sighed and slid down in her chair. Mercury plopped down in the seat beside her.

"Not feeling any better?" Mercury asked.

She shook her head.

"I thought I was, but standing in that line just made it a bit worse. Remind me never to have Jager again," she groaned.

Mercury scowled. "Ugh. No wonder you feel shitty. That's some frat boy shit."

Joelle chuckled. "I know. They were just giving everyone shots, and everyone was so nice. No one brought up the Astera shit for once. It was nice just to—"

"Not feel like a freak?" Mercury asked.

Joelle gave him a sidelong glance. "*Blend in*. Get back to being a *real* college student."

"Well, I'm glad you're getting back to life. Might be hard though, with this new accessory you'll have to wear," Mercury teased.

"I know. But I figured if I just camouflage it with a bunch of other silver chains, I can make it work."

"You trying to be out in these streets looking like the female Mr. T?"

Joelle laughed and swatted his arm. Mercury's heart skipped.

"Well, what do you plan to do? You're not exactly the jewelry type."

He glanced down and smiled. "Oh? You think I can't make it work? C'mon. I'm the son of the most fashionable member of the Witches' Council. There's no way I can leave my house looking dusty, especially since we live together."

Joelle laughed again, but the smile faded from her face. "How's it going with your dad? Is it weird living in the new space?"

His shoulders tensed. "It's hard to get used to. But we're making it work."

"I'm glad. I haven't even seen the new place yet. I've just been so busy with school and everything."

"Well, why don't you come through some time during the week? I'll give you a tour, and we can have some drinks or—"

She made a face.

"Or not," he said, holding his hands up in surrender.

"I made that face about having drinks, dummy. And I'd love to see your new spot, but I'm just so swamped with school."

Of course, he thought.

She told Mercury about her workload, how coming back from Astera put her behind in all her classes. Mercury listened and nodded, and though he knew it wasn't her intention to make him feel guilty, he felt it, nonetheless. As he watched her count off on her hands how many assignments she had, and as he tried to offer substitutions for times they could get together, Mercury began to feel something else, too—insecurity.

"Well, sounds like you've got a hell of a semester happening. But I think a break could help you not feel so burned out. What about Thursday night?"

She shook her head. "I've got a study group."

"Okay, well . . . maybe Friday?"

"I don't think this week will work."

"Alright. Well, maybe I'll catch you for breakfast or something one day? You start class around eleven, right?"

Joelle groaned and Mercury felt a twinge of embarrassment. Was she trying to put him off?

"This semester is just going to be a really busy time. Maybe we can meet up after?"

He knew she still had a few weeks of school left. Yet, he nodded and looked down at the number in his hands, not wanting to look back at her or look up at Sloane, who sat on his right side. Not for the first time that day, he found himself wishing he could be anywhere else in the world.

Seconds later, his name was called.

———

He clutched the dog tag in his hand as he walked out of the W.A.S. building ten minutes later, the California sun sitting high in the sky. The woman behind the counter hadn't even looked up at him, instead staring at her computer and chewing gum. The only time she looked at him was to verify his driver's license.

"Why does your name sound familiar? Mercury Amell," she wondered.

"Because I fought a lot of vampires," Mercury replied. "And won."

She rolled her eyes and slid his license back to him. She grabbed a dog tag and, after scanning the back of the tag, dropped it onto the counter in front of him.

"Have a nice day," she said, her voice icy.

"You, too," he replied, matching her vitriol.

The tag felt heavy in his hands, and the chain already itched like it was silver-plated instead of sterling.

Figures they'd spring for the cheap shit, Mercury thought.

He was looking down at the tag when the door opened onto an

even larger crowd of protestors than before. Several of them shouted at him as he walked out of the door, many of them seemingly recognizing him and the group. They thrust their signs up and shouted that they deserved to wear the chain, saying they were dangerous and should be put down. The protestors crowded the walkway before them. They seemed to be harassing the witches that walked out as the security guard stood there, nonchalant.

Mercury looked over to see Joelle walking out of the building with her head down and her hoodie up. Her brother walked ahead of her, his head held high.

He flipped several protestors off and shouted back at them.

"If I'm dangerous, you all are positively primeval. Get the fuck out of the way before I turn you into a turnip."

Ellis pushed to the front of the group, cutting in front of Mercury.

"C'mon, we just want to get to our car," he shouted.

"Put your fucking tag on," a twentysomething blonde woman shouted. "You must put it on for me now."

"I don't have to do shit for you, lady," Ellis bellowed.

Mercury shoved Ellis forward, wanting to stop him before he clashed with anyone. He then felt a firm hand on his shoulder.

"You've got to put your tags on before you leave the premises," the security guard instructed.

"Why? It's not like I don't know I have to have it on me at all times, *sir*," Mercury replied.

"Just put the fucking thing on, witch," the security guard demanded. His hand fell back to the black bag on his holster.

What's in the bag? Mercury thought.

Mercury looked between him and the crowd. They were still shouting, their faces contorted into scowls. Several of them had their phones pointed toward Mercury and the security guard. Mercury faced his friends who stood looking toward him.

He glanced down at the hideous tag in his hand, his thumb tracing the yellow hexe symbol. They were color-coded based on their element, letting the public know from which element they drew magic. To Mercury, it seemed as if they were too preoccupied with what powers witches had and which element they wielded for them to be thinking they were so dangerous.

Fine, I'll give you what you want, he thought.

Mercury made eye contact with the guard and smiled widely. He stared at him as he slid the tag around his neck. Once he did, he popped the collar of his jean jacket.

"That good for you, sir?" Mercury asked, keeping his smile on his face. The guard scowled but waved them along.

Sloane, Griffin, and Ellis followed suit, each of them performing a final move as if to say fuck off. Sloane flipped her ponytail, her long black hair brushing the guard's chest. Ellis lit two marijuana cigarettes, breathing deeply. He handed one to Griffin, who inhaled and exhaled the smoke toward the crowd.

"Have a good day, assholes," Ellis said.

Griffin walked forward, flipping the crowd off over his back. Joelle put the chain around her hoodie then slid her sunglasses on. They strutted toward their car, ignoring the chants and calls for their ruin.

Despite the tag at his throat, and the metal scratching his neck, Mercury felt alive.

Congress Passes Blood Laws

By Cordelia Edwards
Staff Writer, *The Vanguard*

Vampires across the country have been dealt a blow today after Congress passed HB192, a bill regulating the very life essence that vampires require to survive. The bill was passed mere weeks after a group of vampires were slaughtered at the year's largest witchy shindig and several months after an investigation into several blood bars, starting with the bust of Lyfe Blud in San Mateo, California.

More recently, a bar in Honolulu called Amago was busted after a former employee, a witch named Lola Atkins, said that the owners were forcing employees to "service" their VIP customers by providing them blood straight from the source. In an interview with local affiliate *Terminus*, Atkins described her work environment, which she said was one of intense pressure to perform.

"There would be nights where I pulled doubles feeling like I'd faint at any moment from the blood loss," Atkins stated. She added that one night she did in fact faint on the job but was able to get back to work after taking her lunch break. However, she mentioned that the owners wrote her up for it and threatened to fire her. Though the thought of working while feeling ill is terrible, and being on your boss's bad side equally stressful, one can't help but wonder why Atkins didn't try to cast a spell to make herself feel better? Surely, her magic would have enabled her to pick herself up by her pointy-toed boots so that she could keep working for the night?

Atkins would go on to say that no server lasted longer than six months at Amago being that the number of bite marks would be too hard to cover up and guests wouldn't want to take a taste. Atkins first broke her story on TikTok after she was let go from the popular midnight club, telling her viewers about her experience and showing several bite marks on her body.

"The owners have no chill when it comes to their employees. They are just expendable to them, even though they need us," Atkins said. Thousands of people have seen, commented on, and shared Atkins' video. It became so popular that it made the rounds to news outlets around the country, including the witch community's haven, *Jonquil*.

For those unaware, HB192 will now regulate the sale and attainment of blood. Consent is required in all bloodletting activities, and the commercial sale of blood is now more regulated than ever. Before businesses can purchase blood, they must ensure it comes from a qualified vendor and has been thoroughly tested against blood-borne pathogens like HIV, Lymphoma, Hepatitis, and more. If a person or business is found to be violating any of these rules, then they will face stiff penalties that may include a fine, jail time, close of business, and more.

Though the need to ensure vampires are safe from the types of blood-borne illnesses that humans carry is essential, the other stipulations severely cripple vampires from accessing the very thing that would keep them alive. Vampire business owners are doubly impacted, as they suffer not only by not getting access to their sustenance, but it also affects their ability to do business. While other outlets have flocked to support Atkins and HB192, we at *The Vanguard* know the truth. We know that this law is the very definition of a hate crime. Other so-called vices like drugs or magic-infused goods and tattoos do not face the same regulations as blood. When will congress recognize that vampires deserve rights, too? When will they realize that they are tax-paying, American citizens who deserve to live, love, and thrive in peace?

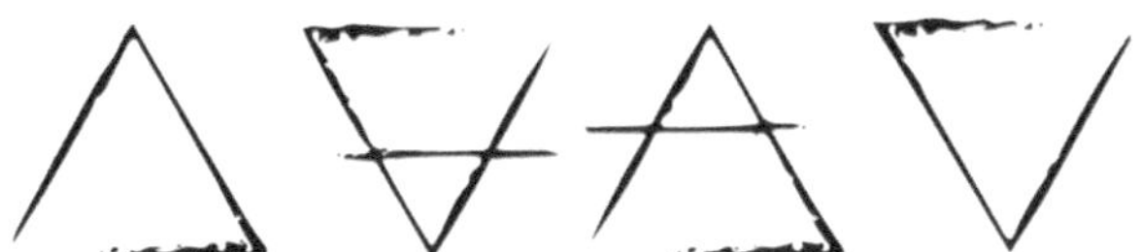

CHAPTER 3

MERCURY STOOD ON THE MAKESHIFT STAGE, BULLHORN IN ONE HAND and the other hand a fist, thrust high into the air. It was only noon in the middle of May, but already the heat caused sweat to trickle down his back. His hair fell in tight coils over his eyes, dancing on his eyelids. The dog tag around his throat itched and burned, and he swallowed constantly, hoping to lubricate his throat. Mercury was so tired and thirsty from talking, but there was so much more to say.

As if on cue, the crowd's cheers died down. Everyone was looking at him, waiting for him to speak. Butterflies raged in his belly, making his stomach churn. His heartbeat raced so loud that it reverberated in his ears, and he wondered if his friends could hear it as they stood beside him on the platform. He opened his mouth but nothing came out.

He glanced at Sloane. He looked at Ellis. He turned the other way to Joelle and Griffin, who nodded at him and smiled.

His mouth opened again. "By now, you all know what the Identity Act is."

Several people in the crowd booed.

Mercury grabbed the tag at his throat and held it up. "How many of you had to go to the Witch Acculturation Services to grab this cheap piece of metal we're all supposed to wear around our necks so humans will feel safer knowing who among them are witches?"

More boos followed, this time mixed with people shouting "fuck the W.A.S." and "the Identity Act is anti-witch!"

Bile rose in Mercury's throat. Acid swam in his stomach.

I can do this, he thought.

"How many of you have struggled at your job or your school since the Identity Act was passed? How many of you have been abused or bullied or have feared for your lives?"

More booing and shouting echoed from the crowd this time, and Mercury balked to see several children and teenagers adding their voices to the chorus. The butterflies in Mercury's stomach flapped harder as he thought of the bullying these children must face every day. For a moment, he was thankful to have grown up before witches had been exposed.

He narrowed his eyes. Across the sea of people, he could see raised signs with the words "separate is not equal," "Reformations not restoration," and "fuck the Identity Act."

Mercury breathed in the warm spring air and released it fully. He brought the bullhorn back to his mouth.

"Today is the day that American witches stand up from our desks, step out from behind the machinery. Our shouts will ring so loud that they'll stretch all the way to the Council house in New York City. They will ring to the summer home of Councilwoman Oliana Murtaza in Miami, where she no doubt sits now, sipping Aperol spritzers and planning her inauguration as President of Kinheld rather than dealing with the very real issues that our community faces today."

The crowd roared.

"Say that shit," someone yelled.

"And to Oliana, to every Kinheld supporter, to the dhampirs, and to Harvey fucking Vael himself, I say this—my brother Troian died at the hands of bloodthirsty vampires who saw his life as inconsequential. I will not be silent. We will not be silent, until our people are safe, equal, and respected!"

More clapping and cheering erupted from the crowd. Mercury began chanting the message he communicated to the world three months ago when he first decided to protest.

"Separate is not equal! Separate is not equal!"

The crowd joined in, harmonizing the words. Mercury glanced at his friends and nodded, and they turned to begin their trek.

They led the crowd alongside the pathway of Venice Beach, where muscle-bound trainers stood in leggings and tight tank tops and stared at them in awe, where starving artists stopped in the middle of a sale to take notice of the procession. All the while Mercury held the bullhorn to his face. All the while he kept his fist pumping up in the air. All the while he kept shouting. By now, his voice was hoarse, but he knew he couldn't stop. These people came because they believed in a common cause, because they believed in him. He would not let them down. Despite the soreness in his throat and the finger cramps from holding the bullhorn, he kept marching and shouting.

The group stopped in front of the newly reconstructed Iron Bird. It smelled like fresh wood and paint, and though Mercury was happy that the only home he'd known had been rebuilt, he knew it would never feel the same without Troian. *My best friend . . . my brother*, he thought.

Mercury stopped in front of the door and stared back at the crowd. Curious eyes returned his stare, eagerly awaiting his next move.

"Here is the spot where my brother was murdered. From the awning that hung just here. He was scared, and he was alone. And I'll never forgive myself for that," Mercury said, his voice cracking.

Sloane and Griffin flanked him, each of them placing a hand on his shoulder. He felt that grief again—the kind that made it hard for him to stand, made it hard for him to focus. He felt his brother's presence here, and Mercury wished with all his heart that his element was water so that he could use blood magic and conjure his brother at will. He blinked away the tears.

"I'll never forgive myself. And I can only hope that my actions at Astera could help avenge his death. And I know that Troian would want us to do whatever it took to ensure our equality. If he were here, he'd be right by my side calling for the same things. Calling for the Witches' Council to stop their stupid plan for a witch reserve and affect the change we need to achieve *real* equality."

Mercury looked over at Sloane, who stood with her head bowed. He could see tears falling from her eyes onto her Reeboks. Ellis stood beside her, eyes covered with Ray Bans and arms crossed against himself.

Mercury quickly faced the crowd. "Thank you all for coming and for your commitment to the revolution, which will not be what?"

"Televised!" the crowd shouted.

"It will not be what?"

"Not be televised!"

Mercury grinned.

"Our next protest is in two weeks, where we'll walk to the Santa Monica Pier. I hope to see all of you there so our cause can stay visible. And between now and then, do whatever you can to help: tweet about it, put it on the 'Gram, TikTok, even Facebook for those of you still on it. Text your friends, your family, anyone who you think would be receptive. But don't forget—the threats to our lives are real. If you're in a situation or see someone in trouble, it is vital that you record it, or take a picture and post it. We have to look out for ourselves and each other . . . because we're family. Blessed be."

Sloane let out a whoop and began to clap. Griffin and Ellis joined in, and Joelle followed soon after. The crowd cheered and clapped, then people began to close in on him. Mercury prepared himself for their questions and their compliments and their concerns.

The events at Astera had made him and his friends overnight celebrities. Before the event he could go anywhere and be left alone. Now, at least one person recognized him everywhere he went. Not everyone was friendly, however. He was shocked at the first rally when a man approached him and shouted at him for his hubris, for putting so many lives in danger. Mercury had to pull himself back from the edge of a panic attack after that experience, which he sometimes relived in an occasional stress dream, witnessing a different outcome every time.

As he stood before the crowd now, he braced himself.

"Mercury, can I take a picture with you?" asked a white woman with blond hair piled into a messy bun.

"What does your father think about this?"

"Why are you rebuilding in the place your brother was murdered?"

Mercury did his best to breathe. He did his best to smile and take pictures and answer their questions. Inside, though, his stomach churned. Bile had risen in his belly and now coated his throat. He resisted the urge to vomit.

"Why didn't you just fight the vampires at the party instead of running away?" asked a woman with tawny skin and honey-blond box braids. She wore a sleeveless black romper with a pair of gold, high-top Chucks. A pair of gold aviator sunglasses covered her eyes; her full lips were painted the same black as her romper. Her tag was tucked into her romper. To Mercury, she looked straight out of a '90s teen movie.

"Excuse me?" Mercury replied.

The woman stepped forward. She held her phone in one hand and pulled her sunglasses off with the other.

"I said why didn't you just fight the UGN brothers at their house instead of driving across the country to fight at Astera?"

The crowd went silent. Hundreds of eyes trained themselves on Mercury.

"I—" he started. He swallowed hard to push the bile back down. "I didn't want to get anyone else involved at the time."

"Well, you did a great job with that, huh?" the woman quipped. Someone snickered.

Mercury's knees wobbled. Suddenly, the ground felt as if it would rise up to meet him. His mind had completely cleared. He looked from the crowd to Griffin, who nodded at him reassuringly.

"Why don't you mind your business, bitch?" Sloane said. She stepped forward from behind him.

Mercury looked at her, wide eyed.

"No, Sloane, it's—"

"Why don't you make me?" the woman taunted.

The crowd stilled, just as Mercury had.

For several seconds, the moment lingered. Then the woman threw her arms up and around Sloane, and the two women giggled.

Mercury exhaled a long breath and bent forward. "What the fuck?"

Sloane pulled away from the woman.

"Mercury, this is Valeria LeFebre, the senior editor at *Jonquil*."

Valeria held out a hand, her jet-black nails making her long fingers look like claws. When Mercury touched her, he could see what she'd done in the days before the rally. She was getting her nails done. She was cooking pasta in a pair of shorts shorter than the ones she currently wore. She was smoking at a table surrounded by three other Black women, each of them wearing a long set of braids. She was talking to a bearded man, his arms crawling in tattoos, about the chance for a big story.

"Nice to meet you, Mercury," Valeria said.

Mercury smiled tightly and took her hand. "What's good?"

The crowd began to dissipate, bored with the lack of conflict. The ones interested in more information about the rallies stood and spoke to the others, who discreetly pulled the stragglers away from Mercury, Sloane, and Valeria.

"Sorry if I scared you with my questions. I'm that ambitious reporter you see in all the movies."

Mercury chuckled, trying not to look affected by the questions. "You're good."

Valeria lifted a brow and smirked. "So, you gave a really good speech today."

"Thank you."

"I've been hearing rumors about Councilwoman Murtaza's plans for a while."

"Really?" Mercury asked, stuffing his hands into his pockets.

Valeria smiled and shrugged. "News travels fast in the Community, what with you Air Hands' ability to scroll through people's memories."

Mercury scratched the back of his head. "What—"

"You all get the same look on your faces whenever you're memory surfing. Can't blame you, though. That power would be so fucking helpful for my articles. Guess I'll just stick with water control."

A Water Hand, Mercury thought.

"My bad, you know how it is, can't always control the power, especially in places like this," Mercury said, gesturing around.

Valeria nodded, knowingly.

Heightened emotions and moments could prevent a witch from maintaining total control of their powers. Though Mercury had been raised to keep control in even the most pressing circumstances, there were moments that challenged him. For a moment, he wondered if that had anything to do with him using fire back at Astera. He shook the image from his mind and turned his attention back to Valeria.

"So, what all have you heard about our head Councilwoman's plans?" Mercury inquired.

Valeria lifted a brow and slid her sunglasses back on. Sloane looked at him and chuckled then looked back down at her phone. Though most people knew that he and Oliana were related, he didn't want to emphasize the relationship if he didn't have to. Besides, calling her Councilwoman helped him compartmentalize his feelings for his aunt, the only one he'd ever known, in his own mind.

As Sloane wandered over to where Joelle stood and began discussing where to go for food, Valeria and Mercury began strolling through the crowd. They passed several people who fist bumped Mercury, offered a high five, or requested a selfie. Throughout it all Valeria remained by Mercury's side. To him, she seemed equally amused and judgmental about the attention he received.

"Well, probably no more than you, nephew."

"Oh, it's like that, huh?"

She smiled.

"I just know that she fought hard to secure that land, that she managed to get Vael to add in provisions for more peaceful relations between witches and vampires, and that she wants to fast-track it all—the goal is to have it ready for entry before the next election."

Mercury pursed his lips. "Yes, the election. The thing we should actually be focusing on instead of trying to get some raggedy land graft."

"Well, some might say she's trying to bring us all peace."

"Well, if you listened to my speech today, you know I'm not one of them. We need true equality, not the equivalent of going back to Africa."

Valeria stared at him over her glasses. "Don't be extra. I'm sure Oliana isn't thinking in those terms."

Mercury stopped walking. "You don't know Oliana like I do."

"That's true. You, uh, willing to spill some tea?"

Valeria turned toward him, pulling her sunglasses off and nestling them on top of her head. She smiled, a dimple forming in her left cheek.

"Not a chance," Mercury replied, though he smiled despite himself. Another group of protestors swarmed him, one of them asking why the next protest was two weeks away instead of the following weekend.

"Permits," he replied flatly.

As they walked away, Valeria stood with her arms crossed.

"Still here, huh?" Mercury observed.

"Thought we were having a chat?" she asked.

"I just figured you'd have left after I told you I wasn't about to air out family drama on Al Gore's internet."

She chuckled. "I know. But if you won't chat about the Amell-Murtaza family secrets, then how about your own?"

His face crumpled. "What?"

"I'd like to do a piece on you, Mercury. On your humble beginnings and rise to power and fame."

Mercury scoffed. "Fame? I don't think so. I'm just someone who can't help but stand up for what's right, even when it could get my ass kicked. That gets people's attention I suppose."

"You've certainly gotten my attention." Valeria smirked.

Mercury smiled and rubbed at his beard.

"Well, I guess this piece could help the movement reach even more witches . . . Okay, I'll do it."

Valeria clapped her hands. "Dope! What's your number?"

Mercury gestured for her cell phone. Valeria fixed her gaze on Mercury as she handed it to him and watched him input his number. Two seconds later, his pocket jingled.

"Got cha." He waved his phone then returned hers after ending the call.

"I'll text you and we'll link up soon," she said.

"Alright, cool," Mercury replied.

She slipped her sunglasses back on and turned to leave. "Stay blessed, Air Hand."

"Stay blessed," he replied.

When she was a safe distance away, Mercury inhaled the air around him and emptied it from his chest. His heart beat fast and try as he might, he couldn't keep a straight face. He couldn't believe that a senior editor—a very attractive senior editor—from his favorite magazines wanted to write an article about him.

This could go viral, he thought, wondering how many people across the nation would read it. Thinking that more people would learn about the movement and possibly join them. He couldn't believe how quickly things were changing. Three months ago when he sent his first tweet opposing Kinheld, he couldn't have imagined it would've gone viral. He never would've thought he'd be organizing and leading a protest against the only aunt he'd ever known. Against someone who he'd looked up to for so long. He felt a twinge of sorrow at the thought of her.

He sighed and looked down at his phone, just as it buzzed. It was a text from Valeria. Mercury shoved down his thoughts of his aunt and pulled open the text.

"You free to link up tomorrow?"

Mercury grinned and replied with the GIF of Snoop Dogg nodding while wearing a top hat.

Valeria responded with a skull emoji. Mercury slid his phone into his back pocket and walked back toward his friends.

"Yo, Mercury, I'm fucking starving. Let's go!" Sloane shouted.

She's right, he thought. *Let's go.*

SUMMERTIME MAGIC

BY SLOANE SALVANERA
STAFF WRITER, *JONQUIL*

I've always wanted to be in the movies.

Not as an actress, wearing clothes someone else picked for me and saying words someone else told me to say. I wanted to be the person in those movies who gets to go on an adventure, who gets to conquer the villain and affect change. As I stood beside my best friend, Mercury Amell, during the recent protest at Venice Beach, I realized my dream had come true.

In the months since our return from Astera, we've launched a movement dedicated to the true equality of witches. Our goals are simple. Witches deserve the same treatment as everyone else and that includes the chance to make it in America. We deserve to strive for equality here instead of a stratified society of only witches elsewhere.

Some may wonder why we're such staunch opposers of the Corvius Accord. After all, it would ensure that witches have their own space away from vampires to make their own laws, their own education system, their own jobs. But these same people fail to see the parallels of this policy to Jim Crow south. The calls for a separation of witches and vampires so that they may be "equal" is nothing but a shady attempt to treat witches even worse than now.

We know this because we've seen the statistics from countries that have tried to implement these types of things before. Those communities statistically receive 46% less government aid and have a 22% higher unemployment rate, a 12% higher high school dropout rate, and a 17% higher crime rate. We know that crime isn't simply a situation of someone behaving badly. There are several factors that impact whether someone will commit a crime, including whether someone has completed high school.

What does all this mean? Perhaps nothing. Perhaps Kinheld will be erected and run as a just and fair society that will receive equal treatment. Perhaps the witches there will receive the same funding for student loans, and the same opportunities for advancement as others.

Or it'll be a dumpster fire. It'll be run like a dictatorship with Councilwoman Oliana Murtaza seeking to run Kinheld in her image. Witches will comply or else, and those that don't will be left out in the cold.

How do we address the rising number of crimes against witches? You may ask. The solution isn't going to be one you like. The solution is to stay and fight. To register people to vote, to explain policy to your family and friends. To protest, to take to the streets and make people listen. To get more people involved, knocking on doors and texting about it, tweeting about it. My abuela always told me that when you want to get something done, you must "make haste while the sun is shining in your backyard." And oh, my friends, how the sun is shining.

CHAPTER 4

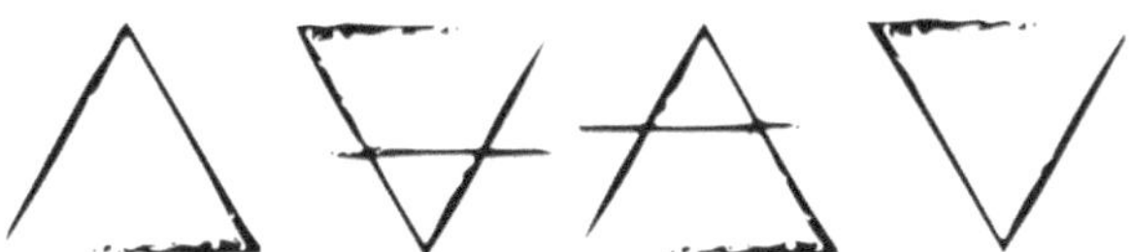

Thirty minutes after the protest wrapped, the group occupied a patio table at Azul, a seafood restaurant with a patio facing the beach. None of them had dined there before, and as his friends quieted to look at the menu, Mercury was glad for a moment of silence.

He spent his whole day talking and being asked questions. He'd been so consumed by other people's energy that he hadn't really had time to restore his own. He especially wanted to steer clear of the post-protest crowd, voting against the popular diners and sports bars in the area.

Mercury absentmindedly scrolled through Twitter, liking and sharing the photos people shared at the protest. He felt vindicated as he looked at the photos of dozens of people taking part in the moment.

He stumbled on a photo that Valeria tweeted and paused. It was one of Mercury standing with the bullhorn close to his mouth, his other hand in the air. His eyes were closed and his mouth was wide open. He liked the photo then clicked on Valeria's profile. Her Twitter handle was @ThatGalVal. Mercury's gaze lingered on her profile picture.

She wore a strapless yellow dress, her hair in two large space buns.

She sat at the edge of a pool, her hands beside her and her back to the camera. She looked toward her left, her eyes shielded by sunglasses with rims as yellow as her dress.

Mercury couldn't look away from the way her shoulders glistened in the sunlight, and he admired how graceful her profile was.

She is gorgeous, he thought.

He followed her immediately.

"Are you ready to order?" the waitress asked, bringing Mercury's focus back to the fore. He looked up at her and smiled then looked back down at the menu.

"I'll take the buffalo chicken wrap," Sloane said.

"I'll have the cobb salad, no dressing," Joelle added.

"Burger, no cheese, no onion, and instead of fries, can I get a side salad?" Griffin requested.

Sloane rolled her eyes at the twins' orders.

"So healthy," she quipped.

The waitress chuckled then looked at Mercury, who was still studying the menu.

"Salmon salad."

She smiled at him and looked toward Ellis.

"I'll do the Cajun pasta."

The waitress walked away with their orders. When she was gone, Sloane lifted her beer in toast.

"Here's to another successful protest."

They clinked their glasses together then savored the contents. Mercury took a sip of his beer, an IPA that he wasn't entirely sure he liked. After placing his drink on the table, he grabbed his phone again and began scrolling.

"So, have you heard from any of the other organizers?" Griffin asked.

Mercury nodded, only half paying attention.

"What did they say? Did they have any notes or have to deal with any assholes trying to stop them?"

He shook his head.

"Yo, you good?" Joelle asked, concern in her eyes.

"Think he's got that reporter chick on his mind," Ellis said.

Sloane pushed him. "Hey, that's my homegirl. Besides, it's not like Merc is exactly available."

Joelle and Mercury traded glances. Mercury smiled but remained silent. After what happened at the W.A.S., he wasn't sure what they had. When neither of them said anything, Sloane narrowed her eyes.

"Did I miss something? Didn't you two get it in at Astera?"

Joelle shook her head and sipped her beer.

Mercury looked down at his beer, wishing the moment would pass.

"Well, I don't remember ever being this uncomfortable," Griffin said. "So, let's talk about something else. Ellis, when's the last time you washed your hair?"

Sloane giggled.

Ellis sneered.

"Seriously, it's gone past goofy stoner and headed into slacker territory."

"Whatever, man. I woke up hella early."

"Yeah, but you also get off work at three," Sloane replied.

As Sloane and Griffin ribbed Ellis about his hair, Mercury tried one last time to catch Joelle's gaze. But she was staring out at the ocean, lost in thought.

***

Though he had grinned upon seeing the notification, Mercury sighed as he read Valeria's text.

"How about The Fountain Bar?"

The Fountain Bar, he thought.

It was a small restaurant in The Grove positioned dead center among various restaurants and shops. It was known for its limited seating and pricey drink selection, and Mercury pursed his lips as he typed. He had hoped they'd meet some place more intimate, quieter. He'd never been interviewed before, but he'd assumed that a restaurant consistently crawling with people may not be the best place. Yet, he told her he was free and they agreed to meet at seven.

He knew parking would be miserable, so he paid the thirty bucks it cost to take an Uber from the Iron Bird to the shopping mall. When he checked his phone, he saw that a video of his speech had gone viral.

"Holy shit," he said under his breath.

It had retweets from more people than he knew. Even *Jonquil* had retweeted it.

His face was warm. He couldn't believe that the movement was resonating with so many people. He thought it would get statewide attention, maybe be picked up by a few major national cities. But now he'd gone *viral.*

Nevertheless, there was just as much pushback as there was support. Some of the more bombastic critics called Mercury an ingrate or threatened to beat him up. Others said Mercury was cutting his nose to spite his face because why wouldn't witches want some land and laws of their own? Why wouldn't they want an escape from Vael's leadership?

The car pulled up in front of the main roundabout, causing Mercury's thoughts to fade.

"Thank you for choosing Uber. Have a great day," the cheery driver stated.

"Thank you," Mercury said.

He slid out of the car and closed the door. As he turned toward the side street that would take him toward the Fountain Bar, he looked at his reflection in the Gap store window. It was a hot day, so he opted for a pair of jeans cut off at the ankle, low-top converse, and a short-sleeve, gauzy white button up. Though he knew this was just an interview, Mercury found himself wondering about his appearance. Had he worn the right thing? Did he look like he was channeling LeBron James or Steve Urkel?

He pushed past his fears as he strolled toward The Fountain Bar. As soon as he approached the restaurant, he spotted Valeria sitting at a corner table, her long, pink nails tapping her phone screen.

Mercury approached the host stand.

"Table for one?" said the host, a spindly blonde man with a baby face and oversized glasses. A wide smile spread across his face, though the gesture didn't reach his eyes.

"No, I'm meeting someone." Mercury gestured toward Valeria's table, and the host nodded.

He looked down at the host stand. The host seemed relieved to have a break from the job and looked back down at his phone. As he passed, Mercury noticed he was reading an article on *The Vanguard*. The author was Cordelia Edwards, and Mercury didn't need to know the article's title to know the angle of the piece.

"Hey," Mercury said when he reached the table.

Valeria smirked as she looked up at him. She wore lipstick almost as pink as her nails. She stood and wrapped her arms around him. She smelled sweet, like honey. Her long, floral-print dress hugged her curves.

Mercury tried to keep his gaze on her face, told himself to just keep looking at her in the eyes.

Get it together, he thought.

They both sat down.

"You good?" she asked. She tapped her phone a few times before placing it between them. "Also, I've got to record this for my interview, cool?"

Mercury nodded.

She smells so good, he thought. *Why does she have to smell so good?*

Mercury looked down at the menu, trying to get his focus back.

"So, what happened after the protest?" she asked.

"We talked about the plans for the next protest over dinner."

"Are those plans something you can share?" she inquired.

Before he could answer, a waitress approached them and welcomed them, asked if they wanted something to drink and if they knew their specials for the day.

Mercury asked for a Modelo. Valeria asked for a Mojito. They agreed to split a plate of truffle fries, and Mercury's heartbeat quickened as the waitress left and Valeria turned her recorder back on.

"We're taking to the ocean walk, going from Muscle Beach and ending at the Santa Monica Pier."

"What's at the pier?" she asked.

Mercury shrugged. "It's where we were able to get a permit. Our goal is eventually to make our presence known outside the Council house."

"Quite the ambitious itinerary," she commented. "What's the end goal for you?"

The waitress set their drinks before them. Mercury thanked her and when she left, he lifted his glass toward Valeria. She returned the gesture then took a sip.

"I think I've been very frank about what the goal is. We want Councilwoman Murtaza to go back to the drawing board and actually try to help witches."

"What are you saying to people who agree with your aunt?"

Mercury winced.

"When I speak to people who agree with *Councilwoman Murtaza,*" he said, emphasizing her name. ". . . I like to remind them that true equality does not come from separation. All you're doing is saying that these two groups can't play together. And inevitably, one group ends up underfunded and underserved. And which group do you think that will be? For all the wealth and access the Council has accumulated worldwide, it still may not be enough to fight against the issues in America."

He sipped his beer.

"You really don't like to admit that she's your aunt, do you?"

Mercury pursed his lips. How could he explain to Valeria how heartbreaking it was to have someone you loved so much, who you admired for so long, now be someone you oppose? Someone who could be so willing to put their own needs ahead of others? He didn't want the article to turn into a sob story about his familial relationships. He wanted this to be about the movement, so he tried to redirect the conversation.

He cleared his throat. "I'd rather focus on her work and how it's harming our community instead of our relationship."

"Hmm. I can't imagine being in your shoes." She sipped her drink then placed it back on the table. "I mean, going against not just your aunt but against the first Black, female Head of Council. Just, *yikes*, you know?"

Mercury was aware of the optics of his decision. To the casual observer, it wasn't a good look. At best he looked insensitive and at worst, he looked sexist, like a man who couldn't stand that a woman was doing something revolutionary.

"It's not like that, and I think you know it, Valeria."

She smiled slyly. "Oh, you know I have to ask these things, Mercury. It's just part of the job."

Valeria grabbed at the fries on the plate, taking several and slipping them into her mouth.

"Yes, well. I'm not going to get into my relationship with Councilwoman Murtaza. All you need to know is that I love my aunt dearly, but I deeply disagree with her decisions as the Head of Council. I want to find a way to address the root of the issue, the fact that Vael has emboldened his followers to commit acts of terror against witches, the fact that we're the ones having to wear these stupid things," Mercury said, pointing to his dog tag.

He hadn't realized that Valeria wasn't wearing her tag around her neck. She'd wound the metal around her petite wrist twice, and the tag dangled delicately. It looked almost normal, were it not for the blue pentagram and hexe.

She asked him what else he planned to do aside from protest. He told her it was his goal to stop the development of Kinheld altogether, but if that couldn't be done, then he'd work to dissuade witches from even going there.

"What if that means they get more pushback from their neighbors? What if staying means they're burned and lynched?"

Mercury flinched at her words. They conjured the images of Troian, of his mother, of things he'd fought so hard to bury. He didn't want to think about them gasping for breath. He didn't want to think about their fear. He blinked away tears and swallowed a gulp of beer, washing down the bile that sat in his throat like a hard lump.

"It won't come to that."

"Can you guarantee it?"

"Of course not. But I feel that these protests aren't just sending a message to Councilwoman Murtaza. They are telling witches everywhere that we don't have to accept things as they are. We can affect change."

Valeria sighed and smiled. "Well, I think that covers the tough questions."

"Really?"

Valeria nodded. She picked at the truffle fries again before responding.

"I'm not just gathering information based on your answers to my questions. I've seen you in action, and I'll be attending the other protests to get the bigger picture. For now, I'd like to switch gears. Have some fun. These questions may seem random, but they help paint the full picture of Mercury."

Mercury nodded.

"Birthday?"

"October 12."

"A Libra. Okay, okay," she said. "Favorite holiday?"

"Ilaris."

"Can't beat the parties," she remarked.

Mercury smiled. Ilaris harkened the start of summer. It fell a few days after Juneteenth, which gave his family extra incentive to celebrate. He smiled thinking about the parties and cookouts of years past —the time when Oliana tried to make macaroni and cheese and ended up burning it, the time when he, Troian, and Faegan got drunk and snuck out to the Walk of Fame. He felt the bittersweetness of love and loss, not just for his brother but for his cousin and his aunt, too.

"Nope."

"Are they having one this year?" she asked.

Mercury nodded. "Dad's already starting to plan the one for the Council."

"Any details you can share?"

Mercury shook his head. "Dad's an expert party planner, and he keeps everything on a need-to-know basis until the last minute. All I know is, it's going to be big."

"I can't wait," Valeria exclaimed. "What are you listening to these days?"

"Mostly west coast shit. A lot of old school: E-40, Tupac, N.W.A. I also listen to The Roots and Led Zeppelin since I'm trying to get my drum skills up."

"Interesting, Valeria said, her eyes sparkling. "How do you take your coffee?"

"Latte."

"Favorite food?"

"Eggs Benedict."

"Seriously?" Valeria chuckled.

Mercury laughed. "Don't be sleeping on eggs benny. It's the ultimate comfort food."

"I guess," she said.

Mercury shook his head and grabbed some fries from the plate.

"Single or taken?"

Mercury paused.

He hadn't expected this question. Did that really matter? More importantly, did he even have a real answer?

"Is this for the article?"

She gave him that smirk again.

"Single," he replied.

"Oh? I thought you and Joelle were a thing. At least that's what Sloane told me," she lifted a brow, taking a long draw from her drink.

"I'm not surprised. Sloane can't keep shit to herself," he laughed. "I'm single, but not exactly looking if that makes sense."

"I see. So, when you are looking," she said, lowering her glasses. "What do you look for?"

Mercury leaned back in his chair, keeping his hand on his drink.

"A Black woman who wants me around but doesn't need me. Funny, smart, beautiful."

"Magical?" she asked, leaning forward.

Mercury glanced at her cleavage and cleared his throat.

"Always."

She smiled at him and tapped her phone, stopping her recording.

"I think that's good enough," she said. "Now we can really enjoy our time."

She tilted her head back and finished her drink.

"Down for another round?"

Mercury smiled. "Absolutely."

CHAPTER 5

Days after his lunch with Valeria at The Fountain Bar, Mercury stood in front of the mirror in his bedroom, grimacing at the way the silver chain clashed with the gold blazer he wore. His hair was freshly lined and his beard was trimmed for the first time in months. Though he felt more like himself, he hated the reason for his elevated style: later that evening, after cocktails and expensive hor d'oeuvres, a witch named Briar Kennedy would be stripped of his powers.

The witch had killed a group of vampires at St. Basil's, a church in Bala Cynwyd. Mercury didn't agree with Briar's decision to open fire on a group of vampires for seemingly no reason. But Mercury also didn't think that stripping Briar of his powers was the right thing to do, either. After all, to be stripped of one's powers didn't simply mean the loss of magic—it meant the loss of contact with the witch community. It meant losing the only identity a person had ever known and being forced into exile.

Mercury's stomach churned as he thought about it. He and his friends had been dangerously close to suffering the same fate not three months ago. He wondered how different things would be for him now if he'd actually lost his powers.

He held out his hand and gestured for his tie. It drifted toward him and Mercury slipped it around his neck, trying to figure out how to tie it. His hands shook.

A knock on his door startled him. He turned to see his father standing in the doorway, dressed in a sleek, peacock blue suit, silky gold shirt beneath it, with a diamond choker at his neck.

"You look good, son," he said.

"Thanks," Mercury replied, still fiddling with his tie. "Why do we have to get dressed for such a shit show anyway?"

"You know I don't need an excuse to dress up. I'll wear a suit and tie to a little league game for goddess' sake," Atlas joked. "But I agree. Dressing up just to watch someone be condemned feels like an insult."

"So why are we doing it?"

"You know your aunt. She's all about optics."

His father crossed the threshold of the room and sat on the edge of Mercury's bed.

"Yeah, well. I wish she spent more time trying to prevent this shit from happening instead of planning and hosting ceremonies for when it does," Mercury remarked.

His father shook his head. "Now that's not just an Oliana thing. You were too young to remember the things that happened under Malcolm. It was a gala or a ceremony or a meeting for everything. A team retreat to discuss whether the Water Hands were claiming too many of the jobs in a certain city. A ceremony to discuss how to plan the next Astera. A black-tie affair just because his daughter graduated middle school."

"Sounds miserable."

"It was. Just like watching you fumble around with that tie. I could have sworn I taught you and your brother how to do this?" his father asked.

Mercury looked down at his shoes. He'd never known how to tie a tie. His father had taught him, yes, but he didn't remember what part of it went over or under or how long it was supposed to be. He'd followed Troian's lead and kept his ties tied and hanging in his closet. When their home burned, Mercury had lost most of his fancier clothes, which he'd kept at his father's instead of in his cramped dorm room closet.

Atlas clicked his tongue and stood. He turned Mercury toward him and grabbed the ends of the tie and began tying it, a smirk on his face as he did so.

"Thanks," Mercury said.

"Of course. You're my son. When you have kids, *if* you decide to have kids, you'll know that the parenting never stops."

Mercury looked upward, hoping to stop the pressure building behind his eyes.

Seconds later, Atlas added the final touches to the tie and patted Mercury on the shoulder.

"Now you're looking extra sharp." His father smiled.

Mercury pulled his father into a hug and relaxed a bit as he felt his father's strong hands wrap around him and pull him close.

When Mercury pulled away, he dabbed at the tears in his eyes.

"I love you, Dad," he said.

"I love you too, Mercury."

Mercury cleared his throat. He gestured to his cell phone and once it was in his hands, he checked to see if he'd gotten a text from any of his friends. None of them had texted him, so he tapped out a message to them as he followed his father out of his room. They locked the door to their apartment and walked downstairs and into the tattoo parlor.

His eyes widened as he spotted his friends already waiting and dressed for the somber occasion. Griffin wore black pants with a green smoking jacket and a set of black loafers with gold paisley print. His dreads were loose and he didn't have his glasses on.

"Are you wearing contacts?" Mercury asked as he gave Griffin a hug.

Griffin nodded. "I just got them; Honore went with me."

"Okay, I see you," Mercury replied.

Joelle scoffed. Mercury looked from her to Griffin and lifted a brow, sensing some tension between the twins. This had became the norm each time someone mentioned Griffin's relationship with the Councilmember.

Griffin shrugged. "I'm not used to them yet."

"Well, you look great tonight."

He looked back toward Joelle. She wore a copper-colored satin dress, her long curls gathered into a high bun. She wore a smokey eye and her cheeks were dusted with gold highlighter.

"You look beautiful," Mercury said.

"Thank you. You don't look so bad yourself," Joelle replied.

He smiled at her and walked to the other side of the shop, where Ellis and Sloane passed her vape between them. He walked into a cloud of kiwi-scented smoke.

"What's good?" he asked.

Sloane stood and held her arms up. She twirled, showing off the bubble gum pink lace dress she wore. Her long hair hung in loose curls. Ellis wore a black leather blazer, white shirt, and matching black dress pants. His black dress boots were pointed and reminded Mercury of a mod.

"Not much. I'm surprised we have to dress up for something like this," Sloane said.

"That's what you're surprised about?" Ellis questioned. "I'm surprised we even got an invite."

"Yeah, why do we get to come to this thing? Three months ago, your aunt wanted to strip our powers and now she invites us to a super exclusive witch event?" Joelle asked.

"It's probably her way of warning you that she's still powerful enough to strip your powers at any time," Atlas interjected. Sloane blanched, and Mercury patted her shoulder.

He walked over to the front desk and set a bottle of cognac down. He grabbed chilled glasses from the small refrigerator beneath the desk then poured a glass for each of them.

After they each grabbed a glass, Mercury's father lifted his.

"Anyway, thank you all for dressing for the occasion. I'm glad I don't have to worry about any of you embarrassing me," he said.

"Thanks Mr. A," Ellis replied, smiling.

"At least sartorially. The night's still young."

Ellis spoke, a wounded look on his face. "Mr. A, I would never—"

"No, no. That wasn't up for debate, Ellis. The night is still young. Let's see if you can get through it without saying anything out of pocket."

"I give him an hour," Griffin said.

"That's generous," Joelle quipped.

"You all are jerks," Ellis responded, though there wasn't a hint of anger in his voice.

"Well, here's to getting through this somber occasion in style," Mercury said.

As their glasses clinked, Mercury feigned a smile, wondering what the night had in store.

THE POWER STRIPPING CEREMONY WAS HELD AT THE COUNCIL HOUSE, an expensive mansion in Benedict Canyon. The road that led to the house curved up a hill lined with trees on either side. The house sat at the top of the hill, and Mercury's eyes widened as he took it in. The circular driveway was surprisingly empty. As they stepped out of their Lyft, Mercury glanced to the right to see a second driveway at the base of a small hill. Several cars had been parked there and two valets stood at the top of the hill, waiting for the next car to park.

The house itself was a sweeping mid-century style mansion. It was three stories high and sprawled out across most of the hill. The front lawn was expertly manicured, and lights lined the walkway that led to the front steps. The massive structure glowed in the moonlight.

"This house is big as hell," Griffin said. "Who lives here?"

"Nobody. At least, not regularly. It's for all of the Council members. Some of the members have multiple homes, like Oliana and Paloma. So this house is where they stay when in town and where a lot of business and events take place," Mercury replied.

Griffin nodded, still taking in the grandiosity of the house.

The interior of the home was more opulent than its exterior. The ceilings were high and the walls and floors were sparkling white. The glass door opened onto a large foyer. Two people dressed in black suits and ties stood at the ready to collect coats. Across from the foyer stood a spiral staircase that led to a catwalk on the second floor. Beyond the staircase was a large great room, where white couches, chairs, and tables idled. The entire rear of the house featured floor to ceiling windows, framed by large gold curtains which hung on gold rods at least fifteen feet high.

They followed the flow of people to the left of the great room, which led to a long hallway. Paintings and photos lined the center of the walls perfectly. Mercury realized it was a wall of current and past council members when he spotted a photo of his mother. His heartbeat skipped.

She wore a sparkling, blue, off-shoulder dress. A three-strand pearl necklace adorned her neck with pearl studs decorating her earlobes. Her hair was styled naturally, her lustrous coils resting atop her shoulders. Long lashes framed her large brown eyes and her dimpled smile showed off the small gap between her front teeth.

She's always so beautiful, Mercury thought. He cleared his throat, trying to rid himself of the bile that collected, trying to suppress the ever-present grief for his mother. Though a great burden to bear, the initial loss of his mother appeared much lighter than the loss he now felt. The brother who had helped him carry that burden no longer existed in the physical world, deepening the piercing wound in his heart.

"This is one of my favorite pictures of your mother," his father said, interrupting his thoughts. He smiled wistfully, and Mercury could tell that in that moment his father was missing her as much as he was.

"I don't think I've ever seen this one."

"This was taken about a year before she died."

"Can I take a picture of it?"

Atlas nodded. "Of course."

Mercury pulled out his phone and snapped a photo. He held the phone in his hands for a moment, rubbing his fingers across the screen.

"Merc, why don't you and your father take one with her? I can take it," Sloane offered.

Mercury looked at his father. He nodded and they stood next to the photo. She nodded when finished.

"Thanks," Mercury said.

Sloane nodded again, her black-painted smile a welcome reprieve from his grief.

Mercury kissed his hand and placed it against the glass of his mother's photo.

"I love you, Mom."

As they stepped away from the photo, the words "I love you, too, son" tickled Mercury's ears. He turned around swiftly, hoping to see his mother in the flesh. Upon seeing her portrait again, he shook the thought away and got swept into the crowd with his father and his friends.

They were funneled into a room even larger than the great room. It looked like it had once been a ballroom, and like the rest of the house, one entire wall was covered in windows. An elevated platform sat in the center of the room, dozens of chairs arranged in a semi-circle around it. A wooden table topped with a grimoire, candles, herbs, and a glass container sat atop the platform. A man dressed in black stood with his back to the windows, a large camera pointed toward the platform.

"Jesus," Mercury breathed. He knew that this was being treated like the event of the season, but he had no idea they were filming it.

"I don't think he's gonna be much help."

Mercury turned to see Valeria standing behind him, dressed in a blood-red halter dress that clung to her figure. Bangle bracelets climbed her left arm and clattered against themselves as she pushed her braids back behind her with long, gold nails. Her braids were twisted into victory rolls.

She's gorgeous, he thought. He surveyed his surroundings, hoping no one with the power of telepathy stood near him.

"Hey," he said, hoping his voice hadn't been too eager.

"Hi," she replied, a wry smile on her face. "Hard to believe all this bougie is just to watch someone lose the best thing about them, huh?"

Mercury nodded. "I knew the Council was extra about everything, but they're filming these now?"

"My sources say that's a new thing. Miss Faegan and her lil' comms initiative. They're gonna live stream it to YouTube and Twitter."

Mercury scanned the room for his cousin but didn't see her. Looking back at the cameraman, he was surprised he hadn't thought that it was her idea. In the months since Astera, Faegan had secured a Council seat, taking the spot left vacant by Effie. Though he was happy for his cousin's success, her presence on the Council disturbed its balance—from its inception the Council always had been made up of one Hand from each element, with the Head of Council as the exception. Faegan was a Water Hand, and so was Mercury's father. Paloma represented fire and Honore, earth, meaning Air Hands like Mercury had no representation. Though Oliana insisted Faegan was a temporary member, according to Mercury's father, she showed no sign of working hard to find a replacement.

"Well, do they have anything to drink here at least?" Valeria asked, pulling Mercury out of his reverie.

"I'm not sure. Let's go find out." He walked back toward the group, who had taken seats in the middle rows. "We're going to find a bar. You want to join us?"

"Hell yes," Sloane said. She shimmied over Ellis, who stared at her as she did so. He then stood and followed her.

"What about you two?"

"I'm good, still recovering from that party last weekend. Thanks, though," Joelle said.

Mercury looked over at Griffin.

"No thanks. I'm waiting for Honore," he grinned.

"Well, if you go, I'll be here by myself."

"So why don't you go with them to the bar?" Griffin asked.

Mercury scratched his head, waiting for the tension between his friends to subside. Joelle rolled her eyes but stood anyway.

"Okay, fine," she pouted. She lifted her dress and shimmied over to them. Mercury looked at Valeria, who stared at Joelle in amusement. When she stood before them, she looked from Mercury to Valeria and back to him, lifting her brows.

"Oh. Uh, Valeria. I know you and Sloane know each other, but this is—"

"Ellis Hall and Joelle Whittaker," she said, shaking their hands. "Pleasure's all mine. Your escapades make for great watercooler talk at the office."

"I thought you all worked remotely?" Joelle asked.

Valeria smiled and turned to walk to the bar, not waiting to see if anyone followed her. Mercury looked back at his friends and proceeded to follow Valeria through the crowd. The room buzzed with energy as more and more witches glided into the room.

"Well, our figurative office. You know, our Slack chat be blowing up with details about your adventures."

"I knew Sloane couldn't keep her mouth shut about the trip," Joelle teased, trying for humor.

Sloane rolled her eyes and clicked her tongue.

"Girl, please. That shit's been public for a while. And with Valeria now going to interview Mercury, it'll be even more public."

"Wait, you're interviewing him?" Joelle's eyelids fluttered rapidly.

Valeria nodded. "We met up the other day. I got an exclusive with the most famous witch in the country over truffle fries and Hennessy shots."

Mercury smiled, his heart skipping a beat. "Yeah, those shots may or may not have been a good idea."

"I'd say they were a great idea," Valeria said, nudging him.

Mercury chuckled. "Well, fine. But I wouldn't say I'm the most famous."

"Mercury, you keep trending. Last weekend, it was the incident at the W.A.S.; this week, it's the protests. Trust me, people know who you are, and those who don't, want to know."

Hesitating, Mercury searched his mind for words but none trickled off his lips. He smiled weakly then continued weaving through the crowd in silence.

The bar occupied the back of the house in a sitting room next to the kitchen. Upon noticing two men in suits and bow ties taking orders and mixing drinks, the group walked toward the shortest line and stood. As they stood in line, Valeria turned toward Joelle.

"So, Sloane tells me you're back at UCLA? It must be hard getting back into the groove of things."

Joelle shrugged. "It hasn't been easy but it's been worth it. I'm back on track with my classes and finals are around the corner."

"I remember the pre-final stress. I'm so happy to be done with all that," she said. "What are you studying?"

"Music," Sloane interjected. "Joelle is a badass musician, and one day she's going to be big and work with the dopest artists."

"Thank you, Sloane," Joelle said, placing a hand on Sloane's arm.

Valeria made an appraising sound. "Well, I happen to know a few musicians myself. My brother, Darius, is a producer. Though he goes by his pseudonym, Mansa Musica."

Joelle's eyes widened. "Wait, that's your brother?"

Valeria nodded.

"He's dope. Why isn't he here tonight? I thought it was mandatory for all witches?"

"He's touring with Lil Nas X."

Joelle's eyes widened even more.

"You know, I can give my brother a call and tell him I met a promising musician that he should look into," Valeria offered. "That is, if you don't mind being around a few more witches."

Joelle shuffled uncomfortably. "I appreciate it, but I want to see if I can figure out the music world without magical help."

"Right," Valeria replied, a bemused expression on her face. "The offer stands if you ever change your mind."

Joelle nodded, tight-lipped.

Valeria turned back toward Sloane and they chatted about their shopping adventure to find their fancy dresses.

"Oh, it was so fun. Valeria took me to this small little boutique that I'd never heard of near Santee Alley," Sloane gushed.

"I told you you'd love it." Valeria smiled proudly.

Mercury looked at Joelle, who stood with her arms crossed and her head down.

"You good?" he asked quietly.

She glanced at him and nodded.

"Just fine," she replied.

Mercury didn't believe her. He was about to ask for clarity when the line dissipated and the bartenders asked for their drink order.

"I'll take E&J on the rocks, please," Mercury asked.

"Same," Valeria said. She looked at Mercury and winked.

"I'll just take a Diet Coke," Joelle said flatly.

"Two tequilas on the rocks," Sloane requested, holding up her index and middle fingers.

The bartenders poured their drinks and handed them over, their eyes scanning the length of the line. Mercury took out his wallet and placed a twenty in the tip jar. The bartender thanked him and turned toward the people behind them.

"Big spender," Valeria teased. She slipped her arm in Mercury's. He looked down at his arm and back at her.

"Well, cheers," he said, lifting his glass.

They clinked their glasses together. Joelle brought her glass to her lips and took a small sip, watching the two of them over the rim of her glass.

They walked back to their section, taking in more of the event's extravagance. Just about everything in the room either glowed or sparkled or shimmered, the perfect setup for a celebration, not the occasion at hand.

Once they arrived at their chairs, they noticed Griffin sitting in the same seat with Honore next to him, holding his neatly manicured hand. Honore stood and smiled at Mercury when he walked into view.

"Well, if it isn't the wunderkind himself," Honore said. He pulled Mercury into a hug.

"Hey, Honore, how's things?" he asked.

Honore shrugged. "I can't complain. Aside from this . . ." Honore gestured.

"Shitshow?" Sloane interjected.

Honore laughed.

"Should have known black tie etiquette wouldn't extend to your conversation," he said as he drew Sloane in for a side hug.

"They could never," she said, grinning.

"But yes, like Sloane said, this shitshow. Aside from that, things are going well. I trust you're doing alright?"

"Yeah. Dad and I are back at The Iron Bird, building our clientele back up."

"Ah, yes. I'm glad you're both back in your own home."

"Yeah, I know Dad is, too." He paused. "It's not the same without Troian, though."

Honore sighed and placed a hand on Mercury's shoulder. "I know. It may never be, but you and your father can create some good memories again."

Mercury nodded, thankful for Honore's positivity.

"So, I also see you've been busy takin' it to the streets."

Mercury chuckled. "Yeah. We figured if there was anything that would get my aunt's attention, it's going viral."

Honore's lip twitched. "Your protests have definitely gotten her attention, trust."

A sharp pain shot through Mercury's stomach.

Wasn't that what he wanted? To get his aunt's attention? A part of him felt guilty, like a child caught out past curfew or doing something they shouldn't be doing.

Mercury sipped his brandy, the warmth of it calming his nerves. "Well, good. Maybe then she'll see there are better ways to protect us witches."

Honore lifted a brow and shrugged. He didn't reply but rather threaded his fingers in Griffin's hand. The two strolled toward the bar.

Joelle scoffed. Mercury turned to her.

"What's wrong?"

"He's so much older than him," she whined as they slid into their seats. Joelle took one near the center of the section, and Mercury pondered whether to sit in the seat right next to her or to leave a space.

"Don't be ageist. He's only ten years older. And isn't Griffin happy?" He dropped into the chair once removed, and for a second, he thought he saw a scowl pass over her face at the empty seat.

"It seems like he is."

"So just relax," Mercury said. He grabbed Joelle's hand and squeezed it. For the first time in weeks, she looked at him as she had when they were at Astera. There was the hint of a smile on her lips, and Mercury desperately wanted to reach for her, wanted to caress her cheek and pull her in for a kiss. His heartbeat raced in that moment.

"Just kiss already," Ellis said, plopping down in one seat over from them.

Joelle looked down at her drink and cleared her throat. When she released Mercury's hand, Mercury scowled at his friend, laying his lonely hand on his thigh.

Sloane pushed at Ellis' shoulder before dropping into the seat between him and Mercury.

"I'm sorry, Merc, Jo. *Someone* doesn't have any manners."

She held out her glass for them to clink against hers.

"Cheers," they said. Each of them sipped their drinks.

"Is this seat taken?" Valeria gestured to the empty chair between Joelle and Mercury as she approached.

"No," Mercury said. Joelle looked away.

Valeria smiled and eased into her seat. She crossed her legs toward Mercury, her petite, golden-heel clad foot brushing against his.

The energy between her and Mercury nearly took his breath away.

"So, how does all of this work, exactly?" Sloane asked.

"I'm not completely sure. Witches have probably heard all the horror stories from our families over the years. Bloodletting, hung by your toes with a tube in your mouth . . ." Mercury began.

"Torture," Mercury and Valeria said at the same time. They both laughed, and Mercury felt the tension leaving his shoulders.

"Yeah, my granny told me that power stripping involved the Iron

Maiden. She threatened Darius and I if we were bad that we were gonna get put in them and left there. When I was a kid and saw the album cover for that band, I freaked," she said.

"If you listened to my grandma, it was that you starved for three days beforehand. She'd always threaten this when Troian and I didn't eat. She'd say, 'do you want to starve for three days and get your powers stripped because you're bad?'"

"So, basically, no one knows how this works?" Joelle interjected.

Mercury looked at her. As he opened his mouth, Valeria spoke.

"Power stripping has been an urban legend for most of us younger witches. I don't know anyone who's actually seen it happen."

"Well, my dad has," Mercury said matter-of-factly.

Valeria rolled her eyes. "We don't all have family members on the Council, sir."

"Oh, it's like that?" Mercury smiled. Valeria chuckled and swatted his arm.

"When was the last power stripping?" Joelle asked, resisting the urge to roll her eyes.

Mercury looked at Valeria.

"Maybe '93?"

"No, '97. It was—"

"Ronnie Deaver," they said in unison.

Joelle smiled tightly and sipped her soda. Mercury looked back at Valeria, who watched him with an amused expression.

"What?"

"Nothing, it's just . . . nice to have someone to talk to about this stuff," she said. "Admittedly, I'm usually the only witch in the room except at work."

Mercury nodded. The experience of being singular described his entire childhood. He was either the only witch, the only Black student, and sometimes both. He cringed at the memories of having to be the representative for two entire races in a room full of little white, non-magical kids.

"Well, now you don't have to worry about that," he replied.

"Can I quote you on that?" she smirked.

Mercury tipped his glass toward her and savored the brown liquor, relishing the oaky taste of the cognac and the way it warmed his belly.

Seconds later, the lights dimmed and the chatter fell in a similar fashion. A spotlight shone on the platform in the center of the room. The light cast the items on the table in a sinister light.

Mercury heard his aunt before he saw her. Her red-bottom heels clicked against the marble floor as she strode toward the platform, her white satin dress grazing the floor as she did so. Around the room, witches stood in reverence of their Head of Council.

She stepped up to the platform and into the spotlight, each step carefully executed. Her dress was a throwback to the 40's, the sleeves gauzy and billowing, ending at her wrists in bedazzled satin cuffs. Her lips were painted wine-red and her hair was expertly coiffed in a large chignon. She looked down at Mercury and smiled, and he returned the gesture briefly.

His father stepped into the room next, the silver at his neck sparkling in the light. He stood to the right of Oliana and clasped his hands in front of him. Paloma strutted toward the platform, her blood red leather dress hugging her body and her dark hair swaying behind her in a long braid. Honore stepped up to the platform from the other side of the room, his mint-green suit and gauzy gold shirt making him look as if he were glowing.

Mercury's cousin Faegan was the last to walk in. Her pale blue tulle dress brushed against the ground as she strutted into the room, hands on her hips. She looked beautiful and under any other circumstance, Mercury would've complimented her. But she was the most vocal advocate for Briar's power stripping. After their last meeting in Astera, when she'd backed her mother's plan for stripping his powers, Mercury didn't need to wonder why.

Each member flanked Oliana, each of them wearing the color of the element from which they drew power: earth, fire, and water. But there was no one wearing yellow, no one there to represent Air Hands.

"Tonight is not a night for celebration but of bearing witness," Oliana spoke, her rich voice echoing throughout the hall. "For tonight, one of our kind, Briar Kennedy, will have his powers stripped for the crime of murder. It is incumbent upon all of us to observe and understand that certain actions in this world have consequences."

She glanced back at Mercury. He looked forward, clenching his teeth. The last thing he needed to show her was that she could get under his skin.

"Each Council member will take part in removing Briar's powers. After tonight, he will be exiled from the warmth of the Fire, the breeze of the Air, the cooling of the Water, and the healing of the Earth."

The room began to chant, "The warmth of the Fire, the breeze of the Air, the cooling of the Water, the healing of the Earth."

Mercury looked toward his friends and nodded, indicating that they were to join in.

After several minutes of chanting, Oliana lifted her hands. The room became silent.

"Now, I know that there are many of you who have never attended such a ceremony before, including my own nephew, Mercury," his aunt gestured toward him and the spotlight shifted, casting a light on him.

Mercury smiled and lifted a hand. He looked at his father, who stared down at his shoes.

"So let me be clear on what Briar's exile means—if any witch, be they born or made, associates with him, allows him safe passage, gives him a job, or engages in any kind of relationship with him, they will be punished. What will happen to them is up to the Council to decide, but know that you may be putting everything from your livelihood to your powers on the line if you decide to help him. Do I make myself clear?"

Murmurs circulated around the room. Several people nodded, including Valeria.

"Good. You may all be seated. Tarit, Jenia, bring Briar in."

Mercury turned to see two witches stand up and nod before exiting the room. The conversation in the room picked back up as they waited. For their part, the Council members spoke amongst themselves, while Oliana stood separately, scrolling through the grimoire on the table.

"I didn't realize just how much a witch could lose if they had their powers stripped," Sloane whispered.

Mercury leaned toward her. "Yeah, it's almost a fate worse than death."

She reached out and squeezed his hand. "I had no idea that this is what would have happened to your father and you."

"All of us," he said.

She shook her head. "None of us had the same ties you do. This would have been a slap on the wrist for us, but for you?"

Mercury's breath hitched. Losing his powers would've been devastating. But it was a devastation he had escaped. By the grace of Honore, Paloma, and Bati—wherever he was—Mercury and his father and his friends got to keep their powers. He had escaped this fate, so why did he still feel so traumatized? Why was there still a panic simmering within him about something that *almost* happened?

Minutes later, the two witches returned with Briar. He was taller than both of them, his red hair sticking up in tufts. His hands were bound with Thurguards. His already pale skin had a yellowish hue, which drew attention to the dark circles beneath his eyes. His breath escaped in shallow spurts as he walked toward the platform. He stepped on stage and the two witches guided him to the center then down into a kneeling position. They tied the magic-repelling ropes at his wrists to two hooks in the floor. Then they stepped off the platform and returned to their seats.

Mercury felt as if he were at the top of a rollercoaster, looking down at the steep drop ahead. He could feel the anxiety buzzing from the other witches in the room, and it gave him an odd sense of community as he realized they were all uncomfortable, anxious about what was about to transpire.

When Mercury's father stepped to his mark on the platform, his back toward Mercury, Mercury gripped the edge of his blazer.

"I am the guardian of water, one too strong to subdue," Atlas began. He held his right hand up as though swearing an oath, and his left hand down at his side, his palm facing Briar. "I am the guardian of blood, sweat, tears, and intuition."

Light emanated from his father's hands. Briar shrunk back, whimpering.

Honore stepped to the left of Mercury's father and faced Briar. "I am the guardian of earth, one too strong to erode. I am the guardian of bone, growth, healing, and hearth."

"I am the guardian of fire, one too strong to contain. I am the guardian of the flesh, of physical strength, of anger and passion," Paloma said, after stepping to the edge of the platform and facing Honore. Briar whimpered again at the light emanating from three of the Council member's hands.

Feeling the intensity of the moment, Mercury's heart pounded against his chest. His temples ached and the spot behind his right eye throbbed. He looked over at his friends. Each of them stood in various states of unrest. Joelle had her arms crossed against herself, her soda in one hand. Griffin stood with his mouth agape. Ellis and Sloane held each other, and when Sloane brought up her drink to take a sip, her hand shook violently. Only Valeria seemed to take in the show with a kind of steely resolve. If Mercury hadn't looked down to see her hands clenched, he would've thought her unfazed.

Mercury was surprised when he heard his cousin speak next.

"I am the guardian of air," she said. She stepped to the spot across from Mercury's father and held her hands in position. "One too strong to anchor. I am the guardian of breath, voice, creativity, and intellect."

No light emanated from her hands. For a moment, everyone stood in awe at the idea that the power stripping might not work. Then, someone shouted.

"You're disrupting the balance!"

"You need an Air Hand!"

"How could you think of performing a ceremony without a true Air Hand?"

"Face crack of the century," Valeria whispered amid the outbursts. "How out of pocket do you think Oliana is about to go right now?"

Mercury scoffed. He knew his aunt. He knew that there was no way she was going to break from her perfect poise to show how put off she was by this setback.

"Don't hold your breath," he replied.

"She should have known better," Valeria said.

"What's happening?" Joelle asked, her voice a whisper amongst the murmur of the crowd.

Each of his friends looked at him, waiting for his answer.

"The balance is off," Mercury explained. "To perform a ceremony, you need a true Hand that represents each of the elements. Only the Head of Council can speak the words representing the soul."

"Why?"

"Because Council heads are imbued with the ability to speak for any element when appointed," Valeria chimed in. She looked at Mercury then back to the platform.

Oliana turned toward the crowd.

"It would seem the goddess requires a little more from us today." Her smile faltered for just a moment, and Mercury thought he could see a hint of fear in her eyes. Part of him wanted to comfort her, but a part of him delighted in her discomfort.

See how it feels for a change, he thought.

"It would seem we need an Air Hand. And I know just the perfect one."

She turned toward Mercury and his mouth went dry. Once again, the spotlight focused on him.

"Nephew, would you be a dear?" she asked, batting her eyes.

"What the fuck?" Sloane mouthed. Ellis' eyes were wide. Griffin and Joelle both leaned toward him, their hands on his sleeve. Even Valeria seemed rattled by Oliana's request.

"Do you have to do this?" Joelle asked.

"I don't—"

"I'm sorry, darling, but we don't have all evening to wait while you confer with your Made Witches," his aunt jeered.

Snickers arose from the crowd. Mercury could feel dozens of eyes on him. His father stared at his aunt. He knew enough not to question the Head of Council in such a public setting. So did Mercury. He knew he couldn't say no even though he wanted to.

"You've got to get up there," Valeria said. "You know if you don't everyone in this room will dog you."

Mercury paused for a second. Even though he wanted nothing more than to throw both middle fingers in the air and walk out, he smiled and stood.

"As you wish," Mercury replied. He buttoned his blazer and stepped up to the platform. The eyes of curious onlookers followed him as he walked to the point where Faegan had been standing. She looked him up and down before stepping down and strutting toward the cameraman.

"While we'd normally prefer people to wear the color of their element when performing this ceremony, I suppose what you're wearing will have to do," Oliana said, gesturing to his jacket.

He looked down, knowing that gold was a fitting color for an Air Hand, and knowing that if his jacket were any brighter, he'd look like a bottle of mustard.

Mercury glanced at his father, who sighed and nodded. He lifted his hands again, reciting the words he'd said not five minutes earlier. All the while, Briar panted heavily. As the light emanated from each of their hands, Mercury took a deep breath and recited the words required of an Air Hand. Words that would take away a witch's most precious asset.

"I am the guardian of air, one too strong to anchor. I am the guardian of breath, voice, creativity, and intellect." He held one hand up and one down, mirroring his father's stance. He tried not to gasp as he witnessed the light emanating from his hands.

Oliana stepped to her point directly in front of Briar.

"And I am the guardian of the soul, one too strong to diminish. I am the guardian of the beginning and the end, the alpha and omega." As soon as Oliana positioned her hands, the light that had emanated from each of them coalesced above Briar.

"We guardians call to the goddess Nephthys. What was once within, bring without," she chanted. "What was once within, bring without."

Each member of the Council added to the chant. Mercury fought the lump rising in his throat, fought the tears welling in his eyes.

"What was once within, bring without."

The light that had lingered above Briar surged toward him. As he threw his head back and screamed, it slithered down his throat. Every pore of his body emanated light. His eyes, mouth, and nostrils glowed. He writhed as they chanted, begging to the goddess for aid.

Suddenly, Briar collapsed forward, in a ragged child's pose, his head touching the floor. A yellow mist seeped out of his body and rose into the air. Oliana stepped toward the table and grabbed the glass jar that had sat upon it. She held it open and whispered a beckoning spell. The mist immediately moved toward the jar and settled within it. Seconds later, it hardened into a shiny, citrine stone.

After Oliana closed the lid and placed the jar back on the table, she nodded. Each of the Council members dropped their hands and stepped backwards.

"Let us test to see if the ceremony worked," she uttered.

"Oliana, you saw the mist like all the rest of us," Paloma stated. "You called Nephthys. She never fails."

Mercury's aunt narrowed her eyes at the Fire Hand and smiled. "There's no harm in being thorough."

Before anyone could see what she'd done, Oliana lifted the skirt of her dress and pulled a knife that had been nestled into her garter belt. She threw it at Briar just as he sat upon his haunches. He lifted his hands, as though he could stop the knife mid-air with his power but nothing happened. The knife stuck in his side, and again Briar yelped as blood seeped from his wound. Gasps filled the room.

"Why?" he whimpered. "Why?"

Oliana clasped her hands. She walked toward him and knelt to look him in the eye. "Because I can."

Briar crumbled to the floor. He heaved and sputtered, and the two witches who had ushered him into the room hustled onto the platform and began untying the knots.

Mercury's knees wobbled. He looked at his father, who looked straight ahead, his face expressionless but his jaw clenched. Paloma and Honore stood with their hands clasped. Honore's mouth was drawn into a thin line.

"Now then," Oliana said, her voice now jovial. "Who's ready for another cocktail?"

The crowd stared at her wide-eyed, eagerly awaiting her next move.

As his aunt stepped off the platform, a barrage of witches flocked toward her. They asked for pictures, asked about plans for Ilaris, and even asked if she planned on attending a few Pride celebrations the following week.

Mercury shook his head at it all, at how quickly they could compartmentalize his aunt's actions. He'd heard the gasps, had seen the horrified faces of the witches around him. Now, it was as though nothing had happened. She was back to being the sun, and they the planets that orbited her. For their part, the witches seemed to ignore the rest of the Council, who stepped off the platform and exited the room without hesitation. Even Faegan rushed out of the room without saying anything to her mother.

"Fuckin' vultures," Mercury said under his breath.

"Well, I guess I better get in line if I want to get a quote from the queen." Valeria gestured toward the cluster of people around Oliana.

"Good luck," he said.

She tilted her head and looked at him, a sly smile spreading across her face.

"What?" Mercury asked. He crossed his arms.

"Want to help a girl out?" she asked.

He narrowed his eyes. He knew what she wanted—if he walked over to the crowd, he could grab his aunt's attention better than she could. He could steal her attention for Valeria. But the last thing he wanted to do was talk to his aunt. She'd bullied him into helping the Council remove Briar's powers. She'd made his friends look like a joke in front of the whole room. And then, she'd stabbed a man when he was already down.

Mercury sighed. "I don't really feel up to talking to her right now."

Valeria groaned. "C'mon, Merc, please? I've got a story due soon, and I just need a quote from her about this."

"We're gonna go get another round," Ellis announced.

Mercury looked over to see his friends clustered together, trying hard not to look like they were listening to his conversation.

"Do you want to join?"

Mercury looked from Valeria to his friends.

Even though he didn't want to talk to his aunt, he didn't want to let Valeria down.

"I'll catch up to you," Mercury said.

Ellis nodded and the group walked out of the double doors toward the rest of the house. Mercury watched them off, hoping Joelle would turn around and steal a glance at him. When he realized she wouldn't, Mercury straightened his blazer. He held out a hand to help Valeria up.

"Thanks," she said, smiling.

Goddamn she's beautiful, he thought.

They sauntered over toward his aunt, the crowd of witches surrounding her seemingly doubled. Mercury stood silently, waiting to catch his aunt's eye. After several moments, she looked over at him and smiled. He nodded and returned the gesture. Just as he suspected, she turned her attention toward him.

"Thank you everyone for your kind words. If you would excuse me for a moment, I need to speak with my nephew, Mercury."

The witches stepped aside to let their Head of Council pass. They turned to look at Mercury, with many of them glaring at him, or sizing him up.

"Hello, Auntie," he uttered when she stepped in front of him.

"Mercury," she rejoiced. She wrapped her long arms around him and for a second, he found himself relaxing in her embrace. He thought about the long weekends he and Troian would spend with Oliana at her New York apartment. How she'd take them all around the city and let them stay up late. How she'd been the one to take them to their first concert to see Drake. Mercury let himself see into her mind. He saw her standing on the landing upstairs just before the ceremony began. She stood alone, her head bowed, breath escaping in hitches, and her hands shaking.

When he pulled back, he looked at his aunt with a slight scowl. Had she really been nervous?

She looked at him, her kohl-rimmed eyes warm and kind.

"You look very handsome tonight," she said. "Did you tie the tie yourself?"

"Thank you," he replied. "No, dad helped me."

His aunt gave him a knowing smile. "I remember you and your brother used to keep them tied so you never had to try to tie them yourselves."

Mercury chuckled at the memory.

"Yeah, those were the days," he replied. He noticed his voice was losing its edge. His anger toward her was dissipating.

"So, who's your friend?"

Mercury blinked, shaken out of his musings.

"This is Valeria LeFebre," he stated. "Valeria, this is my aunt Oliana Murtaza."

"It's so wonderful to meet you," she exclaimed.

"Likewise," Oliana replied.

"Valeria's a senior editor at *Jonquil*."

"Oh? That's right. I thought I recognized your name somewhere. Are you here on official business then?"

Valeria nodded. "I'd love to ask you a few questions about the ceremony. I'll make it quick, I promise."

Oliana chuckled. "Sure. Why don't you head to the bar and grab yourself another cocktail. I'll meet you out there, and we can adjourn to a quieter place."

Valeria nodded enthusiastically.

"That would be great. Thank you!" She squeezed Mercury's shoulder before walking away.

As he turned in Valeria's direction, his aunt looped her arm in his and stepped forward. She guided him through the crowd and out of the room.

"So, Mercury, how have you been?"

"I've been okay; it's been weird adjusting to . . . all the new changes."

"Yes, I can imagine. Losing a sibling is one of the hardest things a person can go through. In many ways they are the first friend you will ever make, and they often know you better than your parents."

He swallowed. "Does it ever get easier?"

"Honey, I think you already know the answer. Losing someone never gets easier. You just get used to it."

They walked outside to the patio, where a second bar sat to the right of the door. His aunt ordered a gin and tonic, and Mercury ordered another E&J.

"But, you fill your days with things to do and then you don't think about it as much."

Mercury sipped his drink as they walked away from the bar and down the steps to the lower patio, where tables and chairs had been set up. Lights were strung from the house to the edge of the property down the hill, giving the yard an ethereal quality.

"Yeah, I've been helping Dad with the shop more and now that I'm a full-time artist, I'm pretty swamped."

"I can imagine. Between that and your protests, you must not have a lot of down time," she replied. It was her turn to sip her drink, but she kept her eyes on him as she did so.

Her words sent a pang through his chest.

"I figured you'd seen the coverage," he said.

"Indeed, I have. I will say, I admire your tenacity. You've always been such an activist."

Mercury smiled tightly.

"Thank you," he replied.

She smiled at him, but it lacked all the warmth that had been there when she smiled at him before.

"Yeah, it's just a pity that your target is the wrong one this time."

"I disagree," he argued, his face now stern. "I don't think Kinheld is a good idea."

"Oh? And why is that?" she said.

To Mercury, it seemed as if she were simply trying to humor him. She crossed her arms and tilted her head, which made Mercury's stomach clench.

"I think we should be trying to dismantle this system and fight for equality for everyone here, instead of sequestering ourselves. I think there's not nearly enough space in this country for a place like Kinheld to be built without displacing the people that are already there."

"Hmm." She shrugged her shoulders. "It's a good thing, then, that I don't need your opinion."

Mercury's grip tightened around his glass.

"Yeah. You don't. But I also don't need your permission to protest."

His aunt took a long draw from her glass. "You're right. You don't. But may I offer you a warning?"

Mercury's heart skipped. "Warning?"

"Yes. Your lil' protests have drawn a lot of attention to the Witches' Council, and not all of it has been good. I know you mean well, but just think about what could happen if the Council is put under such a microscope."

"I'm not—"

"Think, really hard, Mercury, about the things the Council has done for its members and non-members alike, all the money spent, all the things covered up." Again, her eyes remained fixed on his as she sipped her cocktail.

Mercury scowled. Before he could respond, she patted him on the arm and started up the steps. She stopped halfway then turned toward him.

"Just some food for thought, nephew. Enjoy your evening."

Mercury waited for a few seconds before following her up the stairs and into the Council House. He searched for his friends, and hoped that when he saw them he didn't look as rattled as he felt.

CHAPTER 6

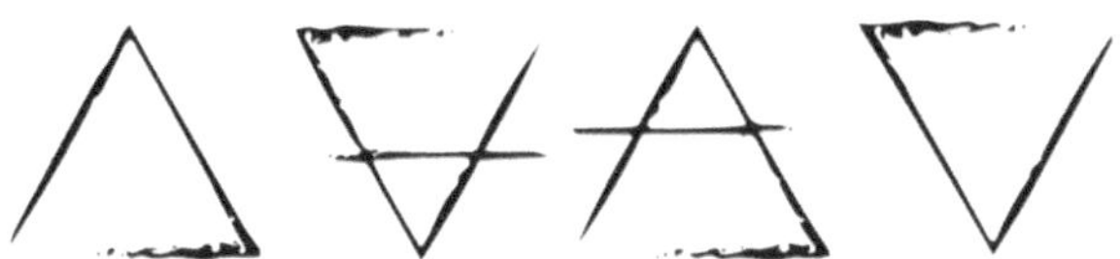

THE NEXT DAY PASSED BY IN A WHIRLWIND. AN INFLUX OF CUSTOMERS came into the Iron Bird, some off the street and some coming from the buzz of Mercury's viral videos. By the end of the day, he'd taken so many photos and spoken to even more people about the movement that his voice was hoarse. His brain was tired, both from the activity of the day and from mulling over what his aunt's warning was all about.

Was she threatening him? Trying to stop him from leading the protests? Or did she want him to stop speaking ill of her while he led them? He thought about talking to his father about it, but when they closed the shop, Mercury could tell that he, too, was exhausted.

Mercury needed a night out, something fun that had nothing to do with magic. Something where he could just be himself.

"Hey, Jo," he texted. Twenty minutes later, his phone buzzed. She responded with a smile emoji.

"Are you free for dinner tonight? I'd like to take you out on an official date, just us. Nothing to do with magic, I promise," he wrote.

He waited with bated breath as he watched the dots moving along the screen while she typed. They started and stopped. Mercury inhaled and waited for the dots to appear. Five minutes later, she started typing again. And a minute after that, her message appeared.

"Sure, but can we make it early? I have a paper to turn in," the text read.

Mercury sighed. He wanted to plan a whole evening for them—dinner by the ocean, a movie, a late-night walk along the beach. He tried to hide his disappointment when he responded and was thankful they were texting and not talking on the phone.

"Yeah, I can make that happen. How about six?"

She responded immediately, a quick "awesome" accompanied by another smile emoji. He told her he was looking forward to their date and she simply responded with "same."

When the bell over the door chimed, Mercury groaned. He looked up and was relieved to see it was only Paloma.

"Hi, Paloma. How are you?" he asked.

"I'm doing well. Your father's hopefully going to finish my half sleeve today. Then maybe after we'll go for dinner." She leaned in and hugged Mercury, and he took in her scent of hibiscus and coconut. Her long dark hair hung loose around her face. She turned toward Mercury's father and planted a kiss on his check.

Mercury's father smiled wryly at her before walking to the hand washing station.

"That's dope," he said. He pulled off his gloves and tossed them in the trash. He stood and stretched, hating the way he started slumping in his chair when he worked.

"How are you?"

"Mercury's got a date tonight," Atlas said. With his hands freshly washed, he walked over and sat on his stool beside Paloma. He turned toward his vanity and slid his hands into a fresh pair of gloves before laying out the colors for her phoenix tattoo.

"Oh? With Joleen?"

"Joelle," Mercury corrected.

"What do you have planned?"

"We're just having an early dinner. She's got a paper due."

Paloma and his father exchanged looks; Mercury didn't need to be a mind reader to know what they were thinking.

"We'll have a much longer date soon; she's just busy with school right now," he added.

"I have no doubt you'll sweep her off her feet, no matter if you're only having dinner or if you do something extravagant. Why don't you start getting ready, son," his father said.

Mercury nodded, not needing another reason to leave his father and his part-time lover alone.

He walked upstairs and pulled a pair of black jeans out of his closet. Going for a more relaxed look, he chose a pink button-up shirt with mini roses on it and black shorts, matching them with a pair of black Chuck Taylors. He'd cut his hair the night before, trimming the sides and leaving the top longer so that the coils sprung up toward the sky. He sprayed on cologne and grabbed his gold watch before leaving the apartment.

They planned to meet at the restaurant in the interest of time, another decision that made Mercury bristle. He'd wanted to pick her up, had asked his father to borrow his car, but she turned him down.

"The restaurant is closer to my dorm anyway," she said.

He took an Uber instead. *So much for some extra alone time.*

Wiping his sweaty palms on his shorts, he stepped out of the car in front of a Japanese restaurant in Westwood. Joelle stood outside, her sunglasses drawn and her fingers moving furiously over her phone. She wore jean shorts, a graphic t-shirt with the Wu-Tang "W" on the front, and black Reeboks. Her hair was wrapped up into a red scarf, leaving the ends to cascade down the side of her face.

"Hey," he said.

She looked up at him and lifted a brow.

"You look great," she complimented.

"Thanks. I'm a bit overdressed." He looked down at his clothes.

"No, no. I'm underdressed. I didn't realize we were doing . . . that." She smiled weakly.

Mercury gestured for her to walk ahead, his attempt to hide the disappointment on his face. When they reached the door, he motioned to pull it open, but she beat him to it.

"Oh, I'm sorry. I didn't know you were—"

"No, that's okay. Let's just—"

They nearly walked into each other.

Get it together, Mercury chided himself as he followed her to the hostess stand.

Joelle asked for a table for two, and the host led them to a corner booth, dimly lit and romantic. They slid into the booth across from each other and after the host dropped the menus, they looked at each other.

"So, uh, how was your day?" he asked.

"Fine," she said. "Just working on a paper, like I said."

"What class is it for?"

"History," she replied. "It's one of my reqs."

Mercury nodded. He always hated taking non-major related classes. He'd already learned spelling, grammar, and algebra. He knew the table of elements and all about World War II. Wasn't the reason a person went to college to get a more specialized education?

"What's the topic of the paper?" he asked.

She shrugged. Their waiter walked over and brought them water.

"What can I get you to drink?" he asked.

"Do you want to split a bottle of wine?" Mercury asked.

She shook her head. "Just a Coke Zero for me, thanks."

Mercury nodded. "I'll have the same."

The waiter walked away, leaving Mercury to glance about the restaurant awkwardly as Joelle turned her attention to the menu.

"So, what's your paper about?" he asked, bringing her attention back to their conversation.

"The lack of intersectionality in the first and second wave feminist movements," she replied.

Mercury nodded.

"That's a good topic. Heavy, though," he said.

She shrugged again. "It's something that's important to me."

Her words pierced his chest. *Unlike me.*

He waited a few seconds before speaking, praying she'd fill the silence. "Well, it was a busy day at the shop today."

"Oh?" She looked up at him over the menu.

"Yeah. Had a lot of customers come in, a few of them drawn in by the video of my speech."

Her brows quirked upward but she remained silent.

"One guy came in for a full-back tattoo. Those take more than one session, but thankfully he didn't have an attitude about it."

"I didn't realize tattoos had to be done in multiple sessions." Joelle set the menu down and steepled her hands.

"Not all of them. Just ones that are big or require a lot of color. My dad is finishing up Paloma's sleeve right now."

"Paloma, she's the one on the Council, right?" She nodded at the waiter as he set their cups down.

"Yeah. She's getting a whole phoenix motif."

"Cool. I don't think I could ever get a tattoo." She looked down at her wrists and smirked. "Well, another tattoo."

Mercury laughed. *Finally, this doesn't feel awkward*, he thought.

"I'm the son of a tattoo parlor owner. It's like a birthright for me," he said.

She laughed. "How many do you have?"

"Seven," he said. "There's the one Dad gave me at Astera, two on my back, this one on the inside of my arm, two on my left leg and one on my right."

"Wow, I didn't realize you had so many."

Mercury smiled. He wanted to be flirtatious and say, "well, if you play your cards right, you might get to see them all someday," but he knew better. He could tell by the way Joelle looked at him, and the casual outfit she wore, that she wasn't on the same page.

Maybe she will be soon, he thought.

"What are you thinking of ordering?" he asked.

She shrugged. "I'm not sure. I've only recently started eating sushi, things like California rolls and stuff. I've never eaten here. What's good?"

"Well, I like the tempura shrimp roll if you're looking for something cooked. If you're open to raw fish, then I'd go with salmon or red snapper nigiri. Those are my go-tos."

She scrunched her nose.

When the waiter strolled over, Joelle ordered miso soup and a California roll.

Mercury wrinkled his nose at her order and turned toward the waiter. He asked for the nigiri rolls, a combo plate of tempura, and extra ginger. The waiter nodded and took their menus.

For a moment, they sat looking around the restaurant. When their eyes met, they smiled but neither one of them spoke.

Ask me something, he thought as she picked up her phone and tapped the screen briefly. He hated feeling as though he were carrying the conversation.

"Are you looking forward to this weekend's protests?" she asked.

Finally, he thought.

"Yeah," he said, his voice almost too excited. "I think this movement could really make a difference."

His aunt's warning rushed back to him suddenly, and for a moment, he ruminated over what she could have meant.

"Yeah, I hope so, too," she said, smiling at him.

Mercury returned the gesture, knocked out of his reverie. He didn't know what else to say.

I guess I spoke too soon. Why is this so awkward? He thought. Why does it feel like every conversation goes nowhere?

"So, what did you think of the ceremony last night?" he asked.

She groaned.

"Not you groaning about it," Mercury laughed.

She lifted a shoulder.

"I didn't mean it like that, just that it was . . . overwhelming. And sad."

Mercury's eyes softened. "Yeah, that's how it felt for me, too."

The waiter set their food down before them just as Joelle began to respond. He smiled politely then asked if they needed anything else. As his eyes bounced from Mercury to Joelle, they both offered him a generic "no thank you" without making eye contact. The waiter nodded then wandered off to another table.

"Do you want to try some of this?" he asked, pointing at the salmon nigiri with his chopsticks. She shook her head, a quick grimace passing across her face.

Damn, is it me? he wondered.

Amid the murmurs in the restaurant, they ate in silence. Each time Mercury tried to ask Joelle something, she responded but didn't ask him a follow-up question. By the end of the night, his heart was beating rapidly and his palms were sweaty, not to mention his stomach being in knots. When he paid for dinner, she thanked him while tapping on her phone.

Mercury pulled out his own device. "So, it's seven fifteen. Do you want to go grab dessert or walk by the beach?"

Joelle tilted her head slightly and shook it. "I'm sorry, Mercury; I can't. I've got a paper due."

"Okay, well, do you want to get together tomorrow or later in the week? We can see a movie, maybe grab burgers or something," he suggested.

A pained look spread across her face.

"I'll still be busy with school shit," she said. "But I'll be there on Saturday for the protest."

Mercury leaned back and nodded. "Yeah, totally. I'm looking forward to it."

They slid out of the booth and walked into the night. As Mercury fantasized about what the night could've been, Joelle called herself an Uber and within minutes, it arrived. She gave Mercury a quick hug before sliding into the car.

Deflated, he sighed and waited for his Uber after watching hers zoom off down the street. He pulled out his phone and texted Sloane to pass the time.

"Just had a date with Jo."

Seconds later, she responded with a GIF of the dinner scene from *Lady and the Tramp.* She added a question mark, and Mercury responded with a quick "no." She replied with a sad face emoji and asked if he wanted to meet up somewhere to talk about it.

"Nah. I'm just gonna head home and binge watch YouTube," he typed.

She sent a sad face emoji.

"Tell me what happened."

As the Uber driver sped onto the highway, Mercury recounted the date to Sloane, mentioning their difference in dress and the way that Joelle didn't seem to want to get together again.

"I don't know. I thought all the signs were there," he said.

"I did, too. Maybe she's just busy with school?"

"Maybe. I'll give it another try maybe next week."

"Good plan! Maybe a daytime thing?"

He responded with the one hundred percent emoji and slipped his phone into his pocket. He wiped his face and sighed, wishing he could be anywhere else.

CHAPTER 7

RELISHING THE BEAUTY OF THE MORNING SKY, MERCURY DUG HIS HANDS into the pockets of his new jean jacket. Though he missed his old one, this new one was growing on him. He'd gotten it from a thrift store. It was worn and molded to his body straight away. The acid wash of it and the stripes on his shoulder made him feel ready for battle.

He stood in the parking lot on Rose Avenue waiting for the rest of the protestors to arrive. He'd been early and spent a great deal of time with his thoughts.

He hadn't heard anything from Joelle since their date. She'd been absent in their group chat and wasn't as active on Instagram. Though he knew she was swamped because of finals, he couldn't help but think she was avoiding him.

Then there was the business of his aunt. Her snarky comments had played on a loop in his mind.

What had she meant? He thought. And more importantly, what would she do if she felt he wasn't heeding her warning?

Valeria and Sloane arrived together shortly after eleven, giddy as a pair of school girls, both wearing sweaters with the *Jonquil* logo.

"Didn't realize you'd be on your press gig today," Mercury said as Sloane wrapped her arms around him.

"The news never sleeps, bruh." She smiled and sat on the hood of the car. She took a joint from her hoodie and sparked it up then passed it to Valeria.

"Good morning, Merc," Valeria said cheerily. Her honey-colored braids were now pink, and the color made her skin look even more gold in the sunlight.

"Hey," he responded. Butterflies fluttered in his stomach as she smiled at him. He smiled back, hoping it didn't look too wide or too eager. She passed the joint to him and he took it, taking a long, smooth puff before passing it to Sloane.

"How many people are you expecting?" Sloane asked.

"Hundred or so," he replied. "The hashtag's been trending all week and more people have retweeted my last tweet than ever."

"Come on, viral tweet!" Valeria exclaimed, snapping her fingers.

Mercury chuckled. As they discussed the logistics of the protest, how they'd walk down Ocean Avenue and take a left on Colorado Street onto the Pier, his heart began pounding faster. Would this protest be as peaceful as it was last time? Would he be able to lead the crowd and gas them up like before? He thought about protests of the past, and what it took to lead them. Though everyone around him told him he had what it took, though they believed in him, though he was going viral, he was still so unsure about his ability to lead a movement of this size.

You can do this, Merc. You've got this, he thought.

He smiled as a car full of protestors pulled into the spot beside him. Five witches emerged from the Kia Soul, each one wearing a shirt that read "Reformations not restoration."

Sloane clicked her tongue. "Whoa, there's merch now? How come you didn't tell me? I would be hocking that shit up and down this walk in my cut offs with my titties out."

Mercury shook his head.

"When would I have had time to make that merch, though?" He turned toward the witches. "Hey, where did you get the tees?"

One of the women hopped out and smiled at him, her blond hair reminiscent of Bridget Bardot. She reached back into the car and handed him one.

"We made them. I hope that's okay?" she asked.

Mercury balked when he realized she was asking him if it was okay that they used his words, the words of the movement he started, on a t-shirt.

"Uh, yeah. Yes, I mean. These are dope," he replied. "Got any more?"

The blonde woman smiled and handed him a handful.

"We made enough for the whole Astera Army." She glanced at Valeria, and after not recognizing her, reached back into the car for another one. "Here's one for your friend as well."

Astera Army? Mercury was dumbfounded. He looked at Sloane, who simply puffed on her joint and lifted a brow.

"Thank you. See you out there," he said.

The group said their goodbyes and headed toward the ocean walk, their pale, skinny arms linked together.

"Astera Army? Oh, that's for sure going in my piece," Valeria said, giggling.

"No the fuck it isn't," Mercury replied.

"That's the geekiest shit," Sloane said. "But these shirts are good quality, so."

She shrugged off her sweatshirt and tied it around her waist. Quickly, she pulled off her tank top and replaced it with the shirt. She scanned the parking lot for any onlookers who might have gotten a sneak peek.

Mercury sighed as he looked down at the shirt. Though he liked the idea of it, he didn't want to wear matching shirts with the group. Instead, he opened his car door and tossed the shirts onto his back seat. When he stood back up, Valeria had changed into the shirt, too, and they both looked at him with raised brows.

"What? I'm comfortable," he fibbed.

Sloane and Valeria traded knowing looks. "Sure, you are," they replied simultaneously.

Twenty minutes later, Joelle and Griffin pulled into the lot, both wearing shades and their hair tied into high buns atop their heads. Joelle opened the backpack she carried, showing off the water bottles within.

"Good looking out," Mercury replied.

"Thank you," she said, not meeting his gaze.

"How's it going?" Mercury asked.

"Oh, you know. We're living the dream," Griffin responded. He pulled his vintage, red cat eye sunglasses off and slipped them into the front pocket of his utility jacket. "Joelle's on edge about finals, and she's mad at me for dropping out."

"You act like it's a good thing to drop out of college," she said before making eye contact with Mercury.

"Sorry."

Mercury held a hand up, waving away her concerns.

"Anyway, we've both been busy. Hey, girl," Joelle said, turning her attention to Sloane. They hugged and Joelle slid next to her atop the car, accepting the joint from Sloane's fingers.

"What's good, twins," Valeria said.

Griffin smiled and hugged her, while Joelle waved and kept her distance.

"Where's Ellis?" Griffin asked, looking from Sloane to Mercury.

"He had to work this AM and said he'd be late," Sloane said.

Mercury nodded.

He looked at his phone and checked the time. It was almost noon. Almost time to start.

"Oh, uh, here are some shirts for you." Mercury opened his car door and grabbed three shirts from the back seat. He handed one to Griffin and one to Joelle. He handed the one for Ellis to Sloane, who rolled her eyes but stood and slid the shirt into the back pocket of her jeans.

"Let's get out there," he said.

His friends nodded and strolled toward the ocean walk, where more people had gathered. Many of them held signs at their side and spoke in clustered groups. When Mercury walked over, several of them looked up at him, excitement and passion in their eyes.

"You good?" Sloane asked.

Mercury nodded. "Yeah, just a little tired. I wish I would have brought some coffee."

Griffin shrugged his backpack off and pulled a cold brew latte out and handed it to him.

"You're a real one," Mercury said, taking the can from him. It was so cold that it made his fingers tingle.

"I made sure we brought provisions for the group. Can't lead a movement if you're dehydrated."

Mercury chuckled.

"I even brought something for you, Val," Griffin said.

"Thanks, bruh. And by group you mean the 'Astera Army?'" Valeria said.

Griffin recoiled. "Uh-huh. Who decided on that nickname because I would like a word?"

Sloane chuckled. She leaned in, lowering her voice conspiratorially. "A couple of Beckys."

Mercury snickered. The woman who made the shirts looked up and smiled at him. Mercury returned the gesture, feeling only slightly guilty that he'd laughed at the joke. He looked back at his friends, who gazed at him with kind but expectant smiles. Mercury breathed in then out and proceeded to walk.

He could feel the group's excitement rising as he put one foot before the other, as he led the way in calling for equal treatment under human and magical laws alike. He nearly lost his footing once he heard their steps in sync with his but he recovered swiftly. His mind drifted to the civil rights protests of the past, wondering how many witches marched alongside great leaders like Dr. Martin Luther King, Jr. afraid to be both Black and magical in America.

A few minutes into their trek, Sloane gestured toward the bullhorn.

Mercury glanced down at the contraption in his hands.

This movement is my legacy, he thought. He put it to his mouth and began to speak. "Separate isn't equal."

"Separate isn't equal," the crowd responded. They chanted the words several times before Mercury changed it up.

"Reformation not restoration."

"Reformation not restoration," the crowd called. After a few rotations, the chant began picking up a beat of its own.

Ref-or-mation not res-toration. Ref-or-mation not res-toration.

Mercury found himself timing his footfalls to the beat.

Sloane and Valeria began dancing to the sound, and Mercury felt the way he'd felt at the beginning of the last protest, when the sound of the crowd and the footsteps and the waves moved inside him.

I can do this, he thought. *Everything's going to work out.*

Everything is going to work out.

Everything—

Icy cold pain shot down his arm. Suddenly, his whole left side was wet. He looked down at the ground where a Big Gulp full of ice and soda lay crushed on the ground.

Mercury looked toward the beach, where a group of vampires stood. The men wore tight swim trunks decorated with the American flag. The women wore string bikinis, barely covering their severely toned bodies. They were laughing and pointing at Mercury and the damage the soda had done to the sleeve of his jean jacket. The women leaned in toward each other and spoke Portuguese. Mercury didn't know much, but he recognized the word "bruxa."

Bruxa. *Witch.*

"What the fuck, butterfingers?" Griffin said.

Mercury hit a double take, surprised by his friend stepping forward. Several witches shouted at the group, who stood and laughed.

"Oops," one of the women said, covering her mouth. The other one began to laugh.

"What the fuck?" several other people shouted.

Someone whipped out their phone and began recording.

"Wow, you see this? These clowns threw their drink at us just for protesting."

"Yeah, these stupid leeches must really want some attention," someone else said.

"Of course, they do. That's why they're wearing those ugly ass swim trunks."

The comment sparked the man in the American swim trunks' attention. The group turned toward the person filming the video.

"Ugly little witch," one of the men barked.

Mercury could feel the tension rising. Despite the numbness in his arm, he had to keep them walking. He had to keep it peaceful.

"C'mon. They're not worth it. Put the phone down."

"But Mercury—"

"Listen to your friend, feio," one of the men shouted.

Mercury sighed. "These clowns just want to go viral. I'm not gonna help them do that, and neither should you. They won't even be a footnote in this movement." He made eye contact with the group before turning and walking away.

His stomach churned as he pushed on. He had to build up the momentum again.

"What are we?"

"Witches," the crowd responded.

"What are we?"

"Witches!"

"Represent!" he said, calling on the group to shout out their element, the source of their magic. "Earth!"

"Earth!"

"Fire!"

"Fire!"

"Water!"

"Water!"

"Air!"

"Air!"

The crowd chanted their elements together, the sound a cacophony as they swarmed the Ocean Avenue walkway. Clouds had settled in, and Mercury tried not to take it as an omen. But as more people walked around them, shouting obscenities, calling them evil and telling them to burn in hell, Mercury couldn't help the foreboding he felt.

"Vael should just lock you all in cages," a woman shouted from atop a yellow beach towel. Mercury could hear people shouting back at her, and when she tried to stand, she was knocked down.

Stop doing that, he thought, wishing he could urge the crowd around him to be more discerning, to not use their magic unless they had to.

"What do we want?" Mercury called.

"Equality," the crowd answered as they turned left on Colorado Avenue.

"What do we want?"

"Equality!"

The pier was crowded. Mercury could see people milling around, holding fried food and cotton candy. As they inched closer, he noticed people turning to look at them, stopping their shopping or game playing. He led the group onto the pier, chanting all the way.

"Represent!" he called again.

The group called their elements as they all stepped onto the pier. The crowds that were already there began turning their attention to the group. Some of them nodded and whooped in solidarity. Others scowled and turned their attention back to their phones. Others turned fully toward the protestors, each wearing similar looks of indignation.

"They are casting a spell on us," someone said.

"They're gonna kill us," another person echoed.

"Stop them!"

Mercury felt a pair of hands grab his right arm. "Let go of me," Mercury shouted, his voice almost a growl.

He turned toward the man and shrugged out of his clammy grasp, only to be grabbed by someone else. More people walked toward them, trying to form a barricade to prevent the group from continuing down the pier.

"You can't block us. We've got a permit to protest here," Joelle yelled.

"Let me see your permit," called a woman wearing an unfortunate bob and powder-blue cargo capris. The people who had gathered behind her nodded and shouted in agreement.

"We don't have to show you anything," Griffin replied. "Move out of the way."

"No, you need to show us your permit," the woman demanded.

"Are you the police?" Valeria questioned.

"You need to show us your permit!" the woman shrieked. "I bet you don't have it and you're just coming onto the pier to cast death spells on us all."

Mercury could feel the crowd's collective hysteria, which only added to his own.

"We have every right to be here, ma'am. We're Americans and we have a right to peacefully protest," Mercury said.

"It's not peaceful! You're casting spells!"

Suddenly, the shouts grew louder. Mercury looked around him to see that the group opposing their protest had grown larger, and now surrounded them in a semi-circle. Bodies clustered around him and he began sweating under his jean jacket, wishing he'd changed his shirt.

He could hear his heart pounding in his ears. He had to diffuse this before it escalated, but how? He looked at Sloane, who was swatting away a short Asian woman with copper hair.

"You're all here to destroy us! Look at her; her shirt even says 'Astera Army,'" the woman said hysterically.

"It's just handmade merch, you dumb bitch," Sloane yelled.

"I don't believe you! You need to leave," the woman shouted.

"Lady, we've got every right to be here; please just get out of the way," Mercury pleaded.

The voices rose in a cacophony. Mercury tried to wiggle out of the space, but each time he stepped toward them, the semi-circle of counter protestors only drew in closer.

They moved closer and closer until a scream rang through the air, piercing through the rising tension.

Mercury shrugged out of a man's arms and ran toward the sound at the back of the pier. Two men were fighting. Mercury tried to pull them apart, but he jumped back amid the flurry of fists and kicks. Someone shouted for the men to stop.

"Keith, stop!" yelled a voice in the crowd.

Mercury and another witch from the protest again tried to pull the men apart. Just as they were about to seize an opening, one of the men grabbed the other and sunk his fangs into his neck.

The man's scream echoed throughout the pier. More people stopped and an even bigger crowd had gathered. Mercury wanted to tell the people who had not five minutes ago been yelling that witches were evil and capable of killing to look at what vampires were capable of.

The man being bitten dug his fingers into the vampire's arms, trying desperately to peel him off. But it was no use. The vampire's grip on the man appeared to be ironclad. The vampire stared at the crowd of protestors. When he made eye contact with Mercury, he could see that his pupils were dilated so wide that his eyes were almost all black.

Shark's eyes, Mercury thought.

Mercury gestured toward the vampire, trying to force him back with his magic. It wasn't enough to break its hold.

"Misputwa," Mercury yelled as he gestured again, sending a bolt of electricity along with his telekinetic push. The vampire yelped as it was forced back.

Mercury dove forward to catch the man the vampire had been feeding on. Blood spurted from his wound as his eyes rolled back in his head. Mercury tore a strip from his t-shirt and wrapped it around the man's neck.

"Where's a healer?" Mercury called, turning toward the crowd of protestors that surrounded him. No one moved. "Stop gawking and help me!"

"Shove over," Ellis commanded. He dropped to his knees and wrapped his hands around the man's neck, seemingly unfazed by the blood on his hands. Seconds later, the blood stopped flowing from the wound. When Ellis moved his hands away, the bite was gone, but the man's neck was still slick with blood.

"Thank you," he whispered. They helped him stand and he looked back toward the vampire, who'd wandered down the boardwalk and had approached another group of people.

"Blessed be," Mercury replied. The man trotted off the pier, rubbing his neck. Mercury turned toward Ellis.

"You know, you could have taken your apron off," he said as he fist bumped Ellis.

"I wanted to show that I'm a man of the people. Besides, it's a good thing I kept it on."

Ellis held his hands out, and Mercury winced at the sight of all the blood. Ellis wiped his hands on his apron, leaving red streaks on the tan fabric.

"Anyone got hand sanitizer?" he asked.

Sloane, Griffin, Joelle, and Valeria had fought their way back to Mercury. Sloane drew Ellis into a tight embrace when she reached him.

"Good to see you, Ellis," Valeria said.

Now with one arm wrapped around Sloane, Ellis smiled in response and asked again for hand sanitizer.

"We ready to get this back on track?" Mercury asked his friends, who nodded emphatically. But then their heads turned quickly, searching for the commotion they heard, another fight breaking out in another part of the crowd.

This time, a man and a woman squabbled. This time, there was no vampire, only a human and a witch, who fought back with magic. Shards of ice surrounded the woman who now wailed for help. She tugged at the icy cage but it wouldn't budge. Several protestors held up their phones and recorded the woman's frantic pleas.

"What were you saying about putting us in cages, bitch?" Sloane giggled as she circled the group.

"Let me out of here! I didn't do anything to you," cried the woman.

"Bullshit, lady. You pushed me then pulled my hair!" the witch replied.

"You all attacked me first!" she yelled, noticing that their fight had caused a scene. "You hear me? You attacked me!"

"Just let her go," Mercury urged. A chorus of boos emerged from the crowd behind him.

"It's what she deserves," another witch stated.

"She deserves worse," Sloane chimed in.

Griffin shouted in agreement.

Mercury sighed. How could he get them to see that this type of violence would only play into the hands of the people calling for their damnation? They were better than this; he had to show them.

"Yeah, I know she does," he began. "But there's no point in people like her getting the attention they crave."

"Mercury—"

"C'mon," he said. The witch rolled his eyes then made a circular motion with his hand. The ice melted all at once, splashing the woman. She screamed and patted her body as though she would find something missing. The pier security guard rushed toward them, his short shorts and oversized windbreaker making him look like a toddler.

"What seems to be the problem?" he asked. His voice was high pitched, and his brow was so furrowed that Mercury wondered if it would get stuck that way. Before Mercury could respond, the woman spoke.

"These witches attacked me!" she screamed, her voice hysterical. Suddenly, she was crying, drawing more attention from the already large crowd.

"You should know better than to trust a middle-aged white woman with a bob," Sloane whispered.

"Yes, I was just standing there and they started pushing at me and saying spells," the woman cried.

Rage simmered inside Mercury's belly. He glared at the woman with narrowed eyes, his fists clenched and lips pursed.

"They approached us first, sir. Just as we walked onto the pier," he interjected.

"So is she right? Did you use any magic?" the guard asked.

Mercury turned toward the witch who used his magic against the woman. He crossed his arms and stood stoically, staring him down until he finally spoke.

"I did, sir," the witch admitted.

The security guard sighed. He looked as if calling this in was the last thing he wanted to do, but still he pulled out his phone and dialed the police. He walked over to the woman and tried to calm her.

As most of the crowd kept their attention on her, Mercury walked over and slid an arm around the witch's shoulder. Mercury could feel him tense up under his touch.

"Do you know that what you did could have completely fucked us?" Mercury whispered into his ear. He surfed the witch's memory, trying to figure out the extent of his powers.

The witch nodded.

"You're a Water Hand, but I know you're really good at persuasion spells," Mercury revealed. The witch stared at him wide-eyed, as if he didn't know that seeing people's memories was one of Mercury's primary powers.

"So what you're going to do is, you're going to tell that security guard, that woman, and the police that only you accosted her. You're going to say that you came with the protestors and that you were defending yourself against their attack but that you did use magic."

The witch hesitated as he watched the crowd. "Okay," he finally relented. Mercury dropped his arm from the witch's shoulder just as the security guard walked back toward them.

"Oh, and one more thing," Mercury added. The witch's pale cheeks turned beet red. "I better not see you at a protest again, you got me? If I do, it's on sight."

Mercury didn't wait for the witch to respond. He turned back toward his friends and began plotting their next move.

CHAPTER 8

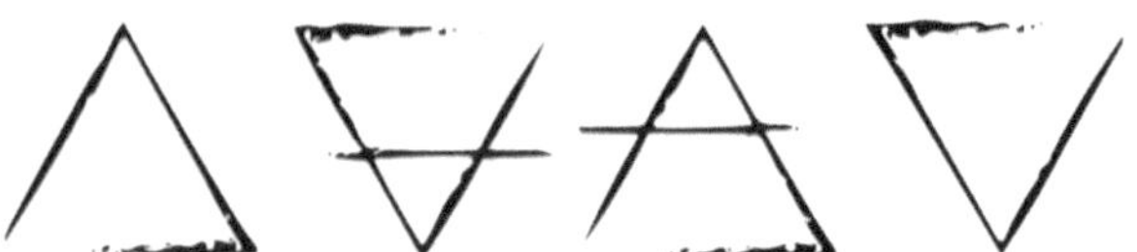

A far cry from the exquisiteness of the Council House, the Witches' Council office was a mid-century modern building across from MacArthur Park. White ramps sprung from the top of the circular building and connected to the concrete; tinted windows stretching from floor to ceiling lined its exterior. To Mercury, it resembled what the architects of the 1960s thought the future would be like. It was gauche, and Mercury knew it was only a matter of time before his aunt would have it rebuilt.

As a kid, Mercury enjoyed visiting the building. It looked like an alien spacecraft on the outside, and the inside housed photos and paintings of the Council and big Witchkind events like Astera. He liked seeing all that history lining the walls, liked looking out over Los Angeles while inside his father's office. At one point in his life, he even dreamed about the possibility of one day having an office of his own. Now, though, all he wanted to do was tear it down.

Though the weather was overcast, the heat was just as oppressive as the day before. Small pools of sweat discolored Mercury's gray t-shirt. Though he tried to hide the growing stains at his armpits, the witch with the Bridget Bardot hair—whose name was, in fact, Bridget—asked if he wanted another "Astera Army" shirt.

At first, he shook his head, but then he looked down at his shirt and noticed the sweat beginning to accumulate along the front of the V-neck.

"Okay, yeah," Mercury conceded. His cheeks were warm as he grabbed the canary yellow shirt with the vintage lettering and changed out of his current shirt. "Thank you."

"No problem, Merc!" Bridget said before drifting back toward her friends.

He looked up to see Joelle and Sloane standing with their phones out, each of them poised to take a picture of him in the shirt.

"C'mon, strike a pose!" Sloane cheered him on.

Mercury pursed his lips. He shook his head and turned toward the park. He heard the camera snap behind him. *Weirdos*, he thought.

MacArthur Park had been a staple of Los Angeles culture since the late 19th century. Trees and bushes and flora lined the edges of the park, and a large lake sat in the middle. Not too long ago, this area was considered a rough part of town, where drug dealing was one of its primary enterprises. When drugs were legalized, MacArthur Park became one of the first areas in the city to offer magic-laced narcotics. This export had once landed thousands of Black and Latinx Angelinos in jail but now that it was legal, it was directly responsible for the gentrification of the neighborhood.

Mercury surveyed the area in disgust of the homogeneity of the newer buildings with their squared-off roofs and corny attempts at edginess. A vegan soul food restaurant featured images from Pulp Fiction on the exterior. A boutique thrift store called Uptown Cheapskate sold clothes that once belonged to MacArthur Park originals at such a high markup that no one in the neighborhood who lived there prior to 2019 could afford.

The Council building had been relocated to this area when the rent was cheap and the area was nondescript. It had been cool then, but now it stuck out like a sore thumb among the new, soulless architecture. Across the park from the Council building stood a drugstore called Para Ben's, some hipster's attempt at humor. It sold everything humans, witches, and vampires needed for a high—from regular grade cocaine to magic-laced brownies to something called Spider-silk, a drug that looked as puffy and inviting as cotton candy that was supposed to give the user extrasensory abilities for a short period of time.

Squinting to shield his eyes from the beaming sunlight, Mercury glanced at his phone. One twenty-three.

Though he wasn't a stickler for time, Mercury was always anxious when it was near call time and the crowd looked thin. He hoped more protestors would arrive as they inched closer to 1:30.

Maybe they heard about what happened yesterday? He thought. A few people had posted videos of the events on the pier across social media, and Mercury wasn't pleased with the reactions. Many people believed that the witches had antagonized both the vampire and the humans on the pier into fighting them. He hoped today would be a better day and that no one acted foolish. *The last thing we need*, he thought, *is another run-in with the police.*

"Are we starting soon?" Joelle asked. She'd been glancing anxiously at her watch for the better part of fifteen minutes. "I've got finals to study for."

Mercury smiled, tight-lipped, attempting to suppress his annoyance. He knew school was important to her, but wasn't this as well? He hated that it seemed as if she were never fully present, always thinking of something else she had to do.

"Yeah, we can start," he said. He grabbed his bullhorn from his backpack and switched it on. He held it to his lips and made a "brrrrrr" sound, rolling his Rs and trying to get the crowd's attention.

"Y'all ready to get this party started?" he shouted. The crowd, which had grown in the last few minutes, clapped and cheered.

"We're here today to give the Witches' Council a piece of our mind. We're here because their bullshit treaty with Vael is nothing more than a smokescreen, something that will prevent Oliana from doing her job which is?"

"To support, uplift, and guide the witch population across the globe," the crowd began, quoting the Witches' Council Statement of

Purpose. "To uphold laws both magical and human and to serve as examples of how to conduct oneself in the world beyond magic."

Mercury clapped at the crowd's recitations. It was a statement that he was all too familiar with, as the child of two Council members.

"That's right. Do we think the Council is honoring their Statement of Purpose?"

"Hell no!"

"I said, do we think the Council is honoring their Statement of Purpose?"

"Hell no!"

"What do we want?"

"Reformation not restoration!"

"Is Kinheld reformation?"

"Hell no!"

"Is Kinheld reformation?"

"Hell no!"

"What do we want?"

"Reformation!"

As the crowd chanted, Mercury inhaled deeply. He could feel their energy rolling over him. He looked around him at the signs thrust high in the air. He noticed the faces of witches from all walks of life, all united for this common purpose.

"Why don't you want a place like Kinheld?"

Mercury turned to see two women standing at the edge of the crowd. They were dressed like extras in an early season of Friends, all baggy overalls and square, striped tops. The blonde one wore small, square-shaped tinted sunglasses, her orange backwards ball cap making her look like a wanna-be Alex Mack. The redhead wore large aviators that covered nearly half of her face. One of them held a clear, plastic cup with the logo of the vegan restaurant. The crimson liquid sloshed over ice as she shook the cup around.

They looked like the type to call your manager. They also looked like vampires who wanted nothing more than to take a witch down.

"Why would we want to go back to the days of segregation?" Mercury replied.

"How is it segregation to have your own plot of land? I'd kill for that," the redhead said.

"Literally," the blonde said. The women chuckled, and several protestors booed.

"Why would you need your own plot of land when everywhere is your plot of land?" Mercury countered.

The crowd chuckled. Someone called out "yeah." Others clapped.

"Ugh, that's such, like, racist thinking," stated the blonde before taking a long swig of her drink. Mercury grimaced, thinking about the blood sloshing around the cup.

"It's not racist; it's true," mentioned someone from the crowd. "You've got land everywhere. No one has ever told you that you can't set up shop somewhere."

The redhead scoffed and lifted her glasses.

She just fed, Mercury thought. He could tell in the way her skin was porcelain-smooth, the way her body was languid, and the way her pupils were dilated.

"Vampires are discriminated against, too, especially women. You don't see us out here protesting."

Mercury rolled his eyes. Fire sparked in his belly and his free hand clenched. He wanted nothing more than to use his magic and push them away, but he took a deep breath and spoke.

"You protest all the time, boo," he mocked. "One of your kind bites a human without consent and suddenly you're at the police precinct arguing that they couldn't help it and maybe humans should be warned. You get told you can't make your employees blood bags and you write think pieces on the restrictions being put on vampires and say it speaks to a broader attempt at PC culture. You knit fang masks for your Dhampirs and march on Washington bitching about the fact that Congress refuses to let you sell and import blood without knowing the source, saying that your needs come before humans' ability to give consent. Get the fuck out of here with this 'you don't see us out here protesting.'"

As the crowd cheered, the vampires pouted.

"Fuck you, witch," the blonde one spat. The pair walked away, headed toward an apartment complex called Ascendance.

"Anyway," Mercury began. The crowd laughed.

"Now, we've got these stupid tags," Mercury said, holding up the dog tag and shaking it. The metal still itched where it touched his skin. Other witches, including Bridget, lifted their tags in the air. "So we're not supposed to practice magic in public. But this is the property of the Council, and thus out of reach of that law."

More cheers and claps filled the air.

"We think the Council could use some help with their decision making, so we're here to call some quarters and make a few suggestions."

Mercury looked out over the crowd. The people clapped and cheered, and he smiled back at them.

"Bridget, would you come up and lead us?"

"Hell yeah!" she squealed. The crowd opened and formed the square with their bodies. Bridget, Mercury, and two other witches took positions at each of the points. They called their elements, with Mercury saying the words of the guardian of Air twice in one month.

"We call upon Bithis to grant us aid. Bring us your cleverness, bring us your allure, bring us your ability of persuasion so we may influence those whose ear we need now," Bridget recited.

Mercury and the other witches repeated the words twice. A light emanated from the group, and a mist hovered over them. They only needed to call upon the god two more times for their wish to be granted.

"Get off me, bitch," Joelle screamed.

Mercury dropped his hands and began inching toward the edge of the circle.

"Don't break the—" Bridget said, but he was already in motion.

Joelle held one hand against her throat, attempting to stop the blood that flowed there from seeping down her cream-colored shirt. With the other hand, she snatched the redhead by her hair, her hand engulfed in the flame of her tattoo. The vampire flailed, and Joelle tossed her down to the ground as hard as she could. A singed clump of hair remained in her hand.

The blonde vampire advanced toward Joelle, but another protestor jumped in the way, pushing her back with his telekinesis. Griffin and Ellis rushed over, and as Griffin comforted his sister, Ellis held out his foot as the blonde witch tried to run toward Joelle. She tripped over his foot and fell into the trash can on the street.

"Oops," Ellis said.

The redhead stood, fangs bared. Before Mercury could get to her, Sloane stepped in front of her.

"Sloane, stop," Mercury yelled. He held up a hand, wanting to push the vampire away from Sloane.

We can't do this again, he thought.

But instead of moving back, the vampire screamed and doubled over.

"What are you doing to her?" the blonde yelled. She ran toward her friend and grabbed her arms.

"He's causing pain," said another witch. "Just like she deserves."

Mercury looked down at his hand.

Causing pain? That wasn't his power. Hell, it wasn't even a power that most Air Hands could have. It belonged to Fire Hands.

What is happening to my powers? He thought, his mind replaying his use of fire against Conner at Astera.

"You're gonna fry for that," the blonde threatened as she stood and pulled her phone out. "I'm calling the cops."

Mercury narrowed his eyes.

"So I can tell them you bit a human on the property of the Witches' Council? You know that's not their jurisdiction," he reminded her.

The blonde ignored him, folding her arms and hitting her keypad.

"Hi? Is this the police?" she asked. "My friend and I have been attacked by a group of witches. They used their magic on us."

The crowd booed the woman and yelled out insults, drowning out her call.

"Shut up!" the vampire yelled as she held the phone away from her mouth.

"If you don't want to end up bald headed like your friend over there, I suggest you shut the fuck up," Sloane threatened, gesturing to the bald patches in the redhead's hair.

The blonde extended her middle finger then returned her attention to the call.

Mercury hurried over to Joelle, who sat on the sidewalk pressing a hand against her neck. Tears streamed down her face and her left foot tapped the ground wildly.

"Are you okay?" Mercury asked.

"What the fuck do you think?" Joelle snarled.

"Sorry, sorry. That was stupid. Let's get Ellis over here to heal you." Just as Mercury turned to wave Ellis over, Joelle shook her head.

"No. I don't want that. I don't want more magic."

"But it's an open wound; you don't want to lose any more blood."

"Don't tell me what I should do," she snapped. "If I hadn't listened to you, I wouldn't be in this place."

Griffin looked down at his feet; Ellis whistled and walked away.

The longer Mercury stared at Joelle, the deeper her words cut. What was once a flesh wound was now inches away from his heart. He couldn't bear anymore damage.

Mercury simply nodded and walked back toward the two vampires, who sat on the retaining wall.

"Please hurry," the blonde woman wailed. "They haven't gone away."

As soon as she hung up the phone, her tears stopped. She wiped her face and slid her sunglasses back over her eyes.

Mercury rolled his.

"Can you believe that bitch?" Sloane walked over to Mercury and stood with a hand on her hip, shaking her head.

"You know they're going to give us a problem," Mercury stated, referring to the police. He gritted his teeth, mentally preparing himself for their questions and attitude.

"I know. And we better get ready," she replied.

Just what I need, he thought.

The vampires ignored the crowd, phones in hand with their live streams capturing the chaos. One of them held her phone out and snapped a picture of them with the protestors in the background.

"Are you fucking kidding me?" Mercury yelled. "You're taking a selfie right now?"

The protestors' shouts rose rapidly, creating a ruckus. They yelled at the vampires, calling them killers and entitled leeches, saying "fuck your fangs" and "I hope you get a bad batch of blood one day."

"As you can see, we're not the ones with the problem." One of the vampires smirked then flipped the camera around to the crowd.

The sound of sirens drowned out their calls.

Mercury and Sloane maneuvered through the crowd back toward Griffin and Joelle. Griffin had torn the sleeves of his shirt and made a makeshift tourniquet and wrapped it around her wound. Joelle leaned on him and wiped the tears that still spilled down her face; Mercury wished he could stop them.

Minutes later, a cop car pulled up and parked across the street at the edge of the park. A tall Black man with short hair and a clean-shaven face stepped out from the driver's side. A short woman with olive skin stepped out of the passenger side, her dark hair tied into a bun and sunglasses covering her eyes despite the overcast weather.

"Looks like this might not be so bad after all," Ellis said. Mercury and Sloane shot him the same look.

"How you figure?" Sloane asked, folding her arms.

His cheeks reddened. "Well, they're both people of color, and most of everyone here is, too, so?"

As the officers approached, Mercury leaned in toward Ellis. "Black cops are sometimes worse than white cops. They often feel like they have to be in order to succeed," he said.

Ellis looked at him, eyes wide.

Mercury patted his friend's shoulder. "Don't worry about it. I'll school you on it later."

"What's the problem here?" the Black officer asked. He stood in the street, one hand resting on his cuffs and the other on his gun.

Mercury focused on the officer, letting his hands go slack at his sides. He hunched slightly and put on a smize, trying his best to look docile, agreeable. *Non-threatening*, he thought.

"Good afternoon, Officer," he began. He kept his voice even, raising it an octave. "We're here protesting outside of the Council building. The women on the retaining wall approached us. They asked some questions—"

"What questions?" the second officer asked. She crossed her arms and tilted her head. Already Mercury knew he'd get nowhere with her.

"They asked why we were protesting Kinheld," he responded.

"Kinheld?" the Black officer asked.

"The plot of land that the head of the Witches' Council, Oliana Murtaza, has secured for American witches."

The female officer snorted. The other officer stared at Mercury, unmoved.

"Then what happened?"

"I answered their questions. They walked away. Minutes later—"

"You said they walked away?"

"Yes, they walked away."

"To where?"

"I don't know, sir." Mercury could feel the anger rising within him, but he did his best not to show it.

"So they walked away then. Why are they here?"

"I don't know, sir."

"What *do* you know, then, huh?" the officer asked. Mercury wanted to smack the smug look off the cop's face. Instead, he forced himself to stand still and looked at the officer.

"I know that they left and came back. Then I heard a scream."

"What were you doing when you heard the scream?"

"I was performing a ritual," Mercury answered.

"Oh? Doing magic out in the open, then?" the male cop smirked. He looked at his partner, who perked up at the mention of magic. No doubt they were looking to catch Mercury and the protestors up with a fine for practicing magic in the open.

"Yes, sir, but on Council property," Mercury explained.

The officer narrowed his eyes.

"All of you?"

"All of us, what?"

"Were all of you on Council property?"

"Everyone who performed the ritual was, yes."

"And each of you is wearing your hexe tags?" the female officer asked.

"Yes, sir," he said. He'd made sure his tag was exposed when he heard the sirens in the distance.

The officer surveyed the crowd, who all stood clumped together on the sidewalk. Everyone who Mercury could see had their tag out and exposed, and though they were silent, their energy radiated with contempt. Mercury looked back at the officers and noticed their discomfort.

"So who screamed?" the female officer asked.

"She is sitting on the sidewalk. She was bitten—"

"Was that part of your spooky ritual?" the officer questioned. "I always knew witches were into sacrifices and shit, especially the Black ones."

Her chuckle sounded off the alarm bells in Mercury's mind. She was baiting him. Mercury knew if he responded to her comment at all, with a word or a glance or a movement, his face would be on the ground in less than a minute.

He breathed deeply, releasing the urge to react. "She was bitten by one of the vampires over there, officers. The redhead."

The officers looked beyond Mercury at the vampires. The Black officer waved his hand, gesturing for them to walk toward him.

"You, girl," he said, speaking to Joelle.

She turned toward him.

"Come over here; we've got some questions."

"Can she answer them here? She's injured and lost a lot of blood," Griffin interjected.

Mercury's heart leaped into his throat. He looked at Griffin, wishing for all his might that he could communicate that he shouldn't have said anything.

"No, she cannot answer them there; she needs to come here. And one more word from you, and I'll fine you for obstruction," the officer threatened.

Griffin clenched his jaw but helped Joelle stand. She stood slowly, wobbling on her feet. She shuffled toward them, but the officer grew impatient. He grabbed her wrist and pulled her toward him. She only whimpered, her words stifled.

"Don't touch her!" Griffin yelled. Seconds later, his cheek connected with the sidewalk as the female officer pressed her knee into his back.

Mercury winced at the sound of his friend groaning and clenched his hands.

If you do anything, they will do worse to you, he thought. *Just stay still.*

His face remained blank and passive. Inside, his emotions raged within him. He was altogether angry and scared, his experience with the Denver police officers rushing back to him in waves.

The crowd of protestors rushed toward them, several of them holding up their phones and pointing them at the cops.

"Get off of him," someone shouted.

"He didn't do anything wrong! Get the fuck off of him," someone else yelled.

"Turn those fucking cameras off," the male officer barked. He strode toward a petite woman, his hand held out for her phone.

Two white, male witches jumped in front of her, standing the officer down.

"You can't confiscate someone's phone for taking a video," one of the witches sassed.

"Yeah, where's your warrant?" the other questioned.

The officer scowled.

"You get out of my way," he ordered.

"No," one of the witches refused. "You can't do this."

"Howard, leave them alone. We got this one here," the female officer said.

For his part, Griffin remained silent, even as his broken glasses looked seconds away from poking him in the eye.

Howard growled and turned back to Joelle.

"Let me see this bite, then," he demanded.

As Joelle tried to take the tourniquet off, her hands shook. Sloane stepped toward her, but Ellis put a hand on her shoulder. He walked toward Joelle, all the while keeping his eyes locked on the officer. He pulled the tourniquet to the side, showing the gaping bite mark.

"That's going to leave one hell of a scar," he remarked, nonchalantly.

Joelle pressed her lips together, trying not to wince from the pain.

With such blatant evidence of wrongdoing, the average person would be certain that the police would make an arrest. But Mercury wasn't the average person, and he knew that the more time ticked by, the lesser the chance of the officers arresting the vampires that attacked Joelle.

"Are you even going to do anything?" inquired one of the protestors. He still had his phone out, this time standing further away but being no less discreet.

"I see nothing that would warrant bringing anyone in," the officer stated finally.

"Are you kidding me?" said the other witch. The other protestors objected, their shouts and moans echoing what Mercury wanted to say.

Instead, he said: "Officer, I'm sure you know that a vampire attack on Council property is a misdemeanor offense."

Howard narrowed his eyes and stepped toward Mercury, so close that their foreheads nearly touched.

"You quoting the law to me, son?" he huffed.

Mercury's mouth went dry. He clenched his fists, his jaw tight.

"You don't think I know that?"

"Officer, I'm just trying to look out for my friend. She was attacked, sir. On Council property. I don't think my aunt, the Head of The Witches' Council, and my father, a Council member, would respond well to LAPD allowing that to happen, sir."

The officer stared into Mercury's eyes for what seemed like forever. He could feel the sweat accumulating at his forehead and under his arms, staining the yellow Astera Army shirt he'd been given. He tried to keep his breath steady.

Troian, lend me your strength, he thought. *I need you.*

As he begged his brother for strength, the officer's hand slid down to his belt. Mercury swallowed, bile forming a lump in his throat. His knees wobbled and he felt as though the ground would quake beneath him.

The crowd's shouts escalated, vicious slurs and insults overpowering one another. The two witches recording the incident had inched closer and were threatening to call the Witches' Council, the ACLU, the NAACP. Mercury felt Sloane's presence looming behind him, knowing that if he asked her to, she'd beat the officers back or die trying.

Finally, the officer stepped back. He gripped the radio at his shoulder and spoke into it, telling dispatch they'd be coming in with two vampires.

"You'd better be lucky you've got so many people here and you're on Council property," the officer said. He let his other hand rest on the black pouch on his belt, the same one that had been on the belt of the security guard at the W.A.S. "If I'd have caught you alone and on the streets, I may not have been so nice."

He faced the vampires, who were standing on the sidewalk filming the exchange. Howard turned toward his colleague and gestured for her to stand. She sighed and gave Griffin one last nudge before standing and walking over to the vampires.

The crowd cheered as they pulled the vampire's arms behind their backs and began Mirandizing them. They yelled "fuck your fangs" as the officers led them to their squad car and slid them into the back seat, both wearing looks of defeat. Then the officers cast one last look at the protestors. Howard shook his head and they both slid into the car.

Mercury released a deep breath as the engine roared. His teeth ached from clenching so hard. His stomach churned from the fear. His head throbbed from all the noise.

"You good, Merc?" Sloane asked, one hand on his shoulder. Mercury waved her off.

"Yeah, yeah. Go check on Griffin," he replied. He leaned over, placing his hands on his knees to steady himself.

"Man, fuck the police!" shouted Ellis.

"Fuck the police, indeed," Mercury agreed in between breaths. Then he staggered to the edge of the sidewalk and vomited.

WITCHES GONE WILD

BY CORDELIA EDWARDS
STAFF WRITER, *THE VANGUARD*

While most Americans kick off summer barbecuing, fishing, and generally enjoying the sun, one group of people spent this Memorial Day weekend staging yet another protest. The witches of the nation rose up and instead of honoring the countless military personnel (some of whom were witches themselves) who gave their lives for these witches' right to complain, they harassed law-abiding citizens at the Santa Monica pier and used magic against a couple of vampires walking home from their local cafe.

Led by a dilettante named Mercury Amell, this group's big gripe is that they aren't treated equally here in America. They see this country not as one where anyone can accomplish their goals but one of struggle, where those like them are "othered". Their leader, a statuesque, well-spoken woman named Oliana Murtaza, recognized the wrongdoing on the part of her people. She witnessed the reckless use of magic, their harassment of humans and vampires, their blatant lies about half of this nation, and decided to do something about it. She sat down with President Harvey Vael, who also saw the need for a healing moment in our nation. Together they developed the Corvius Accord, which would grant American witches their own slice of paradise. This land, called Kinheld, would be run completely by Ms. Murtaza and the other members of the Council.

Witches would have their own schools, their own businesses, and their own laws with which to govern. When I read about the Corvius Accord, I was happy that a people who wanted for so long to be able to live on their own terms would soon be able to do so. Imagine my surprise, then, when I learned that a rather large contingent of them, led by Amell, were so diametrically opposed to the idea that they were protesting in front of the Council building. I was surprised further still when I learned that not only is Amell himself one of the witches involved in the L.A. Riots that led to the mass attack at Astera, but he also is the nephew of Ms. Murtaza and the son of another Witches' Council member. When we talk about privilege, rarely do we talk about the audacity of someone who has the means and ability to have their concerns heard because of their proximity to such power yet decides to take to the streets and harass American citizens.

The behavior of witches like Amell is nothing new. We've seen some who are so full of contempt for what they perceive as injustices before. We've seen it with Briar Kennedy, the witch responsible for the Bala Cynwyd massacre. And we've seen it in witches like Ama Deus, who, if you recall, harassed an officer as he was doing his job and set another on fire, sending him to the hospital with near-fatal burns.

Witches in America have surely gone wild. They claim that the statistics of witch-killings have increased, but what about killers of vampires? What about Briar Kennedy and Justin McDaniel (who kidnapped and strangled two vampire nursing students) and Erin Haynes (who killed her roommate with a wooden stake when she found out she was a vampire)? What about the witches who commit crime after crime each year? According to Pew, witches committed 15% of all robberies, 8% of all rapes, and 23% of all murders last year. And because we know crimes like rape and murder tend to happen within one's own community, it stands to reason that witches are committing these crimes against other witches—the very people they claim to be fighting for.

CHAPTER 9

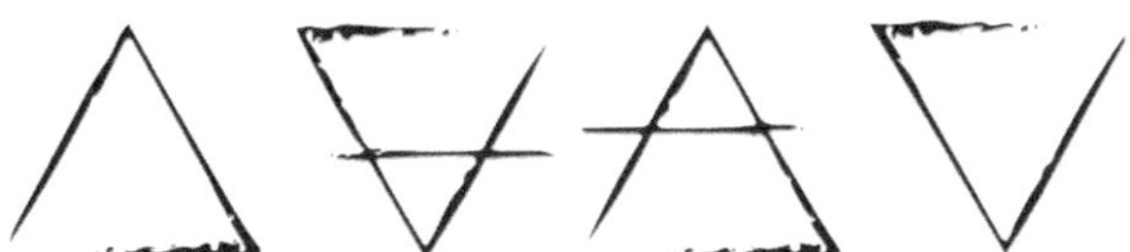

Mercury's father was born on the second of June, and for as long as Mercury could remember, he held his birthday party on the first Saturday of the month. The parties always had a different theme; last year it was solid gold. Mercury remembered laughing at Troian as he dressed in a gold catsuit, his muscular body only emphasizing the flimsy fabric.

This year's theme was afterlife. In the past, Mercury had been excited about the chance to dress up and celebrate. He'd gleefully found a costume or a suit to go with the occasion. This year, however, he felt as if he were just going through the motions as he raided the racks at a consignment store with Sloane and Griffin. He spent most of their outing lost in his thoughts, giving an occasional chuckle, nod or affirmation as he feigned his interest in their conversation. Each time he opened his mouth to ask Griffin about Joelle, he decided against it and busied himself among the clothing racks instead.

Eventually, Mercury found something he could use—a white tunic, gold belt, and a braided gold headband. He went to Target and bought gold bangles and white felt, which he cut into wings and fastened onto his shoes and headband.

He was slipping the last bangle bracelet onto his wrist when the doorbell rang.

Before he could get to the door, Ellis stepped in, wearing a shiny black robe and carrying a foam scythe. Mercury crossed his arms as he took in his friend's costume, which looked to him like a cheap one bought on discount at Spirit Halloween.

"For real?" he said.

Ellis lowered the hood. "What? I didn't want to spring for something expensive. It's not like your dad has the same theme each year," Ellis replied.

He walked over to the counter and grabbed a bottle of Jose Cuervo. Ellis tilted the bottle, gesturing toward Mercury. Once Mercury nodded, Ellis searched the cabinets for two glasses.

"True, but you're going to be hot as hell in that. Plus, it looks cheap as fuck."

"Mmm, okay, brand whore," Ellis quipped.

Mercury scoffed. "I know you're not calling me the brand whore. Ain't you the one who wears those ugly-ass, distressed t-shirts that cost like five hundred dollars?"

Ellis grimaced as he set the glasses on the countertop. "Not anymore."

He poured their tequila, his mouth set in a grim line. Mercury realized his mistake and felt his heart sink. The day after they returned from Astera, Ellis' parents had given him an ultimatum: get the tattoo removed and lose Mercury's number or be cut off. They'd been deeply embarrassed by Ellis, having to laughingly excuse his behavior while having drinks with their vampire friends. When Ellis told them to go fuck themselves, his parents made good on their promise. His BMW SUV had been seized, his cards canceled, and his clothes left on the front lawn. He moved into a room near The Iron Bird and got a job at Pothead the following week.

"I'm sorry, El."

"That's okay." Ellis downed his drink. "I've still got better style than you."

Mercury rolled his eyes but smiled as he sipped his drink.

"Like hell you do," Sloane said, stepping into the apartment like she was stepping onto the runway. She wore a long white dress and veil, gold jewelry adorning her neck. Her makeup was done impeccably, her lips blood red and black streaks, like tears, streaming down her face.

Mercury nodded at her. "You look good."

"You, too. I'm glad the tunic worked for you." Sloane crossed the kitchen and grabbed the empty glass from Ellis' hands and refilled it.

"Yeah, me, too. I didn't want to have to figure something else out on the day of."

"Well, you should have gotten your stuff early, like I did," Ellis said, holding his arms out.

Sloane scoffed and swiped his arm. "Wearing something left over from last Halloween doesn't count."

Mercury laughed.

"The twins coming?" Ellis asked.

Mercury flinched. Though Griffin's communication hadn't changed despite being slammed to the ground and cracking a tooth at the last protest, Joelle barely responded to Mercury's texts, often leaving him on read.

"I don't know," he replied, staring down into his glass.

"Hopefully, they'll get here soon. I'm ready to get lit after all the stories you've told me about your dad's parties," Sloane squealed.

Mercury smiled. He thought about his father's thirty-fifth birthday party and its theme—shades of blue. Though Mercury hadn't been old enough to drink, Troian had let him sip a little from his flask. Mercury spent most of the night on the dance floor with Faegan, but he remembered how wild his father and his friends had gotten. By the end of the night, his father was dancing shirtless on top of the bar.

"Be prepared. People tend to get wild."

"Sounds like my type of party," Sloane teased.

Minutes later, a knock sounded at the door.

"Come in," Mercury yelled. The Whittaker twins stepped through the door, wearing outfits the complete opposite of each other. Griffin, head to toe in black, wore a decadent pair of ram's horns on his head.

His locs had been freshly twisted and his face was heavily contoured. Long, fluffy lashes brushed against his cheeks when he blinked. Joelle glided toward the group, her high-necked lace dress trailing behind her. A pair of shimmery gold wings jutted out of the back of the dress, and her long hair was parted down the middle and hung in glossy coils down her back.

"You two look great," Mercury said.

Joelle smiled tightly. "Well, this was my backup. I had to change what I was going to wear after last weekend."

Mercury looked at Griffin, who simply shrugged and leaned against the counter.

"Well, you look stunning. Tequila?" Sloane asked, holding up her glass.

Joelle waved her hand. "We're good. I think it's probably best to wait until the party."

"Speak for yourself. I'll have a small glass," Griffin interjected.

Joelle pursed her lips.

Mercury glanced at Sloane then back at his cup. He tilted his head back and finished his drink in one gulp. His belly felt warm from the alcohol, his body languid.

"Nah. We should probably go."

He ushered the group out of the apartment and down the stairs. The shop had been locked down a few hours before, so they walked out of the back entrance and onto the street. They noticed other small groups walking up to the neighboring bars and nightclubs, ready to get their weekend started.

As the neon signs illuminated the sidewalk, he pulled his phone out of his pocket and requested a Lyft. Ten minutes later, a black SUV pulled up in front of them, and they all slid in. Joelle sat beside Sloane and Ellis, holding her wings in her hands. Mercury and Griffin sat in the rear seats. Once the last door slammed, the car pulled away.

"Okay, let's take photos before we get trashed." Sloane pulled out her phone and leaned against Ellis.

Joelle sighed but squeezed into the frame. Mercury and Griffin leaned over their seat. Mercury slid an arm around his friend and smiled, feeling altogether happy and anxious.

"Okay, another one—the lighting was off," Joelle said.

"It wasn't that bad," Ellis countered.

"Says you. Remember, we need more lighting." She gestured toward Mercury and Griffin.

Sloane chuckled. She turned up the flash on her phone then lifted her arm and snapped a photo, the light making Mercury blink.

"This is good. What do you think?" she said. She turned and showed them the photo. After everyone nodded their approval, Sloane opened Instagram.

"What should the caption be? Boozing with my bitches?" she said in a nasally voice.

"Hashtag blessed!" Joelle said.

"Hashtag live laugh love," Griffin suggested.

Sloane shook her head. "Okay, okay. How about this: the four elements of my life. Hashtag earth air fire water."

Mercury groaned at the sentimentality but still felt a swell of love for his friend.

"Whatever, posting it, bitch."

She pressed "post" and set her phone in her lap. Ellis wrapped his arm around her.

"So, who all's gonna be at this shindig?" Griffin asked.

Mercury searched his thoughts for a moment.

"Well, all of the Council. Some of my dad's friends. The owners of Pothead and the bakery down the street. Valeria."

"Oh? She's coming?" Joelle asked, turning her head toward the rear seat.

"Why wouldn't she?" Mercury asked.

Joelle didn't respond. She faced forward and gazed out the window instead.

Mercury glanced at Griffin. He shrugged then looked down at his phone, where he double tapped the photo they took and kept scrolling.

"What's wrong with Valeria?" Sloane asked. There was an edge to her voice that Mercury caught, but no one else seemed to notice.

"Nothing, she's just . . . around a lot lately."

"Well, she's going to be doing that piece on me," Mercury explained. "We met up. She's cool."

Griffin and Ellis said their congrats, with Ellis adding that he was surprised more outlets weren't interested in profiling him.

"You're like the 2022 Dr. Martin Luther King Jr.," Ellis said.

"That's a reach, but okay," Mercury chuckled.

"I didn't know that she was doing a piece on you." Joelle looked over her shoulder at Mercury. "Why didn't you mention it before?"

"I did, at the power stripping ceremony. You probably just forgot, what with the protests and . . . everything. You've been busy."

"I can't help that I have a life outside of all of this," Joelle started. She opened her mouth to say more but Griffin touched her shoulder.

"We're here," he said. "Perhaps you two can chat about this later?"

Mercury sighed. "There's nothing else to talk about."

He slid out of the car before Joelle could respond. Why was she mad? What right did she have to dislike Valeria, to feel as if he owed her an explanation for not telling her things?

Why is she so hot and cold? Mercury thought.

He stepped onto the long, gold carpet that trailed up the steps to the Council House. As he ascended the steps, several witches nodded at him. He responded in kind, not speaking their names or waving their way. Many of them were part of the movement against Kinheld but were adamant about staying anonymous.

"This is a level of extra I don't think I've ever seen," Griffin remarked, his eyes drinking in the view.

"Oh, you mean Astera wasn't extra enough for you?" Mercury replied.

"Nah. This tops it for sure."

The carpet continued as they walked into the house. The walls were draped in white gauzy fabric, strings of light threaded throughout. It smelled like honeysuckle, and Mercury wondered what poor intern had to schlep to Bath and Body Works to get enough plug-ins to fill the entire home.

Once they stepped onto the patio, even Mercury was in awe. The trees were draped in the same gauze and lights were strung on every branch. Fire pits were perched on each step, and tables formed a circle around the patio area. In the center of a large group of cheaply costumed witches stood his father.

"Who wants a drink?" Ellis asked.

Sloane raised her hand, and Griffin followed suit.

"Sure," Joelle replied. She looked toward Mercury.

"I'll be back. I'm going to holler at my dad right quick," he announced.

He trotted down the steps before anyone could respond. Had he done something wrong by inviting Valeria? Was Joelle genuinely mad at him? He felt as though she'd been giving him so many mixed signals lately. Every time he was near her, he could feel her pulling away, wanting to be somewhere else, but then when he didn't include her or when she was the last to know, she was angry. And after their date, Mercury was sure she didn't have *any* feelings for him. So why was she still pressed?

Get your head in the game, he thought. *Stay focused.*

He put on a smile just as he reached the edge of the circle of witches surrounding his father.

"Okay, golden god," Mercury said, inspecting his father appraisingly. His long, gold tunic and robe fit his body and stopped at his feet. His eyes were circled in gold eyeshadow, his cheeks shimmering.

"Mercury, son! Don't you look sharp," his father exclaimed. He extended his arm and the crowd parted. Atlas excused himself from the group of people and wrapped his arm around Mercury's shoulder. "Let's get you a drink."

When they were out of earshot, he added: "You have no idea how happy I am that you saved me from those vultures."

"Really, Dad? Vultures?"

His father scoffed and rolled his eyes. "They accosted me as I was about to grab my long island. For twenty minutes, I had to stand and listen to them jabber about some proposed policies to add to next week's session."

"Isn't that part of the job of being a Council member?"

His father gave him a sidelong glance. "Tuh. Tonight, I am not Atlas Amell, Council Member. Tonight, I am Atlas Amell, *birthday boy*, who wants to turn up and find some trade."

Mercury frowned. "Can you still call yourself a 'boy' if you're almost fifty?"

His father patted him on the shoulder. "You are shady."

"Learned from the best."

"Ha! You got that right." Atlas turned, scanning the area. "Your crew here?"

Mercury gestured to the group, who all had seemingly gotten their drinks and were now standing beside the bar. When they noticed Mercury and his father stepping toward the bar, they walked over.

"Happy birthday, Mr. A!" Sloane smiled and threw her arms around him.

He chuckled and wrapped his arms around her.

"Thank you, Sloane," he said.

"Yeah, happy birthday!" Ellis greeted him, lifting his glass.

"Can't toast without a glass, son," Mercury's father said.

The father and son turned to the bar and ordered their drinks. After toasting, the group moved to a table to the right of the bar, gazing at the view below.

"I'm glad you all came through with some nice-looking costumes, though, Ellis . . . yours does look seconds away from ripping," Atlas commented.

Ellis groaned. "Is everyone going to drag me for this?"

Mercury laughed and the rest of the group joined him. For a while, they sat and sipped their drinks, joking with each other about their costumes or past moments of embarrassment. Mercury found himself relaxing even more as he began to feel his gin and tonic. He was languid, his lips beginning to numb.

"Be careful, son."

Mercury turned in the direction of the voice, the same voice he had heard before the power stripping ceremony: his mother's voice.

He looked up to find Valeria joining them, taking sips of a margarita and wearing a long leather dress, black platform boots, and a spiked mask that enclosed her whole head. Her eye makeup was smokey and she'd powered her face with white powder. Mercury's eyes widened as he saw her approach.

"Is that a Hellraiser costume?"

Valeria smiled and nodded. "It's one of my favorite movies."

"I didn't picture you as a horror fan," Mercury said before realizing how offensive it must have sounded. "I'm sorry, I—"

She waved him off, her jet-black nails sharper than before. "Don't worry about it. You've still got a lot to learn about me, but that'll come in time."

Mercury lifted a brow. When he heard someone clearing their throat, Mercury looked back to see his father standing just behind his chair.

"You're looking especially spooky this evening, Valeria. I like it," he said as he hugged her.

"Thank you, Councilman Amell. Happy birthday."

"Please. Call me Atlas. And thank you." He sipped his drink. "I'm going to go mingle. I hope you enjoy," he said to them all before smiling and walking away.

Dinner consisted of a buffet of finger foods. While standing in line, Mercury wondered which late night spot he would hit up for some real food. He rolled his eyes at all the different types of cheese laid out on the table, yet he filled his plates with brie and gouda and an assortment of other appetizers.

The group engaged in casual conversation during dinner, with Valeria and Sloane gushing about the happenings at *Jonquil*. As Ellis and Griffin asked Valeria about her upcoming feature on Mercury, Mercury noticed Joelle contributed the least to the conversation. She spent most of her time eating while scrolling on her phone.

After dinner, a server wheeled the birthday cake out to the patio. Mercury and his friends gathered with the rest of the crowd as his father stood before the three-tiered confection. Gold icing dripped down the sides, and the edges were ringed with gold-covered strawberries. At the top sat a ring of white candles, the flames illuminating his father's face.

"How opulent," Valeria teased.

Mercury chuckled. "Yeah, that's Atlas Amell for you."

His father grinned as the crowd began singing happy birthday, many of them buzzed and off-key. When they finished, Mercury raised his glass in toast.

"It's not every day that we get to celebrate someone like you, Dad," Mercury began. "Though I know if you had it your way, we'd celebrate you all the time."

"You're damn right," his father said.

Several people laughed, causing a soft roar.

"But today is your day. And I am happy to lift my glass and celebrate a man who is so unapologetically himself that he gives everyone around him the courage to be the same. A man who knows what's right and isn't afraid to stand for it, fight for it, day in and day out. A man who taught me how to be a person of integrity, compassion, and pride. And also, how to be the best damned witch I could be. Happy birthday, Dad. I thank the goddess every day that I got you as a father."

His father dabbed a tear from his eye, leaving streaks of gold paint on his cheek.

"I love you, son. Thank you."

"To Atlas!" Mercury shouted.

"To Atlas!" The crowd responded. Everyone savored their drinks, and the music resumed. His father blew out the candles, the crowd rejoicing in his honor.

Mercury went to his father and hugged him, breathing in the smell of Black Opium perfume. Mercury pulled away from his father and he nodded, patting him on his chest. The crowd parted and as Mercury made his way back to his friends, several people complimented him on his speech, including Councilwoman Murtaza.

"I've forgotten how eloquent you are," his aunt said as she glided toward him. She wore a fiery red double-breasted suit, the pants long and hitting the ground as she walked. Her long hair was braided into a sleek faux hawk style braid that snaked down her back. Her smokey makeup complimented her dark brown eyes, highlighted by a pair of red horns affixed to the top of her head.

"Thank you, Auntie," he replied. "Is the devil wearing Prada tonight?"

Oliana tilted her head back and laughed. "Mugler, actually."

Faegan stood by her side, dressed in a gauzy grey gown with chains strung from her wrists. She held a Long Island iced tea in one hand and tapped on her phone with the other.

"Faegan," Mercury said.

"Hey." Her eyes remained locked on her phone, her acrylic nails moving furiously over the screen.

Mercury rolled his eyes.

"You look well," Oliana interjected, diverting the attention back to herself. She looped her arm in Mercury's. "Come with me to the bar."

Mercury smiled, his mouth closed. The thought of being near his aunt for any longer than he had to be made his skin crawl. How could she act so normal, like she hadn't covertly threatened him the last time they spoke? Like she hadn't added insult to injury when she stripped Briar's powers by stabbing him, like she hadn't tried to have his powers stripped. Instead of saying what was on his mind, though, Mercury asked: "Is there something you wanted to speak about?"

"You know, there was a time where you considered me your favorite aunt," Oliana recalled.

Mercury fought the instinct to scoff. Like at the ceremony, he was all too aware of how he needed to behave. He tapped his fingers against his empty glass.

"Well, I was a kid then."

It was his aunt who scoffed this time. "When you know better, you do better, I suppose."

She asked the bartender for Bourbon, neat. As she stood waiting for her drink, several witches approached her, wanting pictures, asking questions. Mercury sighed at the annoyance of it all.

Does this have to happen every time? He thought, thinking back to the power stripping ceremony and all the fanfare she received at Astera.

"Well, this was fun." Mercury said, motioning to leave.

"Oh, Mercury, you can spare some more time for your aunt. I'm sure your friends will be just fine." She gestured to the group, all of whom were on the dance floor. It looked as if they were having a good time; even Joelle appeared to have loosened up.

Mercury sighed and followed his aunt up the steps and into the Council house, his heart beating to the pace of his steps. She led him down a long hall and into a drawing room, where Paloma, Honore, and his father sat.

Faegan trailed behind them. Paloma, who'd come to the party dressed as a mummy, complete with a facekini, sat on the couch. Honore wore a suit and top hat. His face was painted as a skull and he swished Bourbon in one hand and leaned against the bookcase. His father sat at the desk, his legs crossed. He leaned back in the desk chair, playing with a small ball of ice.

Oliana closed the door behind them.

"Dad?" Mercury began. His father looked up at him, a hint of sadness in his eyes. "Am I about to get merked?"

Oliana chuckled. "Always with the jokes, Mercury. I love that about you. No, no one is going to get killed. At least not at this meeting."

No one laughed.

"Why am I here then? Why is Dad in here when he should be celebrating his birthday?"

"Mercury, I've gathered the Council together to discuss these protests you insist on having."

Now, he did sigh. Now, he rolled his eyes. He crossed his arms and sat on the coffee table, cursing himself for not steeling himself against his aunt and her machinations. He'd been right that her comment to him after the power stripping ceremony had been a threat. He'd been foolish to forget about it, though, and now he feared she wouldn't warn him again.

"We spoke about this after the ceremony, Auntie. I told you I didn't agree with your decision to strike up a peace treaty with Vael, so I decided to do something about it."

Oliana stood against the door. Her nails thrummed against her glass, the sound sending a shiver down Mercury's spine.

"That would be fine, dear, if it weren't for two very obvious things." She took a sip of her drink and placed it on the bookshelf beside her. Then she strode over to Mercury and sat beside him. Instinctively, he tensed up, his jaw clenching. He sat up straight and stared her in the eyes.

"And what would those be?"

"Well, the first is that you're my nephew, and you're his son," she said pointing toward his father.

Atlas played with his beard.

"Not only is it not a good look to have someone so tied to the Council to be opposed to this ruling, but it hurts our feelings. Isn't that right, Atlas?"

She looked over at Atlas and Mercury followed her gaze. Though he knew his father was for Mercury exercising his right to free speech, he also knew his father had to play the game. Atlas simply nodded, his jaw tight.

"You see? Do you want to hurt your father's feelings like this? Do you want to hurt *my* feelings?"

"Can you stop sounding like Culture Club and get to your next point?" Mercury said.

A darkness passed over her eyes as she narrowed them. She placed one hand on his arm and suddenly, Mercury felt his whole body tingling and a wave of invisible fire rushing through him. He groaned as sweat beaded on his forehead.

"Oliana, it is not necessary to use your magic on my son," his father asserted. He was standing now, both hands clenched.

"Please, dial down the anger, Oliana. We only wanted to talk to him," Paloma said.

Honore also stood, his hands by his sides.

His aunt sucked in a breath and released him. Mercury coughed and gasped, leaning forward. His father ran to his side and picked him up, lifting his chin and checking him out.

"Fine, fine. You're right. I'm sorry, Mercury. That was extreme of me."

Mercury gawked at her. She still sat, leaning back, her hands on the coffee table. To Mercury, she didn't look sorry but delighted that she'd caused pain. He wanted to tell her to go fuck herself, but he knew better. She was already on the offensive.

"I accept your apology, Auntie. Thank you," He looked at his father and nodded. He responded in kind and resumed his place behind the desk, though he didn't sit down.

"Where were we?" she asked. "Oh, that's right. My next point is that after all the Council has done for you, this antagonism is a slap in the face."

Mercury opened his mouth to ask what the hell the Council had done for him. Though they had voted to allow him and his friends keep their magic, they had almost stripped his father's powers, too, and he was one of the longest standing members of the Council. Nevertheless, he kept his mouth shut, crossing his arms so tightly across his chest that his shirt pulled.

"I can see in your eyes that you'd like some clarification on that last point, so allow me." Oliana stood and walked around the room. "We made sure your family was taken care of after your mother died. We helped secure you a scholarship to get into UCLA, which you have squandered now that you've dropped out. We helped rebuild your father's tattoo parlor, which was destroyed by you and your brother, may he rest in power, because of your temper."

"All of those things sound like what would have happened anyway, given that my father is a member of the Council, and my mother was one, too, before she was killed," Mercury said, looking Oliana in the eye. He glanced around the room at the other Council members, each of them wearing matching expressions of unease. "Everyone knows that children of the Council are awarded scholarships. And Everyone knows that if a Council member chooses to have another livelihood and that livelihood is threatened, the

Council steps in. So, whether the Iron Bird being destroyed was caused by a spell or a wildfire, you all would have picked up the tab anyway."

"Careful, Mercury," Honore warned. "You're treading some unsafe water here."

"Thank you, Honore." Oliana clasped her hands behind her back. "Indeed, you are. While all of the things you've said are true, I've got a few more facts for you."

She stopped pacing and turned toward her nephew.

"So how about this—you and your brother illegally gave magic to humans, an offense that is punishable by power stripping. Though you said it was a necessary evil, the time that you spent marking them is time that could have been spent loading up a car and starting your journey to Astera. It certainly might have ended better for everyone, including your brother."

Atlas slammed his hand on the desk. "Oliana, that's enough. I'll not have you speaking ill of my sons this way, especially as Troian is no longer here to defend himself."

Though he knew his father was on his side, the comment still stung. Tears sprung into Mercury's eyes.

Oliana held a hand up at his father. "You're right. He isn't here to defend himself because *this* son has a temper and his tactical skills are severely lacking."

Mercury attempted to stand up, but his aunt knelt in front of him.

"Speaking of temper," she said. She looked up at him. "It was *your* temper that caused you to murder that human, Delanie. And though you're right about the Council taking care of its progeny, we usually draw the line at murder. So how do you think you've been able to skate by all these months without incident? Without LAPD busting through your door and shooting first only to ask questions of you later?"

A tear slid down Mercury's cheek. His stomach churned as he clenched and unclenched his fists. His cheeks were hot, sweat beading on his forehead and trailing down his back.

"It's because the Council covered up the fact that you killed that girl in cold blood. You used one of the deadliest spells on her that there is, leaving her to burn to death in agony."

"Oliana, that's—"

"Atlas, you're going to get enough of interrupting me. Know your place, Councilman."

Mercury's father gritted his teeth and slid back from his chair. He stared out the window, looking out toward the front of the property, his chest rising and falling rapidly.

"Now," she said, grabbing Mercury's chin. "We can continue to keep this secret forever. No one has to know about this beyond us in this room and your magic-tinged friends. We can even invest in some therapy for you, as I heard you've been having some nightmares."

Mercury looked up at his father. Had he told Oliana about all the nights Mercury woke up crying out for Troian, calling out to himself to stop before he used the death spell? All those nights of having to take showers at three in the morning and having to change his sheets after he'd soaked through them? Emotions flooded his body like a raging river.

"Or, you can keep protesting. You can keep telling the world that the Council is bad for witches and this new direction is the wrong one. You can keep getting Twitter famous, and then someday, someone will drop a tip off to the LAPD that a certain witch was responsible for that murder at that party, not the vampires like all the reports say. Maybe they'll investigate first or maybe . . ."

She didn't have to finish her sentence for Mercury to understand what she meant.

"You wouldn't," Mercury quavered. "That would implicate the Council, that you've all been covering it up for me. You'd be accessories."

"Oh, honey, no. You see, that would implicate your friends. All of you combined have the juice to alter a memory here, change some camera footage there, threaten a poisoning or a knife fight. Do you really want to put their lives in danger *again?*"

Though his eyes burned with tears, Mercury wouldn't let her see him break. He just trembled, looking down at the aunt that he once loved more than anything.

"Just think about it, my love," she said, caressing his chin. "I know you've got a protest scheduled for this coming weekend. Plenty of time to spread the word and cancel it."

She smirked at Mercury before standing and strutting out of the room. Faegan and Paloma followed closely after. Mercury could hear Paloma calling his aunt's name and trying to get her attention. Honore stood at the door for several moments, uncertain of what to do.

His father walked over to him and tried to draw him into a hug.

"No, it's okay, just go," he said.

"Mercury."

"No, just go. I need a minute," he yelled. He looked at his father. Tears welled in his deep, brown eyes. "Please."

His father kissed his forehead and stood. Once Honore walked out of the room, Mercury's father exited shortly after.

With the silence of the room louder than ever, Mercury sat there, replaying every wrong move in his mind. Even though he thought he had lost everything when he lost his brother, he realized he now had even more to lose: his freedom and his friends' freedom. Desperately wanting to drown out the noise, he motioned toward the door, but his legs went numb. As he slunk to the floor, he heard cries in the distance, cries that resembled those of a wounded animal. Only when he touched the dampness on his face did he recognize the sobs as his own.

CHAPTER 10

Facing away from the front windows of the Iron Bird, Mercury sat on a chrome barstool, upper body hunched over a white man with '80s hair, boardshorts, and sandals.

He tried not to cringe as the man and his girlfriend, whose vibe was equally tacky, stepped into the shop minutes earlier. He gritted his teeth when the man told him he wanted the symbols of the four elements tattooed on his forearm.

"Oh?" Mercury said then, knowing full well the man didn't have any magic in him and that he smelled more vanilla than a carton of Haagen-Daaz. But he wanted to see how much the man knew about magic, so he asked: "What's your element?"

The blonde man scoffed and looked at his girlfriend quizzically.

"I don't know about all that. I just think these symbols look dope." He turned to his girlfriend, who was twisting strands of her blond hair around her finger. "Don't they look so dope?"

The exchange made Mercury feel more on edge than he'd already felt. He breathed deeply to quiet the small tremors erupting over his body.

He'd left the party after Oliana's threat, telling his friends that he'd had too much to drink and needed to take a Lyft home so that he could pass out in his own bed. He didn't know if they hadn't believed him. He didn't care. He only wanted to be in his room in his bed, burrowed under the sheets. He did his best to stave off a panic attack, but the tears flowed off and on for the rest of the night.

Now, as he watched this couple, both of them blissfully unaware of their appropriation, annoyance rose within him. He blinked slowly and sighed as the couple beamed at each other. He wanted to reach across the desk and slap the smug smile off the blonde man's face, sending him and his girlfriend running. He wanted to cuss at them, tell them how ridiculous humans looked with magical symbols on them, say that they had no fucking business wearing his culture, his life, his magic as accessories.

But, he knew they had to pay the bills. He knew that one bad word from the blonde man in front of him and they could lose more business than they already had. His protests, though important, had driven away those in the magical community who agreed with Oliana, as well as humans and vampires who didn't want to get in the line of fire.

"So, so *dope*," the girlfriend agreed, breaking Mercury out of his anxiety-fueled fog. "Which is which?"

Mercury pointed at the row of triangles in the booklet. He pointed to the triangle facing up, the one with the line cutting through the top third.

"This is air," he said. He pointed to the one beside it, an inverted triangle with the line in the lower third. "This is water."

"This is earth, and this is fire," he continued, pointing first to the upright triangle representing earth then the inverted one representing fire. *Oliana's element*, he thought.

"Cool. I want them big, like, really big. Can I get them here?" the blonde man gestured to his calves. Mercury nodded.

"And I want them outlined in color."

"But, like, what would be the color for air? White?"

That feeling again, like fire in the pit of his stomach. He suppressed the urge to scream and simply said: "It's yellow."

"Well, that's really dumb. Why not white?" the girl questioned.

Mercury turned his back toward them and walked them into the main parlor, gesturing to his chair.

"I don't know. Witches are just *weird*." The blonde man shrugged.

Mercury tightened his jaw as he sat down, hating the way the man leaned into the word "weird" like he'd just bitten into sour candy. The girlfriend chuckled at this, and Mercury took a deep, measured breath to ground himself.

He plopped down on the chrome stool and put gloves on, retreating into his head as the couple sat and chattered about what to eat for lunch, about whether they'd go whale watching this weekend, and about whether he thought the new glasses she wanted to get were so retro.

The door to the shop dinged shortly after, a much-needed distraction from the obnoxious couple. Mercury looked up as Sloane entered. Her pink high-top Chuck Taylors matched the pink denim shorts she wore. Her top, jet black with a white, vintage kitten on it, read "pet the kitty" in cursive lettering. Her long, black hair had been weaved into two French braids, the ends snaking over her shoulders.

"Aye," she said to him as she peeled her sunglasses off. She held a tray with two iced coffees and a paper bag in her other hand. "Brought coffees and grub."

"Thanks," Mercury replied, nodding at her. She smiled at the customers as she took her position behind the desk. After booting up the shop's laptop, she pulled a copy of *Fairy Dust and Stripper Heels* from her purse and buried her nose in it.

Mercury set about tattooing the customer's left calf. Each passing minute fueled his anxiety. Between the couple's inane conversation and the knowledge that this idiot wouldn't even remember which element was which, colors be damned, it was all he could do not to snap when he heard his phone buzz.

He paused, looking up from the start of earth when he noticed a message from Bridget, the t-shirt creator, asking about the next protest.

"What's the itinerary for this Saturday's protest? Do we bring the same signs? Are we standing outside of the Council building or are we marching?"

I already posted about this on Twitter yesterday, Mercury thought. His cheeks were hot, and his ears rang.

"Hey, Merc, did you see Bridget's text?" Sloane asked.

Mercury looked up at her, shaking his head slightly, and turned his attention back to the tattoo. More messages popped up on his phone, causing the metal hand cart that held the colors and various gear to rattle. He sighed. He couldn't touch his phone; he was already gloved up.

Just leave me alone, Mercury thought. *I don't have the energy for this.*

"Do I need to bring more t-shirts?" Bridget asked.

"That would be good, but please think of a name other than 'Astera Army.'" Griffin wrote.

"What should it be? Let's brainstorm," Bridget asked.

Mercury breathed in then out, attempting to block out the distractions around him. He tried to keep his focus on the tattoo, knowing that a fuck up would be permanent. He was on to fire now, and as he traced the lines with red ink, he tried to keep his hands steady.

Sloane chuckled then took a long draw from her vape pen. The smell of strawberries filled the shop.

"Ha! Like Astera Alliance is any better," Sloane said. "You see this shit?"

"Nah," Mercury replied, hoping his response would register with her. She shook her head and laughed again, her phone pinging every few minutes.

Turn your ringer off, Mercury thought. *Just shut the fuck up.*

He urged himself to focus. He had only two symbols left. He tried his best to tell himself to stay calm, but inside he was screaming.

"Halfway done," Mercury uttered, though more to himself than anyone else. He dipped the needle into the blue pot sitting on the table and began etching the symbol of water on the man's other calf.

"So, I was thinking we should do Thai after this. Or maybe Japanese? I'm really feeling like, a total Asian-y vibe," the girlfriend said.

"Yes, let's do Thai. I'm in the mood for Udon," the man responded.

Sloane scoffed.

Mercury looked up to see the couple glance at each other before turning back to their discussion.

"Or maybe we should just get some brunch. Is that place down the street good?"

The girlfriend tapped Mercury on the shoulder. He flinched, turning the gun off quickly before it glided off course.

He looked up at her. "Yes?"

"Is that place down the street good? I think it's called, like, Coffee Pot or something?"

Mercury smiled tightly. "Pot Head," he replied.

"Right," she said. "So is it good, though?"

"Yeah, the food is good."

"But what's on the menu? Is it like breakfast-y or like, lunch stuff like sandwiches? Do they have any—"

"Ma'am," Sloane interjected. "I don't know if you know this, but Google is free."

Mercury looked from Sloane to the woman then back to the tattoo.

The woman scoffed and pursed her lips, glancing down at her phone.

Sloane rolled her eyes and picked up her novel.

Mercury moved on to the final symbol, air, and he inhaled deeper than he had before. His phone still rang. The couple still chittered about food, and Sloane still provided commentary on the messages they received. He felt the tension settle in his shoulders. *Just one more and I'll be done. Just one more.*

"All set," he announced twenty minutes later when he finished the final symbol. He covered the tattoos with gauze and told the man how to properly care for the tattoo, how long to keep putting lotion on it, and what to do if it felt infected.

"Thanks," the man said as he slid off the chair. He walked to the counter without another word, his girlfriend following him.

He paid Sloane then walked out of the parlor. The girlfriend cast one final look back at them before turning left toward House of Tofu.

"Hipster trash," Sloane said while watching the couple disappear down the sidewalk.

Mercury smiled briefly then turned his attention back to cleaning his needles.

"Did you see the thread in What's App?"

"I was a little busy," Mercury said, gesturing to the table.

"Oh, well. We're trying to think of a new name instead of Astera Army. Poor thing, Bridget is trying to hold onto it but Griffin and I keep telling her, like, baby, you gotta let that go."

Mercury stood and wiped down the chair as Sloane spoke at length about different names. His heart thumped wildly at the thought of their eagerness for the next protest. His aunt's threat loomed large, making his chest feel tight and his palms feel sweaty.

"Do you like any of these names, Merc?" Sloane asked.

"Uh, they're okay," he said.

Please just stop, he thought. He wanted nothing more than to burrow into his bed and sleep. *If I'm asleep*, he thought, *I don't have to make decisions. No one is depending on me when I sleep.*

"But, do you have one you prefer?" she asked.

"No, not really."

"But, like, which one—"

"I don't give a shit," Mercury snapped.

Sloane knitted her brows.

"What the hell, Merc?" She scowled at him; Mercury couldn't help the shame washing over him. "What's wrong with you?"

"Nothing," he said. He turned his back toward her and began straightening his station. "I'm fine."

There was a part of him that wanted to break and tell Sloane everything. He wanted to tell her about Oliana's threat, tell her that his aunt didn't give a fuck about him and that she planned on turning him in and implicating them in the cover up. But he knew what she'd do if he did. She'd yell at him for lying about why he left the party and for not telling her the second it happened. She'd cuss and want to speak to Oliana in person, and last, and perhaps worst of all, she'd want to tell the rest of the group. Then the process would start over again.

I can't let them know, Mercury thought. *I'll take care of it. But how?*

"Uh huh," Sloane said. She scoffed and inhaled the vapor from her pen.

"Really, I'm fine."

"If you say so. We've got a lot of planning to do this week in preparation for this next protest. It's going to be the biggest one yet."

Mercury nodded.

"Yup," he agreed halfheartedly. He walked over to the desk and grabbed the iced coffee she'd gotten him. He sipped at it, but the second the coffee hit his stomach, he could feel the acid rising, making his stomach churn. He could see his friend examining him, her expertly lined eyes squinting as she looked him up and down.

"I know what's wrong," she said.

Mercury's heart leapt. There was no way she could know what was happening, could she?

"Oh?" he said, playing dumb.

"Yeah. You're nervous. You're leading this big-ass movement that's growing and growing and for the last few months you haven't really slowed down. All this must have you feeling overwhelmed."

Mercury nodded. He sighed and leaned against the desk.

"Yeah, I am. There's so much to do, so much more I'm responsible for."

"Well, that's why we're here," she assured him, holding up her phone. "You've got a team behind you. We won't let you fuck this up."

Mercury chuckled. "I know. But it's not just that it's . . . at the party, something happened."

She cocked her head. "Oh?"

"Yeah. Oliana pulled me to the side and—"

The door to the shop dinged again. Mercury turned to see his father step into the shop, wearing a floral suit and Ray Bans.

"Hey, kids." Atlas pulled his shades down and slid them into his pocket with his right hand. He held his briefcase in his left one.

"Hey, Mr. A." Sloane extended a fist and he bumped it. "Council meeting?"

Atlas rolled his eyes. "Unfortunately. I love my job, I love your aunt, but fuck do those people talk too much."

Sloane giggled.

"What did you talk about?" Mercury asked. He looked at his father, who eyed him briefly before looking down at his phone.

"Plans for Ilaris, plans to lobby for or against bills in the house. Kinheld, a few things we discussed last weekend."

The threat, Mercury thought.

"Sounds like so much fun," Sloane said sarcastically.

Atlas laughed. "It was the highlight of my week. Anyway, I'm off to change. I'll be back down shortly."

He walked up the stairs toward their apartment. Mercury watched him curiously, wondering what information his father hadn't shared.

"What were you saying, Mercury? About Oliana," Sloane said, interrupting his thoughts.

"Oh," he replied, turning away from the staircase. "She was just a nightmare. Said something about my costume not fitting the theme, that I ought to know better since my dad was the host."

"Ugh, gross. I wish she'd get off her high horse. She was a much better person before Vael was in office," Sloane remarked.

Mercury nodded. "Yeah, she was."

A lot of things were better back then.

Quotes on a Protest

By Sloane Salvanera
Staff Writer, *Jonquil*

President Harvey Vael gave a speech in the Rose Garden on Tuesday addressing the wave of protests in the City of Angels that led to several incidents of violence. With a collection of human, dhampir, and harridan journalists in front of him, the President told the American people that the protestors who have taken to the streets in opposition of Kinheld, the newly sanctioned plot of land where American witches will be relocated, are nothing more than "derelicts, provoking fights because they do not want to follow the laws of the land."

Of course, we know that Vael really wanted to use a stronger phrase than derelicts to describe witches and their allies fighting for equality. But as the blood-sucker-in-chief took the time to pontificate at length about the merit of the protests (or "riots" as Vael has dubbed them), he added:

"Any witch using magic at one of these riots, because that's what they are, riots, will be arrested. Anyone caught using magic against officers or other members of law enforcement will be dealt with harshly. Their punishment will be swift and unforgiving."

Most of the journalists huddled in the recently renovated Rose Garden (now no longer filled with roses but instead with foxglove, dahlias, and night-blooming jasmine) lobbed softball questions at the President in regard to his statements. The only one to ask for clarification on said punishment was the *Los Angeles Times'* White House Correspondent, Kareem Jeffries. After telling the President that his comments sounded threatening, Jeffries asked what the punishment would entail, and whether or not vampires caught in the vicinity biting people without consent would also receive the same kind of punishment.

"Witches are prohibited by law from using their magic in public, regardless of the circumstance. I trust that they know that simply marching and conducting themselves respectfully is in their best interest, just like I trust that vampires know to ask for consent before drawing blood. This isn't the dark ages," Vael stated.

The President wasn't the only powerful person to condemn the protests. Celebrities, political pundits, and TikTok trolls all ranted about the merit of the complaint many witches across the nation have. Some call the protestors "greedy," others have said they're "cutting off their nose to spite their face."

"We all want our voices to be heard," said Senator Ezekiel Frank (D-Iowa), a vampire senator and rumored 2024 presidential candidate. "But stoking violence and causing dissension isn't the way to get your point across. It makes support for Councilwoman Murtaza's decision to take her magical kin to their own land all the more likely. If witches, vampires, and humans can't get along, well, somebody has to go."

Senator Amelia Squire (D-Hawaii) is another rumored presidential candidate who spoke out about the protests. Squire, who would be the first known-witch to run for president, denounced the protests, calling them "divisive," and accusing the protest's leader, Mercury Amell (who happens to be the nephew of Councilwoman Murtaza) of "cannibalizing the movement" toward equity and peace among witches, humans, and vampires.

But no one has been more frank about the protests against Kinheld than the architect of the Corvius Accord herself, Councilwoman Oliana Murtaza. In an interview with Gayle King, Murtaza sat down in the Council's opulent home in Benedict Canyon. When asked about what she thought of the protests themselves, Murtaza was blunt.

"I think they are an insult to everything the Council and I have worked for," she said.

She went on to say that she understood feeling voiceless, and that disagreeing with the powers that be are what turned her first into an activist and then into a political powerhouse. But, she added, resorting to violence only "sullies the message."

"People aren't going to take your plight seriously if you can't even walk two miles across the beach without conflict." Murtaza is referring to the second protest in Los Angeles, where a group of protestors clashed with human and vampire tourists on the Santa Monica pier.

"How does it make you feel that the main architect of this opposition and violence is your own nephew?" King asked.

Murtaza demurred. She tearfully replied: "I treated Mercury like he was my own child, especially after my sister, Kessia, was murdered. I can't understand how someone who has seen so much violence and injustice in their life would want to perpetuate it."

The Councilwoman added that she "still loves [Mercury]," and that she plans to be there with "open arms and an open heart" when he changes his mind.

"How do you know he will?" King asked.

"Because I know my nephew more than almost anyone else in this world. He'll come around and see that what we're doing will benefit us all."

CHAPTER 11

THE NEXT DAY, MERCURY SAT BEHIND HIS DRUM KIT, STICKS IN HAND. IT was the second hour of his jam session with Ellis. At first, Mercury had been excited when Ellis texted him and asked if he wanted to play music. He'd been longing to spend time with his friends doing anything other than protesting. But it seemed Ellis had something else in mind. He'd spent nearly the whole first hour talking about the coverage the protests were receiving, both good and bad. He asked what the full plan was for the upcoming one, where they'd meet, and if he knew how many people would be in attendance.

For his part, Mercury answered as vaguely as he could. He kept trying to shift the conversation back to music, hoping his friend would get the hint that he wanted a protest-free day.

They were in the middle of playing "Love Will Tear Us Apart" when Ellis stopped abruptly.

"You good?" Mercury asked. His friend balanced the mint green guitar on his knee, one of the last things his father bought him before cutting him off. He pulled off his striped beanie and ran a hand through his unruly brown hair.

"Are you even still interested in this movement?" Ellis asked. He looked at Mercury, his hazel eyes inquisitive.

138

Mercury's stomach throbbed. He knew that sooner or later someone other than Sloane would ask him about the protests, about why he'd stopped responding to the messages about it on social media, or why he'd been so vague in the group chat. Because he'd thought it would be Griffin, Ellis' comment caught him off guard. He stared at his friend, searching his brain for words to say.

"Uh, of course I am," Mercury lied; even he didn't believe himself. He smiled but knew it wouldn't do. Ellis knew him too well, had seen all his bullshit attempts at obfuscation before. As if reading his mind, his friend raised a thick brow and pursed his lips.

"I call bullshit."

"Whatever, man. I've just been tired lately." He said, twiddling the drumsticks between his fingers.

"You know who's tired? Me. I'm having to work double shifts just to cover the rent on a 400 square foot apartment that could barely fit a family of ants. You've got it made," Ellis fussed.

Mercury sighed. How could he explain to his friend that he didn't mean physically tired? It was his essence, his very being that was struggling to make it through each moment.

Oliana's threat, whether serious or not, had done its job. Every day for a week, he'd considered typing in the group text that the movement against Kinheld was over and they should just focus on other things. He couldn't eat; he wasn't really sleeping. The nightmares he'd had of Delanie after Astera were now replaced with ones of police busting down his door. In some, they handcuffed him with Thurguards and he felt all his magic slowly drain out of him. In others, they simply shot him. Those were the ones that forced Mercury awake and kept him up for the rest of the night.

Mercury shivered in spite of himself.

"Well, I don't know what to say about all that," he replied. "Me saying I'm tired isn't a knock on you. I'm just . . . tired."

"So go grab one of Marta's special mixes," Ellis suggested, referring to the Adderall sugar cookies his blue-haired neighbor made.

Mercury shook his head in protest.

"They aren't bad. They get me through my shifts sometimes. And if you need to level out, well." Ellis pulled his vape from his hoodie and took a long pull. The sticky, dank smell of weed filled the room. He passed it to his friend, and Mercury sighed before pressing the tiny vape to his lips and inhaling.

"It's not like that," Mercury spoke, holding the weed smoke in his lungs.

"Well, what is it like?"

Mercury dropped his head as he blew out the blueberry-flavored smoke. For the first time in a while, he was afraid to look into his friend's eyes. What would he find there if he told him he was planning to pull out of the protests?

"I just . . . I'm just wondering if the protests are still a good idea."

Ellis' eyes shot up, his mouth hovering near the edge of the vape.

"What?" Ellis asked. "Why?"

A pang in Mercury's stomach again. He set the sticks down, wiping his palms on his jeans.

"They've gotten violent. I can't risk something bad happening again."

"Yeah, they've been violent, but they've also been making an impact."

"I know you've been there to help soften the blow, but you and the other white allies aren't going to be around forever. Someone could get killed."

"People will be killed regardless."

"Exactly. So why risk it?"

Ellis narrowed his eyes and spoke, his hands moving wildly. "Don't you want change? Don't you want equality? You said yourself separate isn't equal and if Oliana goes unchallenged and gets her way, Kinheld will be built, witches will be relocated, and who knows what'll happen then. Are you ready to give up on things already?

Mercury sighed. "It's not like that."

"Well, what is it like?" Ellis questioned.

Mercury shook his head. "C'mon. Let's talk about this later. You called because you wanted to jam, not bump your gums about this protest shit."

"'Protest shit?'" Ellis leaned forward.

"Yeah, protest shit," Mercury said. His voice was loud, and the anxiety he felt had been replaced by anger. Who the fuck was Ellis to lecture him? Hadn't he bitched the entire time they drove to Astera? Didn't he spend the whole trip holding their fate over Mercury's head? He was with Sloane now, and he said he bore no ill will toward Mercury, but Mercury knew there was some part of him that hated Mercury for putting him in that position, for his parents taking away their wealth and leaving him with nothing.

"I don't know why you're so pressed about this. It ain't even your fight."

Ellis scowled at him. "What the fuck do you mean it's not my fight?"

"I mean, you're not born this way. You're just a Made witch. You're not a real witch."

Ellis set the guitar down and stood. "Oh? I'm not a *real* witch? Why the fuck do I have to wear this dog tag then?"

He grabbed the tag from behind his shirt and held it up.

Stop this, Mercury thought. *Just tell Ellis the truth.*

But he couldn't. He was so damn mad and scared, not just for himself but for his father and his friends. They were all he had. He couldn't tell them the truth and risk them trying to save him. He doubled down instead.

"That dog tag doesn't make it real. And you never really wanted this anyway. You're just trying to hijack this movement so you can look down. But you're not a real witch, none of you are, and you all should just stop trying," Mercury fumed. His voice had gotten so loud that it reverberated throughout his room.

Ellis shook his head. He slipped his beanie on and gave Mercury one last look.

Please don't go, Mercury thought. But his jaw remained clenched.

I'm doing this to save you, he thought. But he crossed his arms against himself.

I'm sorry, he thought. Yet he remained silent as Ellis unplugged the guitar and slipped it into its case. Ellis zipped it up and slung it over his shoulder, his face expressionless.

"You know, Mercury. You can be a real piece of shit sometimes."

Ellis opened Mercury's bedroom door and slipped out. Mercury gawked at the door, wondering who would be next to leave his life.

He eased behind his kit and sighed just as his father walked into his room.

With his eyebrow raised, Atlas asked, "Mercury, what did you do?"

***

STILL SITTING BEHIND HIS DRUM SET, HE TOLD HIS FATHER WHAT happened. When Atlas tried to argue with him about why alienating his friends wasn't a good idea, and about how telling the truth was the only way to relieve him of his anxiety, Mercury snapped.

"What does it matter to you, anyway? If I tell the truth, then Oliana will come for me and I'll be arrested. I should think my silence is better for you in the long run."

"Not if it means you blowing up your life and losing the things you're trying to fight for."

"You have no ground here, Dad. You're as much a part of the system as she is," Mercury spat, his hands trembling. He set the drum sticks down and stood then rushed past his father into the kitchen. Atlas followed him.

Mercury's stomach roiled. His whole body vibrated with his anger and though he wanted to collapse into his father's arms and never leave the apartment, Mercury lashed out. "What would you do if she tried to make good on her threat, huh? Would you end your career trying to save me? Or would you stand there silent like a good dog after she yells at you to stay in your place again?"

A loud pop echoed throughout the room. His father had slapped him only once before.

It was when he was sixteen and angry because Troian was seemingly the center of everyone's universe. He'd felt like he was nothing, like he didn't even exist. He'd been jealous of his brother's powers, of the easy way he could talk to women, of how he seemed so poised to take over his father's empire. When he'd picked a fight with his older brother and his father broke them up, Mercury told him the intervention didn't matter because he'd just take Troian's side because he was the golden boy and Mercury was nothing to him. A mistake. The one who should have died instead of his mother.

He'd felt the sting of his father's palm then, and it left his cheek as hot and throbbing as it did now. In the present, Atlas strode toward Mercury and gripped his head in his hands.

"You listen to me," he began. "There will always be people in your life who will do everything they can to stop you from doing what you're meant to do. If you give in to those people, if you believe what they're telling you, they win. You lose."

"Dad, this isn't the same as some dweebs on the internet trying to troll me." Tears welled in Mercury's eyes as spoke. "If she goes to the police, I could die."

His voice broke at those final words. As his father's eyes met his, Mercury could see that his father knew down to his bones the fear and anguish that only came with being seen as dangerous to the very people who swore oaths of protection. He knew because Mercury remembered his parents sitting him and Troian down to have "the talk".

He remembered shivering despite the heat of a Los Angeles summer day and feeling rudderless as his parents gave them the checklist of things to do and to avoid when dealing with the police.

"Don't make any sudden movements."

"Ask for permission to retrieve your items."

"Keep your hands where they can see them."

He also knew because the bruises Mercury sustained from the encounter with the police in Denver had not just been physical. Mercury had been lucky that time—his friends had come to his aid and sprung him from jail just as that group of badged-up vampires cornered him. He doubted he'd have the same luck again.

Atlas drew him into an embrace and Mercury let the tears fall down his cheeks, his arms wrapping around his father. He leaned into his magic and surfed his father's memories, finding the ones of him and Troian as children, back when his mother was still alive. He wished he could curl up in the memory and let it envelop him like a blanket. He wished he could stay there, basking in its warmth and comfort.

But his father pulled away and Mercury was standing in their kitchen, shivering and sweaty.

"Nothing is going to happen to you," his father assured him.

"You can't make a promise like that; you know better," Mercury replied.

He noticed his father's eyes were glassy.

"I'm saying it as much to you as I am to the goddesses," his father said. "If I could shield you from all of the pain this universe has to offer, I'd do it in a heartbeat."

"I know." Mercury sniffled. "But I've got to do what I have to do to keep everyone safe. So I'm going to cancel it."

"Mercury—"

"Maybe Oliana was right. Maybe this is the best thing to do." He pulled out of his father's arms and hurried out of the apartment and the tattoo parlor before he could respond.

Atlas stood there speechless, his heart sinking to the pit of his stomach.

For the first ten minutes, Mercury found himself wandering aimlessly along the sidewalk, not even acknowledging the people who called out to him from across the street. He even blocked out the sound of the traffic and other passersby as his thoughts ravished his mind. Somehow, he landed safely in a quaint café, sipping on a latte and ruminating over his plan for the next hour.

First, he told the group. He Facetimed them, not wanting to tell them his plans via text, even though he couldn't bear to see their faces. Ellis didn't respond to the request, which Mercury supposed was just as well. He'd already known what Mercury would say.

"So you're just going to give up because a few witches can't handle their shit?" Sloane spoke first.

Joelle winced at Sloane's comment, bringing a hand to the wound on her neck.

"Mercury, I don't think you realize how big this movement has gotten. We can make some real changes. We can't stop now," Griffin pleaded.

Mercury repeated the same reasons over and over again: "I don't want it to get violent." "I don't want the police called." "Maybe let's let things cool down."

"You've been quiet, J," Sloane said, shifting the attention away from her best friend. "What do you think?"

Joelle looked up, flustered.

"So I'm the tie breaker now?"

Sloane rolled her eyes. Joelle paused.

"Did your camera freeze or something?" Sloane quipped.

Another pause.

"I think . . . Mercury is right." Joelle's voice broke.

Mercury wasn't surprised to find that Joelle agreed with him. After all, she'd been the one out of all of them most affected by the violence at the recent protests.

Sloane scoffed and rolled her eyes again.

"Of course you do," she said. Ellis placed a hand on her shoulder and Sloane pursed her lips and huffed.

Joelle looked down at her hands before speaking again.

"I know you're more than willing to deal with violence for the cause but after what happened last time," Joelle quavered. She pulled her hair over to her right side, exposing the left side of her neck, the skin still puckered and bruised.

Mercury sucked in a breath.

"I don't want to go through this again."

Sloane's lips were no longer pursed but her eyes were hard as she stared back into the camera.

"Fine. You both want to abandon the movement, that's your prerogative. I, however, am not going to just tap out because I'm scared of a little violence. It's not the first time I've had to stand up for myself, and it sure as shit won't be the last."

Silence followed her words.

"I guess that's it then," Griffin said, interrupting the silence.

Mercury's eyes bounced between Griffin and Joelle. Each of them wore expressions as if they were bracing for his response. Joelle was on his side. And even though the violence of the last protest had been an excuse, it still felt nice to have someone agree with him, especially Joelle.

"I still don't think it's a good idea to do this protest. I'm going to call it off."

Sloane took a long draw from her iced coffee.

"You can't stop us from going," she argued as she placed the cup back on the table.

"Well, I could," Mercury said, hoping it wouldn't come to him using a suggestion spell on his friends.

Griffin shook his head and turned toward his computer to type something. Joelle pressed her lips together, her eyes watery.

"It's okay, Mercury. I know you're just thinking of our safety."

"Uh huh," Sloane said. She leaned forward and pressed her finger to the phone. She dropped off the call, leaving only Griffin and Joelle on the line.

"I didn't want it to be this way," Mercury spoke, more to Griffin than to his sister. His friend coiled the top half of his locs into a bun at the top of his head, leaving the bottom section to hang over his shoulders.

"None of us did, but it's for the best," Joelle lamented. She looked at Griffin, who was looking anywhere except the screen. She turned back toward Mercury and waved before ending the call.

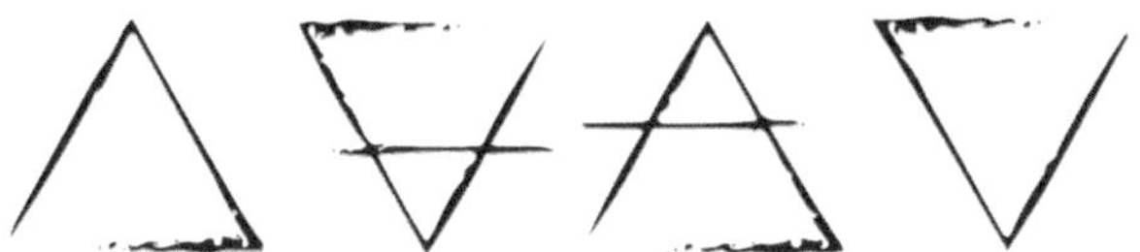

CHAPTER 12

ON THE NIGHT BEFORE WHAT WAS SUPPOSED TO BE THE PROTEST, Mercury tossed and turned.

He went live on Instagram after he spoke to the group, telling everyone that the protests were canceled indefinitely. He'd lost count of the number of comments that came in asking why, telling him that he was stopping too soon, and worse, accusing him of using the protests for clout. Afterward, he posted the video on Twitter and TikTok. His notifications skyrocketed so much that he turned his phone off. Even though he knew the madness would be there when he returned, he needed to feel as if it didn't exist for a while.

But even without the constant trill of his phone, his brain was still thick with noise. Thoughts streamed in and around his brain so quickly that he couldn't grasp one long enough to focus on it.

As he lay on his side, trying to soothe the burning feeling in his throat, Mercury thought about the moment in Astera when flames escaped from his hands and he burned Conner off of him before using the death spell. He wondered if his use of a different power had been a fluke, or if something else was to blame.

His mind worked over these things for hours and hours, until he saw the light of the morning shining through his curtains. He got out of bed and changed out of his sweat-soaked t-shirt and shorts into another set. He slid his feet into his Nikes and slowly walked out the door, closing it behind him.

"Bloqendis," he said, waving his hand behind him to lock the door. He turned right once he reached the street level and began jogging, headed for the beach. The sky was pink and there were barely any people crawling the beaches yet, and the steady sound of the waves crashing gave him something to focus on as he pushed himself to put one foot after another and another. As the wind whisked across his face, he wanted to believe his troubles had gone with it.

He ran for over an hour before pushing his way back into the apartment, out of breath and more sweat-drenched than he'd been when he woke up.

Mercury showered then climbed into bed, grabbing his phone and pulling up spells gone wrong with the volume down. Thirty minutes later, his father found him like this, a video of a group of teens trying to summon Bloody Mary but actually summoning the ghost of one of their dead, outspoken aunts in the process.

"Why you kids spend so much time with your head in your phones is beyond me," he said. He crossed into the bedroom and held out a coffee mug with the words "Gimme the coffee and no one gets hurt" written on the side.

Mercury sprang up, instantly relaxing at the feel of the warm cup in his hands and the smell of the latte drifting toward his nostrils.

"Are you going to tell me why you look like you do?" his father asked.

Mercury steadied himself against his headboard. "I canceled the protests. Now Sloane, Ellis, and Griffin hate me, not to mention the responses I'm getting online. They hate me. Say I'm doing all this for clout."

"Well, only you can know if you're doing the right thing, but people are going to have something to say regardless."

Mercury groaned. "Where is this sage-like advice coming from? Yesterday you were seconds away from telling me about myself when it came to canceling this protest, and now you're okay with me canceling it?"

His father crossed his arms.

"If I were to tell you that you were wrong, what would you be able to do about it now?"

"Nothing."

"And if I were to say you made the right call, what about it then?"

Mercury shrugged.

"No, don't do that. You have an answer."

"I would still feel fucked up about it all."

"That's how you'll feel either way," his father explained. "I figured the best thing I can do is just give you your space and let you know you made the right decision for you in the moment. You did the best you could."

Mercury sighed then sat up, wiping at his face with his hands.

"Now come on. Let's get brunch."

AN HOUR LATER, THEY SAT AT THE BAR OF A SMALL DINER ON VERMONT Avenue. Mercury ordered the avocado Eggs Benedict and a Bloody Mary. Normally, he'd be enjoying his favorite breakfast and the possibility of a weekend turn up with his father. But the acidity of the tomato juice soured his stomach. The sauce was runny today, a combination of the egg yolk and the hollandaise sauce that normally wouldn't bother him but now made him grimace. The avocado was overripe, and it turned to a brown mush on his plate. Even the smell of the diner itself, eggs and maple syrup and strong coffee, made Mercury's head swim. He sipped water as his father flirted with the waiter, asking for another round of drinks for them.

"Can I actually have coffee instead?" Mercury asked, knowing that it likely wouldn't make his stomach feel better but that his father would endlessly ask him if he was okay if he just sat sipping water.

The waiter nodded at him and smiled at his father before walking away. His father turned his attention back to him.

"Are you feeling better?" Atlas asked before taking a sip from his mimosa.

Mercury breathed in the stale air around him then released it. "I don't really know what to feel," he said.

His father nodded.

The waiter returned with his coffee. Mercury grabbed it when it hit the bar in front of him, wrapping his fingers around it for warmth though it wasn't a cold day. The second his fingers hit the cup, the television above the bar chimed with a breaking news report.

The headline was simple, only eight words, but it was enough to make him nearly fall off his bar stool.

"Jonquil Writer Freddie Karr's Death Ruled A Suicide."

Suicide? Mercury thought as murmurs filled the restaurant.

He'd never met Freddie, but from everything he knew and from what Valeria had told him, he didn't seem capable of such an act. Mercury knew he was receiving a surplus of hate mail and death threats—Freddie wrote and spoke candidly about the messages he received. Hell, he even posted the messages in his Instagram stories and TikTok videos and responded to them with witty rebuttals. Though he seemed to joke about it, was it possible that the hate had gotten to him?

No, Mercury thought. *Fuck that. This is the police we're talking about.*

They were the world's most dangerous gang. They'd planted evidence, falsely arrested and accused people. Hell, they'd even shot people for speaking out against them. Never mind covering up or closing cases of Black and Brown people dying. Did he really believe they wouldn't stoop low enough to cover up such a high-profile case?

He searched for the Witches' Council Twitter and was surprised to find a perfunctory message Faegan likely crafted. The timestamp read "2 mins ago".

"The members of the Witches' Council once again extend their thoughts and prayers to the family of Freddie Karr during this trying time. Losing a loved one is never easy, no matter the circumstance, and we wish healing and peace to everyone who was touched by Freddie's light."

Mercury grimaced at the message's sterility. There was no anecdote about Freddie's contributions to the community, nor was there even a link to the interview he did with Oliana earlier in the year. It looked like the kind of message copied and pasted from a marketing website on how social media managers can convey grief and sensitivity for an event the company didn't really care about.

"Dad, did you know about the ruling on Freddie's death?" he asked. He eyed his father, taking in the slight arch of his right eyebrow and small twitch of his lips just before he lifted his glass to his mouth.

"I didn't, but I'm just devastated. The last thing this world needed was to lose another talent like his. And the things he did for our community . . ."

His father trailed off, clenching his jaw. Mercury knew his father was talking about his community threefold, of course. Freddie wasn't just a witch; he was also a Black, Queer man—three communities touched by Freddie and mourning his loss.

Mercury knew he should be sympathetic, shove down his anger at his cousin and aunt, and comfort his dad in that moment. But those small, imperceptible tells his father gave just before he sipped his cocktail told Mercury that he knew more than what he was saying. And it pissed Mercury off. His blood boiled.

"Do you really believe he committed suicide? Does the Council?"

"Mercury," his father warned.

"Are you not going to answer my question?"

His father sighed. "Mercury, please. We were having a wonderful brunch. Let's not ruin that."

"Ruin it?" he questioned, his voice louder than he intended. The couple beside them looked over at him, their hackles raising at the sound of a Black man raising his voice. His father narrowed his eyes as he glared at him.

"Whether I believe that Freddie ended his own life or that he was murdered doesn't make a difference. He is gone, and the Council cannot change that."

"But it's bullshit. He didn't kill himself."

"And you know that, how?" Atlas lifted a brow at his son. "You don't have the kind of magic that lets you see the dead."

Mercury bristled at his father's shade. He took a sip of coffee, trying to swallow all the mean shit he wanted to say. Instead of choosing violence, he turned to his phone and pulled up an article about Freddie's death. He retweeted it, typing: "Smells like pig shit to me."

He added the hashtags "rest in power," "no justice no peace," and "Freddie didn't kill himself."

He'd gotten several notifications over the last few minutes. Avoiding conversation with his father, he swiped through them, seeing tag after tag for articles about Freddie, with people writing either that the witch deserved to die or the generic reply of "this is why we march."

One notification stood out to him. He hovered his finger over the post as he read the caption then lowered the sound on his phone and began playing the video. He could hear people singing in the background, could hear someone playing a beat on a set of drums. The videographer panned the camera around, showing the people marching alongside them singing and chanting and thrusting signs in the air. A woman stopped to dance, her body moving in time to the beat of a steel drum set.

The woman who'd been dancing dropped low, twerking and clapping. Despite the cheers and the jubilation the group felt, the videographer panned to the left, showing a group of people walking toward them swiftly.

Within seconds, they reached the woman who'd been dancing. One of them, a man in a leather vest with hair reminiscent of a '90s boy band member, pushed the woman so hard that she fell to the ground. There was a sharp thwacking sound as her body connected with the ground, and the videographer pointed the phone down, showing the woman on the ground, blood trickling from her head. Screams rang out, and several people dropped to their knees to shield the woman and offer her aid. The video whipped back to the man who'd pushed her, whose smile was purposefully wide to show off his fangs.

Mercury's heart bellowed from his chest. His ears throbbed and it took all his strength to keep his face blank instead of tossing his phone across the bar and yelling.

At first, he found himself wondering how the protest had still continued despite him cross-posting his cancellation video across social media. Then he caught himself; did it really matter? People were protesting for a cause he brought to the fore and though he wasn't there, the violence still persisted.

I can't stay here, he thought. *I can't stand by.*

He scanned the cafe. The seeming normalcy of everyone there, even his father, only added to his frustration. He felt as if he were losing his mind, as if his very being threatened to bust out of the seams.

For the last few days, he'd been tormented, paralyzed by Oliana's threat. He still remembered the feeling of those iron bars of the jail in Colorado, still had moments of his heart beating triple time when he thought of the sound the bars made as they swung open wildly and the officers stepped in ready to bite. He didn't want to feel that helpless ever again. He didn't want to feel so out of control, goddess help him; he didn't want to feel so weak. So *human*.

But something crystallized in him just then. Freddie's death getting barely a five-minute breaking news segment, the underwhelming response from the higher ups of the magic community, including his aunt, was unsettling. Where was the support? Where was the follow through with the Council's mission of supporting and seeking justice for all witchkind?

Seeing the woman knocked to the ground in the video shook him further. Another life affected by the Council's inability to act. Another person terrorized by vampires who have carte blanche to do whatever the hell they wanted with little to no repercussion.

It was clear to him, as he turned back to his father, swilling mimosas and fawning over the overpriced French toast, that no one in the upper echelons of Witchkind was going to do a goddess-damned thing.

He peered out the window, gazing down at the people waiting for a table or walking about the city. He wondered if they had any idea what was happening. Did they know that across the city from where they sat addictively scrolling on their phones and taking their brunch-time selfies a revolution was underway?

We all we got, he thought. *Only us.*

He clenched his fists, his grip tightening around his phone. He knew what he had to do.

"I've gotta hit the restroom."

His father nodded, his eyes focused on the news, which was now covering President Vael discussing his Supreme Court replacements.

Mercury excused himself then strolled to the back of the restaurant. He glanced back at his father, whose eyes remained glued on the television. When he was sure he was out of sight, he scurried to the door and out of the restaurant.

MERCURY NOW FACED THE EDGE OF THE BLOCK, TURNING THE CORNER and walking up a set of stairs into the shopping center. He remembered seeing a Bath and Body Works when he was here last with Sloane and Griffin.

He hustled through the crowd, his fists still clenched. He tried to control his breath, hoping he could stop it from escaping in ragged spurts. People stared at him as they passed him, no doubt sensing his anxious energy. He was trying to remember the words to the teleportation spell, something about summoning Eshu, when the blue and white checkered sign caught his eye.

The brightly lit store swarmed with people. He inhaled deeply and looked around, making sure no one saw him as he slid his dog tags beneath his shirt.

He rushed into the store, the scent of peonies and imitation vanilla flooding his nostrils. He winced as he walked, searching aimlessly for the candles. He knew he wouldn't have any luck with finding candles that were the colors he needed, but he figured the gods would forgive him if he used white candles with containers that were the right colors.

He needed one blue one, to appease water, and two yellow to appease air.

Mercury groaned as he assessed his options. The only blue candle was one called "Endless Weekend". The scent—mandarin, magnolia, and so much fake coconut it made Mercury's nose itch—had been his ex-girlfriend's favorite. He supposed her taste in smell was one of the reasons why they broke up.

He grabbed it off the shelf before reaching for the two yellow candles he'd need. His choice was either Pineapple Mango or something called Island Margarita, which smelled like a green skittle mixed with more fake coconut.

"Aww, hell," he groaned. As he was about to grab two candles off the shelf, a high-pitch voice sounded from his left.

"Would you like a basket?" an employee asked.

Mercury startled, trying not to wince as he turned toward her.

"Nah, I'm good," he replied. "I'm just getting these."

"Oh, good choices. Island Margarita is my favorite. Are they for a special someone?" she asked.

She smiled at him, her cheeks dimpling in the corners. She was a beautiful woman, petite with a mane of wavy purple hair, her edges laid perfectly and her lashes fluttering seductively. In any other circumstance, Mercury would've put on the charm and been happy to receive the attention. Hell, he might've even asked for her Instagram handle to learn more about her. But he was against the clock, and his only saving grace were disgusting candles and trying to surf his own memories to find the teleportation spell.

"No, I just needed a pick me up," he said. "Thank you."

"Well, if you need any help now or in the future, I'm Mia," she offered.

Mercury smiled at the woman and nodded, thankful his hands were full. He turned to see a line of people standing before the checkout counter. There was only one person working the register in the middle of the Saturday rush.

"Shit," he muttered. He eyed his surroundings. He'd hoped he hadn't had to use his magic just yet, and he wished he'd taken that basket from Mia. Instead of hoping and wishing, he cleared his throat and whispered a spell, looking around to make sure no one was focused on him.

"Nyxia, kiyuvidar ippio," he mumbled. He repeated it once more, and one by one the people before him walked back to where they'd been in the store before deciding to check out. He'd been careful, not wanting to turn away all the people in line. He waited behind three women giggling over their discount New Years' Eve scents before placing his items on the counter.

The clerk didn't smile at him or address him as he stepped forward, her eyes staying on the merchandise. He was thankful; he had no desire to make idle small talk. He just had one question.

"Do you have any lighters?" he asked. "Or matches?"

She looked up at him and raised a brow.

"I'm all out." He smiled his most charming smile. She rolled her eyes and slid a pack of Mother's Day themed matches into the bag. "Thanks."

With her eyes still fixed on the candles, her lips remained closed.

Mercury checked out and grabbed the bag, hustling out the store as fast as he'd walked in. He'd spent too much time there. He looked at his phone, another ten minutes gone. He searched for a place where he could complete the ritual, hoping to find an empty men's room.

He walked past several stores, weaving in and out of crowds of people strolling casually through the mall.

With each step, his anxiety rose. Now, he was irritable. He groaned as he was caught behind people aimlessly sipping Frappuccinos and gazing at store fronts as though the same ten clothing and makeup stores weren't in every mall in the city.

"Move," he said under his breath.

He couldn't use his magic here, but he kept repeating the spell to move in his mind.

Imixu. Imixu. Imixu.

Finally, he found a long corridor with restrooms at the end.

He entered the family restroom, just as a man and his toddler were strolling up.

"Sorry," Mercury said, locking the door.

"Jerk," the man called before kicking the door.

He didn't hear them walking away, and Mercury hoped they weren't standing and waiting for him to finish. He crossed himself against the smell of the restroom and grimaced at the dirty floors.

His eyes roamed the facilities until he spotted his target. He laid the candles out on the diaper changing station, wondering how often the custodians sanitized the germ-filled contraption.

Mercury set the blue one down first, then the two yellow ones just below it, forming the edge of an arrow.

He then pulled the matches out of the bag. He ripped two free and struck it against the cover of the matchbook. His nose wrinkled at the candles' scent, but it was the smoke he needed. It was what would carry him along to his destination.

Mercury yanked his belt off, hoping the prongs were sharp enough to cut. He filled his chest with air then ran the prongs along the palm of his hand, pushing lightly.

"Fuck," he cried out as a trail of blood dripped from the wound.

He squeezed his hand over the Endless Weekend candle. The flame turned blue for just a second, and Mercury sighed with relief. The candles would work after all.

He then traced a finger along the cut and drew the symbols for water, air, and spirit on the plastic of the changing station. Finally, he drew a line down his forehead, nose, lips, and chin. The line ended in an arrow at the top of his clavicle.

He breathed in the smoke and tried to focus on his friends. He didn't know exactly where they were, but he figured he could teleport to them if he kept them in his mind's eye.

He cleared his throat, hoping he'd be able to get the spell correct.

"Here goes nothing," he said. He opened his mouth to speak, but there was a knock on the door.

"One second," Mercury shouted.

"Sir, the family restrooms are only for people with kids," stated a deep, impatient voice.

Fuck, Mercury thought. The man with the toddler must have gotten the security guard.

"I'm sorry; I'm almost done."

"Sir, you need to come out as soon as possible; there are people with families who need to use the changing station."

"Yup, almost done." Mercury leaned over and flushed the toilet.

"Okay, you can do this," Mercury whispered. He closed his eyes and pressed one hand to his head and the other to his heart.

"Eshu, endu, meyloctu. I call upon you, with the offering of water and air, carry me to my loved ones. Carry me on the wind of the candle smoke, take this blood and the body it flows within, take me and my mind and my spirit. I am now here, but I open my eyes there, Eshu, endu, meyloctu. Carry me."

Mercury repeated the spell again, but already he could feel himself fracturing, part of his being carried on the smoke. He tried to keep his focus even as he felt his spirit begin to float on the smoke.

The spell had to be recited three times, once for spirit, once for the mind, and once for the body. Forgetting or being unable to complete the ritual could mean that a part of him could be stuck in the restroom. He'd been told horror stories about the teleportation ritual when he was a kid. He thought at first it was Troian trying to scare him, but then he'd seen one of the former Council members try it at one of his father's parties. He was a Fire Hand, brash and boastful, and he'd forgotten to say it three times. He'd ended up fractured, his spirit outside his body and away from his mind. Not even the head of Council, Malcolm—at that time the world's most accomplished Water Hand—had been able to put him back together. The man spent the rest of his life alone in his apartment, unable to handle the constant feeling of being unwhole, of feeling every emotion, every connection a little less.

"Eshu, endu, meyloctu. I call upon you, with the offering of water and air, carry me to my loved ones. Carry me on the wind of the candle smoke, take this blood and the body it flows within, take me and my head and my spirit. I am now here, but I open my eyes there, Eshu, endu, meyloctu. Carry me."

He kept his eyes closed but he could feel his body lightening.

"Sir, you've got to come out of there now."

Mercury didn't respond; he couldn't break concentration. He wouldn't become fractured, not like this. He wouldn't end with two thirds of himself on a street in Los Angeles and his mind in a dirty family restroom in a mall.

"Eshu, endu, meyloctu—"

"Is that smoke? He's burning something in there!" exclaimed the father.

Mercury heard the jangle of keys and the sound of a shoulder hitting the door.

"I don't get paid enough for this shit," the security guard grumbled. "If you don't come out of there, I'm going to come in there and kick your ass, then I'm calling the cops."

More and more of his body was going and being displaced by the spell. He could feel asphalt beneath his shoes, could reach out and touch bodies around him. He just had to finish the spell one more time. Just once more.

"Eshu, endu, meyloctu," Mercury started again. His voice sounded so far away from him. He was breathing heavily. He thought he was sweating, but he couldn't feel it. All at once he heard keys and pounding and shouting and ice shattering against the ground. There was a car horn blaring and a baby crying. He moaned at the pain of being unwhole. "I call upon you, with the offering of water and air, carry me to my loved ones. Carry me on the wind of the candle smoke, take this blood and the body it flows within, take me and my head and my spirit."

The door opened. Mercury didn't look.

"What the fuck?" said the father, his child crying. The security guard rushed toward Mercury, trying to grab for something that wasn't altogether there. No doubt he saw through Mercury to the table and the candles and the symbols.

"A fucking witch," the guard uttered. "I'll be damned. They're so sick, they're performing Satanic sacrifices in restrooms where kids are changed."

He grabbed for Mercury again, his hand strong and nearly enough to yank Mercury back. Mercury could feel it just as he felt the heat of the sun on his face.

"I am now here—"

"I'm calling the police! I'm going to tell them this witch was trying to curse my child," the father said. Mercury heard more people behind the father now, a crowd gathered and seeing magic in action.

"But I open my eyes there—"

"What is he doing? Why can I see through him?"

"Blow out the candles; that'll stop whatever he's doing," called out another, someone with a raspy voice.

Mercury couldn't move; he couldn't open his eyes. He had to finish the ritual even as he felt the air move and the security guard lean down to blow the candles out. If he succeeded before Mercury finished the ritual, it was over for him. He'd never be whole again.

"Eshu, endu, meyloctu," Mercury shouted fast.

And then, as the man opened his mouth to blow, Mercury cried: "Carry me."

CHAPTER 13

WHEN MERCURY OPENED HIS EYES, HE FOUND HIMSELF STANDING ON Hollywood Boulevard.

He looked down at his hands, squeezing them to make sure he was all there. He pushed at his wound with a finger and was delighted when a sharp feeling of pain rang through him.

"I'm whole," he breathed. "I'm whole."

He tilted his head back and smiled, letting the warmth of the sun pour over him.

"Move out the way, asshole."

Mercury was pushed forward, his focus now ripped from the sky to the street around him. Someone on a bike with a large sign that read "all witches must burn" sped past him, hitting him in the arm with the sign.

"Hey, fuck you!" Mercury yelled after him. The man turned around and flipped him off before swerving to avoid a yellow cab. Mercury smiled, thankful that sometimes karma was that bitch.

He browsed his surroundings. His friends were still on Hollywood Boulevard, only a block or two away from Regan Phillips' star, which was supposed to be the start of the protest.

It had been Griffin's idea to start the final protest there, on the three-month anniversary of the actor's death. Though he wasn't a witch, he was a harridan, and it only made sense to show up and show out for such an ardent supporter of the witch community. Then, they'd march to the Witches' Council Building. Mercury would give a speech, and they'd stand there and protest until a member of the Council came out and addressed them.

"We are prepared to stay outside of the Council Building overnight," they'd written on Twitter. "All protestors should come correct, with their own supplies, snacks, and the right pair of shoes."

It was two o'clock, and they should've already moved out of the Hollywood Walk of Fame area.

He'd been dropped on the sidewalk, next to a woman who was trying to soothe her baby from crying. He smiled at the woman as he stepped away.

"Where are they?" he asked. The spell was supposed to take him to who or what he visualized. He'd thought of Sloane, yet he didn't see her there. The march moved in front of him, a mass of signs and bodies and shouts. For a moment, Mercury stood in awe of how many people showed out. The group moved like a mass down the street, too many to count. He wondered if some of them were people who, like him, found the ruling on Freddie Karr's death to be suspect.

Amid the shouts for reformations, of calls for separate not being equal, he heard a call of justice for the murdered journalist.

"Say his name!"

"Freddie Karr!"

"Say his name!"

"Freddie Karr!"

Mercury couldn't see the person holding the bullhorn, but he knew that voice almost as well as his own.

He walked toward the protest, excusing himself as he weaved between people, until he found his friends in the middle of the crowd. Sloane held the bullhorn in her hands, her red lips pressed against it.

"What are we here for?"

"Justice!"

"What are we here for?"

"Equality!"

"What are we here for?"

"Reformation!" Mercury shouted. The crowd around him whooped when they saw he had joined them.

Sloane looked over at him and lowered the bullhorn. Her lips were pursed and her eyebrow raised. Her eyes traveled from his head to his shoes then back up again. Several seconds of silence passed before she turned toward Ellis and Griffin.

"I guess you called it, Griffin."

Griffin smiled as he lowered his sunglasses.

"Mmhmm," he said. "So, who's gonna run me my money first?"

Ellis blushed. He glanced at Mercury as he dug deep in his pocket and grabbed a twenty. Sloane followed suit.

"You bet that I wouldn't come?" he asked.

Ellis and Sloane looked at each other. "Yeah."

"And Griffin was the only one who thought I would?"

"Yeah," his friends said in unison.

Mercury felt a pang in his stomach.

"I'm . . . I'm sorry I let you down," he apologized. "I've been dealing with some things and I . . ."

He looked up at the sky, at the never-ending turquoise, unblemished by clouds. He blinked back tears as he turned back to his friends.

"Just know I'm here now. I'm not going to let you down again."

"I know you won't." Sloane smiled. "I might not be so forgiving the next time you do."

Ellis nodded.

"Thanks for believing in me," Mercury said to Griffin.

Griffin fist bumped him. "You're leading a movement that's gotten bigger than all of us. I don't blame you for being shook."

"Yeah," Mercury agreed, nodding.

"Alright, enough sappy shit. You, Mercury, have a protest to lead," Sloane said.

She handed him the bullhorn. Mercury gripped it, and a wave of peace passed over him as he held it. As he pressed the talk button, he smiled, feeling giddy and almost manic.

I am exactly where I belong, he thought.

He glanced over his shoulder at Sloane then brought the bullhorn to his lips.

"What's poppin', Los Angeles?"

The crowd roared. He heard people shouting his name, whooping at his presence.

"I'm sorry I'm tardy to the party, but you know what they say— better late than never!"

More cheers and clapping. Mercury wiped his forehead with the back of his hand, already sweating from the midafternoon summer sun.

"I didn't get to see all of you before we set off, so I need y'all to do something for me." He looked around, smiling at the people with whom he made eye contact. He noticed his friends walking, their strides lighter than they'd been when he first touched down. "Can I get a roll call one time for the one time?"

He could feel the crowd's energy as they marched; he could feel the magic filling the streets as they passed the Pantages Theatre.

"Where my Fire Hands at?" Mercury called. The crowd responded in kind, and he could see some of the fire Hands walking ahead of him lifting their hands in the air, fire caressing their fingertips. He could hear Sloane beside him making a "brrrr" sound.

"What about my Earth Hands?"

The wielders of the earth whooped. Mercury heard Ellis and Griffin shout beside him. Griffin pulled his glasses' cleaning cloth from his pocket and held it in his hand. For a second, he closed his palm, and when he opened it, a butterfly flew from his hands and into the sky.

"Water Hands, I know you got no trouble showing up and showing out!" Mercury yelled.

The water hands shouted "you know!" back to him. Mercury turned to his left, and suddenly Valeria was standing there. She smiled and whooped along with the Water Hands. Valeria lifted both her hands up and clenched her fists. Two icy shards slipped out of her wrists and she sent them flying over the heads of the protestors.

"And last, but certainly not least, let's make some noise Air Hands!"

A smaller portion of the crowd shouted, but Mercury's shout into the bullhorn sounded out loud for his fellow Hands who drew their magic from the air.

"Let me hear your element!"

As the crowd shouted their respective elements, Mercury turned toward Valeria.

"Nice to see you," he said, giving her a hug. "You missed the last one."

She nodded. "Doing some field work. I was sad to miss it; Sloane told me it was quite eventful."

Mercury turned back toward Sloane, who shrugged.

"I'm glad you're here."

"I'm happy to be here. I was doing some interviews with people in the crowd. They seem to be really engaged in this movement. Mercury, I think you've really got something here."

Mercury smiled at the compliment, butterflies in his stomach.

"Thank you. I really think we can change the world."

"That's a real tall order, Merc," Ellis said.

Mercury turned toward his friend, his eyes widened. That was the first thing he'd said to him in days.

"You're probably right," Mercury replied. "Let's just start with Los Angeles then."

Ellis looked at him conspiratorially, and Mercury fist bumped him. He hadn't realized how weighed down he felt by Ellis' silence until it ended. The weight he'd been carrying for the last few days felt lighter. He could release the breath he'd been holding in.

You've still got Oliana to contend with, he thought, and suddenly his breath seized. He took a deep breath, then another. He tried to center himself, knowing he had no choice but to be all in. He had no choice but to be brave.

They passed Grauman's Chinese Theatre. Though his breath had stabilized, he was still warring with himself. He brought the bullhorn to his lips again.

"Reformation!"

"Not restoration!"

"Reformation!"

"Not restoration!"

"Is separate equal?" he asked.

"No!" the crowd replied.

"Is separate equal?"

"Hell no!" he heard Sloane shout.

"Fuck no!" Valeria yelled. She'd migrated toward Sloane, and now they walked arm in arm, their free hands' fists up in the air.

"Now, I know we've all heard the news about Freddie," Mercury said.

The crowd booed.

"It's disgusting, and that's why we have to keep his name in our mouths." He inhaled a deep breath and as he exhaled, he shouted: "Say his name!"

"Freddie Karr!"

"Say his name!"

"Freddie Karr!"

"Say his muthafuckin' name!"

"Freddie Karr!"

Amid the shouts, someone in the crowd started singing "Hell You Talmbout".

Mercury joined in with the rest of the crowd, singing the names of all the witches slain by police. He was unsurprised to find that many of them were Black. His voice broke as he added Freddie's name to that list.

He nodded to his friends, gesturing for them to move to the front of the crowd. As the protestors thrust their signs in the air and clapped and stomped along to the song, they danced their way to the front, all the while singing.

Once at the front, Mercury instantly felt cooler. The sweat that accumulated on his forehead and at his armpits made him shiver momentarily.

The song was over.

They marched in silence for a moment, passing North Sycamore Ave. He looked toward Valeria, who walked backward taking photos of the crowd. When she turned forward, Mercury could see her posting them on *Jonquil's* Instagram.

"How many people are back there?" he asked.

"It's at least a hundred, maybe more," she said. She lifted her phone and pointed the camera toward him.

"Nah," Mercury refused, holding his hand out.

"C'mon. We need a photo of the face of the movement."

Mercury shook his head. "I don't want this to be about me."

"Don't be so shy, Merc. Quit acting like you ain't a whole lotta handsome."

Mercury rubbed at his beard and nodded. "You might be right."

They both chuckled.

"Give me 'defiant leader on the front lines,'" she instructed.

Mercury sighed and looked at the camera, his left brow slightly raised and his teeth clenched. She tapped her phone three times before nodding.

"Now, let me get a few of you in action."

Mercury lifted a fist and shouted: "Do we want Kinheld?"

"No!" the crowd behind him roared.

"Do we need Kinheld?" he asked.

"Fuck no!" they replied.

"What do we want?"

"Equality!"

"When do we want it?"

"Now!"

"What do we want?"

"Equality!"

"When do we want it?"

"Now!"

Gone was the anxiety he'd felt moments ago. Now, he was back to feeling invincible, awed by the momentum of the crowd. He carried that feeling as he called upon them again to say Freddie's name. He carried that feeling as they thrust their fists into the air, as the summer sun made his shirt sticky on his back, as he saw the bystanders on the street filming them as they walked, some shouting their support and others condemning them.

He spotted people with signs saying witches must burn. He spotted signs that had photos of a witch hanging from a noose, and a sign saying that they would avenge Conner's death. Though his breath hitched as he saw the sign with Conner's name, he shoved down the anxiety and covered it in power because he wasn't alone. There he was out in front of this movement that had such momentum that it was getting the attention of the head of the Witches' Council, of celebrities, senators, and even the President.

Charged from the energy of the protest, they turned left on LaBrea, which they would take all the way to the Council Building. Mercury turned to gaze at the crowd behind him.

"Mercury!"

The alarm in Sloane's voice nearly made him trip. He looked toward her, seeing the fear in her eyes. He turned, facing back toward the street before them, and what he saw took his breath away. He stopped walking. There in the middle of the street, beside a luxury apartment complex, stood a line of police officers in riot gear.

They held clear shields before them, and behind them sat two large Hummers, which were armed with gunners up top. An officer sat in each vehicle at the wheel, while another sat arming the gun atop the vehicle. They wore sunglasses but Mercury could sense their disdain from yards away. A dozen "what the fucks" rang out as the protestors behind him collided with him and others in the front of the line.

"What do we do?" Sloane asked.

"Is there another way to the Council Building?" Griffin questioned.

"Are you filming this?" Ellis asked Valeria.

Mercury turned toward his friends. Each of them wore matching expressions of fear, including Valeria who stood with her phone in one hand and the other over her mouth.

He took a step forward, mostly to give himself space from the crowd that was bunched up behind him. He knew there would be a police presence at their protest. They were walking down one of the busiest streets in Los Angeles and headed toward an official building. Cops typically posted on protest routes during large marches but this wasn't that. This wasn't monitoring to make sure things didn't get out of hand. This was intimidation, and likely a response to the events of the previous protest.

Mercury recalled some of what President Vael said in his speech the Monday after the protest:

"These people aren't patriots walking in the spirit of free speech and assembly. They're derelicts, provoking fights because they don't want to follow the laws of the land. Any witch using magic at one of these riots, because that's what they are, riots, will be arrested. Anyone caught using magic against officers or other members of law enforcement will be dealt with harshly. Their punishment will be swift, and unforgiving."

Their punishment will be swift and unforgiving, Mercury thought, wondering if this was the start of that punishment.

But he couldn't let the protestors behind him know he was afraid. He couldn't look like he wasn't figuring out a plan, so he closed his eyes and asked for Troian and his mother to lend him strength. He let out a deep breath and plastered a cool smile on his face.

"Good afternoon, officers," Mercury said, his voice booming through the bullhorn. The cops didn't react. They stood there like an immutable line. Just as Mercury was about to speak again, one of the officers in the car spoke into his radio.

"Your protest ends here. You can go no further. You need to disperse now and go back to your vehicles."

Mercury looked back at the crowd. He could see the worried looks on their faces.

"Officers, we have a permit to walk from the Hollywood Walk of Fame to the Witches' Council Building," he explained.

Mercury could barely finish his sentence before the officer replied:

"This is a direct order from the mayor of Los Angeles. "Your protest ends here, and you can go no further. You must disperse. I don't care if you go back to your car or your fucking broomsticks, but you've got to get out of the street."

Fucking broomsticks. Mercury's eyes narrowed at the words.

"Actually, we all left our broomsticks at home, sir," Mercury quipped.

Sloane gripped his arm. "Why the fuck are you taunting him?"

He could hear chatter behind him. He could hear and feel people stepping forward to stand beside him.

"We have a permit," Mercury said. He checked himself as soon as he did. He knew better than to assume that a piece of paper meant anything to these bullies. He sucked in a breath.

"What do we do?" someone asked.

"There has to be another way to get to the Council Building," someone else stated. "I'm going to Google it."

As several people pulled out their phones to check for an alternate route, others lifted their phones to record the scene. Mercury was thankful for their presence but their phones made him feel all the more nervous. No one filmed interactions with police anymore to ensure that everything went smoothly. It was always for evidence of wrongdoing, so when the person cornered by the cop ends up fucked up or dead, there's a record that they didn't do anything worthy of brutality.

"Only way to get there is to take the freeway or go through the 'burbs. I doubt those bougies will be cool with a mass of witches stomping through their grounds," someone mentioned.

Mercury clenched his teeth. There was nothing they could do but turn around.

"Let's head back. We can plan for another protest just outside the Council Building, or we can carpool now and get there," he decided.

Immediately, he was met with boos.

A tall man stepped forward, a scowl on his face.

"So what, we're just going to quit?"

"No, that's not what we're doing. We're just going with a plan B."

"We're not even gonna try to do anything? We're more powerful than they are," the man said.

Mercury could see people in the crowd agreeing with him. They nodded their heads, looking at this man with the same belief and adoration as they had with Mercury. He tried to ignore how much that stung.

"Do you see how many fucking police there are? They've got tanks," Mercury warned.

"Yeah, but we've got more power among us all than a goddamn bomb," a petite, pink-haired woman argued.

"Okay, just calm down, we—"

"Did you just tell me to calm down?" she asked. This only stoked the crowd's anger. Mercury licked his lips and turned toward his friends. He looked at them pleadingly, feeling as if he'd lose control of the crowd any second.

"You know damn well he didn't mean anything by that," Sloane said, stepping into the crowd. "We may have all the power, but that's not the point. We need people to be on our side, especially those without magic."

"Fuck those without magic," the man snapped.

More claps and confirmation from the crowd followed.

"We can't accomplish anything without them as allies," Ellis said.

The man sneered at Ellis. "Why the fuck are we even listening to these two anyway? They're only magical because of their fucking tattoos."

"Yeah," the crowd shouted.

"Fuck them," someone yelled.

"Let's keep going," another added.

Mercury could barely control his breath. He glanced at the street then looked back up just as quickly as his vision spun, and he felt as though the ground would rupture beneath his feet.

He held his hands up and stepped toward the tall man.

"I hear what you're saying, bruh. I really do. But we've got to be strategic about this shit. Our movement has already caught the public eye, and not all of the attention has been good. We can get more done if we take this L so we can move forward."

The man crossed his arms and scoffed. "There wouldn't be so much drama if you weren't stumbling around this shit like a kid."

"Ooooohhh," several people said.

"What?"

"I'm saying you ain't running this shit properly. Hell, you didn't even show up on time."

The sound of clapping and "yeahs" and "what the fuck" pierced Mercury through the chest. He was so close to losing them.

"Look, I know I'm not perfect. But I care about this movement more than anything. I don't want to see anyone get hurt."

"You have five minutes to turn back to where you came from," shouted the officer.

Mercury looked back at him. In the time they'd been talking, the police line had advanced. They were mere feet from them now.

"Well, while you're standing there wanting to be passive, we're showing the world that witches are cowards. Is that really what you want to show them?"

Mercury opened his mouth but the man stepped around him.

"Fuck you," the man shouted. "You and your Made witches can turn back around and call an Uber. We're going to teach these assholes better than to fuck with witches."

The man strode forward, and the protestors mirrored his steps. Mercury stepped back quickly, narrowly avoiding getting trampled over by the crowd.

He glanced at his friends. Ellis, Griffin, and Sloane stood, slack jawed and defeated. Valeria was nowhere in sight.

"Where's Valeria?" Mercury asked.

Sloane shrugged. Tears streaked down below her sunglasses as she cried silently.

Mercury wiped his face. The stranger had read him so completely that all he wanted to do was curl into a ball.

"What do we do now?" Griffin started.

"I don't fucking know," Mercury snarled. "Fuck!"

Griffin held his hands up.

"Did that fucking chud just take over your fucking movement?" Ellis asked, his pale cheeks flushed and his eyes wild.

"I—"

Mercury heard arguing.

Then feet shuffling.

Someone screamed.

The sound of breaking glass rang through the air.

Mercury stared at his friends before turning toward the sound. Though most of the crowd blocked them, Mercury could see the police line had advanced to meet the crowd. Without checking to see if his friends were following him, he darted onto the sidewalk. He could see the police pushing most of the crowd back as they shouted and screamed. A woman wailed, sobs wracking her body.

As he inched closer, the smell of magnolia and sulphur filled his nostrils.

His stomach dropped as he inched closer to the front of the crowd.

The tall man who'd led the crowd toward the police lay in the street, clawing at his throat, his fingers already tearing gashes into his skin. His eyes rolled back in his head. His mouth hung open as though he were screaming, but no sound came out.

"Holy shit," Mercury said. He took a step backward and felt a body behind him. He gasped and turned to see Griffin standing behind him, Sloane and Ellis standing on either side.

"What the fuck happened?" Sloane asked.

"A fucking potion," Mercury explained.

"Did he get hit accidently?" Griffin asked.

"I don't know," Mercury responded. When he saw another officer in the line lift a gloved hand with a glass jar in his hand, his eyes widened.

The cop tossed the potion over his shield. It hit a woman in the chest, a purple liquid swirling around her. She screeched as her chest caved in.

Bergasca, Mercury thought. A potion to break bones on contact.

He looked back at the man on the ground. His face was purple. He was dead.

Nefastle, the breath taker.

Every part of his being wanted to turn and run the other way, but he knew he couldn't let his people be slaughtered. As the police line pushed them back further, the witches began using their powers. A teenager with large glasses and stubble tossed a fireball over an officer's shield. As the officer caught flame, the cop beside him pushed the teen to the ground with his shield and crushed a glass jar into his stomach. Grey smoke swirled up, stealing the teen's breath. Mercury looked away, knowing the fate he was to suffer.

"We have to pull them back," he shouted. "We've got to get them to safety."

His friends nodded.

"Griffin, Sloane, you take that side," Mercury ordered, pointing toward the other side of the street. "Ellis and I will stay here."

"Be careful," Griffin uttered.

"Please don't die, either of you," Sloane said, her voice breaking.

They turned and ran.

Mercury looked at Ellis and took a deep breath. Ellis tugged on the sides of his mint-green beanie. Fear loomed in his eyes, but Mercury could see his friend trying to be strong.

"Okay," he said.

"Okay," Mercury replied.

They rushed into the crowd, shouting at them to fall back. Mercury's shoulder connected with someone's back and when the person turned and pushed him, he fell back into another protestor.

"Fall back!" he shouted.

But no one listened. Someone with the power of lightning hurled bolts at the officers, sending two of them into the air. Mercury's ears rang as he made his way toward the front of the line. The air was thick with smoke. The smell of sulphur and magnolia mixed with the deep smell of anais, used in the Bergasca potion. He coughed as he tried to shout at the protestors, urging them to stop using magic and fall back.

Someone stepped on his foot, and Mercury grunted as he stumbled to the side. He narrowly missed a cop who was beating someone, Mercury guessed a harridan, with a club. Mercury extended his hand and gestured, sending the officer back and into a tree.

"Run!" Mercury yelled at the kid. As he ran, Mercury turned back to the scene. Shouts and cries and groans filled the air as the witches and the police officers clashed.

A witch with the power to control weather stretched their hands to the sky. Gone was the sun, replaced by dark clouds fat with rain. Thunder clapped above them, the sound making Mercury's ears ring. Then a torrential rain began, putting out the fires but sending the scene further into chaos. Mercury stepped to his left, shoving an officer back just as he was about to step onto a fallen woman's face.

"Gimibresu," he shouted. The officer moaned, dropping his shield and clutching his stomach. As blood poured from his mouth, Mercury helped the woman up and gently pushed her toward the sidewalk. He turned in a circle, seeing bodies lying on the streets in various states of distress. Some had been hit by potions, others were on their stomachs, hands cuffed behind their back. He didn't see his friends anywhere.

"Ellis!" Mercury yelled. Another thunderclap sounded above. "Sloane! Griffin! Val!"

An officer hurled a potion at him, and Mercury motioned it to the side. He coughed as the smell of peppermint flooded his senses. The potion had made contact with another protestor.

"Oh no," Mercury whispered.

Green smoke swirled around the protestor. Seconds later, every inch of their skin scabbed over. The protestor fell to their knees scratching at their skin.

Ivarick, Mercury thought. *Skin poison. How the fuck did they get so many potions?*

He didn't have time to think. An officer charged him and Mercury pushed him with all his force. The second his hand connected with the officer's body, he saw a memory of him, sitting in a chair at the precinct. He saw a situation room, where officers huddled discussing a plan to stop the protest. "Operation Bathsheba" it was called. He saw boxes with the name Spalding Wellness. He could smell the peppermint and magnolia and anais and brine from the potions. There was one more scent, one Mercury couldn't place but one that set all the alarm bells off in his head.

In the here and now, Mercury dodged the officer's club. He gestured, sending the officer back and bumping against another cop. They fell to the ground, and Mercury turned in time to reach out as an officer pushed Sloane to the ground with his shield. From Mercury's hand a long chain of ivy wrapped around the officer's legs. He fell forward, his face shield breaking, shards piercing his skin.

"How the fuck did you do that?" Sloane asked.

Mercury looked down at his hands in wonder. Again, he'd used a power that wasn't Air-based. *What's happening to me?* He thought.

He pointed at Sloane with his fingers then closed his hand, pulling his friend up. She nodded at him as her fists clenched. Two perfectly sharpened daggers ejected from the skin on her forearms.

She charged at another cop who'd dropped his shield. As Mercury dodged potions and picked up protestors from the ground, gunshots boomed like fireworks in the distance.

"Be careful!" Mercury shouted. "If you have a forcefield, use it!"

Mercury inhaled the dense air and summoned his shield. Unlike the night at the UGN party, Mercury was only covering himself. His energy wasn't as drained, so he charged forward, pushing a cop to the ground and pulling his plastic shield from his hands. The officer reached for a pouch on his belt but Mercury snatched it from him. It looked like the one he'd seen on the cop at the Witches' Council building and the security guard at the W.A.S.

"Sonevardu," Mercury said. Instantly, the officer fell asleep. Mercury opened the pouch and gasped at the arsenal within. There was Nefastle, Bergasca, and Ivarick. There were two more, and as Mercury ran his hands over them, his body went cold. The liquid within one of them was as purple as a plum. Mercury gazed at the people on the sidewalk, laying dutifully with their wrists bound. *Claudust*, Mercury thought.

The other one was as black as night. He smelled the same scent he'd had before. This time he recognized it. Mushrooms slightly past their expiration date.

Hellefax. The widowmaker. It was a potion so archaic that Mercury had only ever read about it used on the unfaithful lover of the Head of the Witches' Council.

How in the hell could these officers have gotten ahold of these potions? What the hell was Spalding Wellness?

Someone bumped into him, setting his forcefield ajar. Mercury tossed the pouch in the air and sent it flying into the gutter with his magic.

He fixed his forcefield and jumped out of the way of one of Sloane's knives. It landed in the leg of an officer, and Mercury and Sloane pushed him to the ground as he set upon Bridget. They were too late, however. The officer had been a vampire, and he'd torn a gash in Bridget's neck. As she gripped her neck, Mercury lifted her to her feet.

"Ellis!" he called. He spotted the green beanie bopping toward him through a cloud of smoke. When his friend reached him, Mercury gestured toward the sidewalk. "Take her over to the sidewalk and heal her."

Ellis wrapped one arm around her waist and grabbed her free hand, guiding her to safety as she whimpered from the pain.

Mercury followed Sloane to the other side of the street, where Griffin had turned an officer's shield into a scorpion. The officer yelped as the stinger pierced his hand.

"Fall back!" Mercury shouted, trying to get the rest of the protestors to move.

Magic enveloped the air. The officers still advanced as the witches spelled them and called their magic forth. A witch gripped an officer's arm and poisoned him, but not before he hit her arm with Bergaska, breaking the bone completely.

Another witch used blood magic to cause a cop's blood vessels to burst. He'd been holding a potion and the witch was too close. As the officer dropped the potion, Ivarick went to work on the witch, covering his body in sores.

What have I done? Mercury thought. *What have I done?*

He exhaled, the energy of holding the forcefield and fighting taking its toll. He lowered his head for a second, letting the force field down. When he looked up, he saw the potion soaring toward him.

"Mercury!" Sloane shrieked, but her voice reached him too late.

He could see the richness of the purple liquid. When it hit his stomach, he could smell the brine of it. He gulped down air as he felt his whole body lock up, one muscle, one bone at a time. His heart pounded erratically as he fell on his side, his head barely cushioned by someone's backpack. Mercury couldn't move. Even his eyelids were stuck open, his eyes fixed on a position across the street. Tears welled in his eyes and spilled down his cheeks. His throat ached. Saliva filled his mouth. *Claudust*, he thought.

He could hear Sloane calling his name. He could see Ellis rushing toward him and could feel his hands on him trying to heal him. Nothing. Already his left hand was going numb from being tucked under his body for so long.

"What the fuck do we do?" Sloane asked, her voice frantic.

"I don't know, but I can't heal him; it isn't working." Ellis panicked.

"We can't leave him here," shouted Griffin.

The trio traded glances then one of them grabbed Mercury's ankle. Another one picked him up by his arms.

They didn't travel far. Mercury heard glass breaking, a loud crack. Suddenly, his feet fell to the ground. The smell of anais wafted to his nose, and more tears flooded Mercury's eyes. He could hear Ellis' cries of pain, could hear an officer shouting at his friend. Then his upper body connected with the pavement. Whoever had held his upper body had let him go.

He heard Sloane's scream seconds later.

"Hey! Don't touch her!" Griffin shouted.

Stop! Mercury thought as the scuffle continued. *Stop hurting them!*

Bodies and broken glass covered the street. Signs, backpacks, and shoes littered the ground. Blood mixed with water from the rainstorm that Mercury only now registered had stopped. He heard another blast, and the sound of a car alarm. He heard a man crying, shouting in agony.

I should have listened to her, Mercury thought.

I should have made sure no one would march, he thought.

I am a failure.

This is a failure.

Before him he noticed Sloane and Griffin walking, their hands behind their back. Sloane's bare legs were covered in dirt, and a large cut stretched down the length of her left thigh. Two officers held Ellis in place as they walked behind them. Ellis hopped on his left leg, his right one hanging awkwardly. Broken.

Across the street, Valeria stood with not one hair out of place.

She now wore a hat and sunglasses; she'd changed her shirt from the Astera Army one she'd worn earlier to something plain. Around her neck rested a lanyard, and as she held her phone up, she twisted from side to side as though surveying the chaos.

No, not surveying it. Filming it.

Valeria had disappeared before the fight and Mercury had forgotten all about her. Now she stood, her clothes pristine, observing carnage and doing nothing.

He couldn't help the rage simmering, and the fact that he couldn't shout made the tears flow even more.

How could you? He thought. *You goddamn vulture.*

Another, rougher set of hands scooped Mercury up and flipped him onto his stomach. The cold plastic of a zip tie cinched his arms together. Someone carried his feet, and another held him up by his hands. As they walked, Mercury surveyed more carnage, more blood. Then he saw the tailgate of a van, heard the doors open, and was placed on his side on a bench seat. One of the officers smiled at him, his fangs yellowing, as he slipped a seatbelt loosely over Mercury's lap.

"Enjoy the ride, witch," he snarled.

He slammed the door as he stepped out.

A hand weaved around Mercury's neck. His heart jumped then

settled after realizing it was Sloane's. She leaned forward, her face dirty and a large cut above her eyebrow.

"It's okay; I've got you," she sobbed.

Ellis, Griffin, and two other protestors sat on the other side of the van, staring at Mercury in disbelief. As the van inched into the street, Mercury's heart rate increased; he could hear someone gasp. He could still hear screaming and the sound of breaking glass as the van sped away.

CHAPTER 14

Having added another offense to his growing rap sheet, Mercury began regaining the ability to move his fingers three hours later. Two hours after that, Mercury's eyelids closed halfway, providing only the slightest relief for his burning eyes.

All the protestors who'd been arrested that day were crammed into two small cells, the spaces no larger than a living room. The other protestors who'd been paralyzed lay on the ground beside him, each of them in various states of regaining mobility. Sloane, Ellis, and Griffin sat on the floor beside him. The magic carved into the bars had zapped their powers, so Sloane's leg still bled, and Ellis' right leg still rested at an odd angle. Sloane and Griffin tried to set Ellis' leg with the cardboard from their signs and strips of fabric from the newest Astera Army shirt that Bridget had made. Ellis grunted each time they touched it.

Though Mercury couldn't see them, he could hear the pain in his friends' voices whenever they spoke.

"How long until we get a phone call?" Ellis asked.

"We'd be lucky to even get one," Sloane said. "We were the last group here, and no one has been let out of these cells."

He heard Ellis shift his weight, then the sound of cardboard scraping against concrete. Mercury wiggled his fingers, attempting to reduce the intense pins and needles feeling. He tried to move his vocal cords and was surprised to find them moving slowly. But no sound came out.

"We're going to be in here all night," Mercury heard someone say.

Someone else groaned. "All night? Try the rest of the weekend. I hope no one had plans because we're gonna be here 'til Kingdom come."

Mercury released a deep breath for the first time since being hit by the Claudust. Once again, he tried to speak yet remained mute.

When will this end? He thought.

His friends leaned over him, watching him closely. Mercury managed a half blink, but when he attempted the movement again, his lids would no longer close.

"Mercury?" Griffin asked.

"He's starting to regain control," Sloane observed. "Let's see if we can sit him up."

Griffin and Sloane stood and pulled at Mercury's shoulders, sitting him upright against the cell bars behind him. Mercury could see the rest of the cell clearly now. An injured body occupied nearly every inch of it. Only one bench occupied the far side of the cell, taken by two women who'd gotten multiple bones broken after being hit by Bergasca.

"Unnnnhhh," Mercury moaned as he nearly fell to the side.

Ellis slid beside him, stabilizing Mercury with his good side.

"Do you think he's going to be like this forever?" Ellis asked, his cheeks still ruddy and his eyes wide. Sloane looked at him with narrowed eyes.

"Of course, not. Don't you see the other people here coming out of this?" She gestured around the cell.

Ellis looked down and tugged at his beanie, now covered in soot and blood. Sloane kneeled before Mercury, her wide, dark eyes assessing him.

"What can you move?" she asked gently, as if speaking to a child.

Mercury wiggled his fingers, and his toes in his shoes. He tried to blink again and though he gestured to lift his shoulders, they barely moved. His eyes burned. His throat felt like it was almost completely swollen shut.

"Can you try healing him again?" Sloane asked Ellis.

"I think you know it's not going to work," he said. "If it could, I would've already healed myself."

Sloane sucked in a breath and rubbed at her face.

"We have to figure out a plan to get out of here."

"What can we do? We don't have our phones or our things. No one is getting a phone call. So unless Joelle or someone from the outside can get to us, we're fucked," Griffin responded.

Sloane leaned her head against the wall and sighed.

They sat like this for hours, long after the sun had set. Sloane began pacing the small square of the jail cell they'd claimed for themselves. Griffin leaned against the bars to Mercury's left, arms crossed and Doc Martens tapping the floor. Ellis shuffled his body frequently, trying to alleviate the pain. By now, most of the people in the cell were sleeping. There'd been no one new added, and the guards simply ignored them if they passed their cell at all. The lights in the cell were almost nonexistent, and when the sun went down, so did their source of light.

When they first arrived, the cell smelled simply of body odor. Now, the smell of urine and rotten eggs filled his nostrils so completely that Mercury gagged occasionally. His hands were mobile now, and so were his ankles. He twisted his feet this way and that, then clenched and unclenched his hands. Still, he couldn't move his head left or right, nor could he use his arms.

"Fuuuuuu," he groaned.

"I know, buddy; I know." Ellis said as he leaned against Mercury to help stabilize him.

There was so much Mercury wanted to say, and it killed him to feel so powerless. He sat with his thoughts as more and more of the cell's occupants fell asleep. His mind flashed to Valeria, and the anger he'd felt as he saw her filming them rose within him again. Then he thought of the voice he heard at his father's birthday party.

"Amell, Salvanera, Hall, Whittaker," a guard called.

Sloane and Griffin stood at the ready. The guard gestured to them and unlocked the cell. "You're free to go. Someone's posted your bail."

"Who?" Sloane asked.

The guard rolled his eyes. "What am I, your secretary? Just get your shit and come on."

"C'mon, man, we gotta get you up," Griffin said to Ellis.

He and Sloane stood and grabbed Ellis beneath his shoulders and helped him up. Then Griffin slung one of Ellis' arms around his shoulder.

"Wait, what about the rest of us?" someone said.

"Did I call your name?" the guard snapped. "If I didn't, get comfortable. Because you'll be here until someone posts your bail."

"Don't we each get a phone call?"

The guard scoffed. "Sure. I'll make a note of that."

Sloane rolled her eyes then turned toward Mercury. "Okay, let's see if you can stand."

She grabbed Mercury's hands and slowly pulled him to his feet. It took him three times to stabilize his legs. She wrapped an arm around his waist and slung one of his arms around her shoulder, slowly helping him put one foot in front of the other.

"What about us? What are we supposed to do?" another person asked as they began to leave the cell. Sloane stared at Mercury for a long while before turning back to the protestor.

"We'll help you; we'll come back for you," Sloane assured.

Mercury grunted. He tried to nod but his head remained paralyzed in place.

The second he stepped outside the confines of the cell, he breathed in the air around him. He was away from the intense smell of body odor and urine and flatulence. He also was away from the magic-draining force of the bars. As the group walked, he could feel his own magic start to buzz inside him again.

They plodded down a long corridor and out a door into a lobby that looked as if it were last remodeled in the mid-80's. Standing on the other side of the reception desk was Mercury's father and Honore.

Both men were dressed in suits, ties, and dress shoes that Mercury knew cost more than the receptionist's monthly pay. While Honore filled out paperwork and spoke with an officer in a mismatched blue suit, his father flirted with the receptionist.

"Now, Gretchen, what a beautiful name," his father said.

The receptionist demurred, playing with a strand of wheat-blond hair.

"I believe it's German, right?"

"Yes. It means 'little pearl,'" she replied.

"Your parents were smart to name you that. It suits you so well. You know pearls are the most delicate, and lucky, of all the gemstones."

His father flashed his most flirtatious smile and the receptionist's eyes lit up.

"Thank you, officer." Honore scribbled one last thing on the paper and handed the clipboard to the cop and smiled. The officer returned the gesture.

"Blessed be," the officer said.

"Blessed be," Honore replied. Then he turned toward the group.

"Well, if it isn't the Astera Army," Honore said, a smirk on his face.

Mercury wished he could roll his eyes.

"You all are free to go." The officer nodded at Honore before walking to the other side of the desk and leaving the room. The guard handed Sloane their belongings before closing the door from where they emerged behind him.

"Mercury?" Gone was the flirtatious Atlas Amell. His smile and the twinkle in his eye were gone, replaced by a frown and deep lines across his forehead. Mercury's heart leapt and he longed to run toward his father and hug him, apologizing for leaving the restaurant without saying goodbye.

"He got hit with a potion the cops were using," Sloane informed them.

Honore and Atlas glanced at each other, alarmed looks on their faces.

"Come, let's get out of here. We can proceed with this conversation at the Iron Bird," Mercury's father stated.

Mercury gestured toward the door.

"Wait. I've got to heal myself and then Mercury," Ellis said.

"Let's just start walking toward the car. You can do it in a moment," his father offered.

Ellis frowned. "But—"

"Boy, if you don't start moving!" Mercury's father spoke through gritted teeth. He looked back toward the receptionist and smiled.

"Let's go, El." Sloane slung her backpack over her shoulder and began walking toward the door. Honore held the door open for them and as they stepped into the night, into fresh air, Mercury inhaled the deepest breath he'd had in hours.

"Thank you," Mercury said, the words muddled.

His father wrapped an arm around him and pulled him into a side hug.

"You're welcome. We've got a lot to talk about this evening."

"Mmm."

"Shhh, it's okay. We'll get you healed and then you can tell me how this protest turned into the shit show it became. But first, let's grab some takeout."

"Mr. A—"

His father held up a hand, interrupting Sloane.

"Save it for the Iron Bird. All I need to know right now is what type of food to order."

They shuffled to the car in silence, and as Mercury slid into the backseat with the help of Sloane and Griffin, he couldn't help the pang of nervousness welling in his belly.

CHAPTER 15

MERCURY'S HEART SANK AS HE WALKED INTO THE IRON BIRD AND FOUND Oliana and Faegan waiting for them at the shop. His aunt sat with her legs crossed, wearing expensive jeans and even more expensive wedges. She sat across the shop from Faegan, who for once wasn't furiously tapping on her phone. Her long, orange maxi dress hit the ground, pooling at her feet.

"Oliana," his father said.

Mercury could hear the edge in his voice, but he knew it had as much to do with Oliana sitting in the shop as it did with Mercury landing himself in jail for the second time in a year.

The car ride had been awkward, all conversation driven by Sloane and Griffin. Honore answered everything in one-word responses and Atlas sounded exasperated with each question asked. They settled on Chinese food, and as they rode toward the Iron Bird, Mercury's stomach ached.

Now, they stood still in the shop's threshold, holding onto containers of steaming hot Chinese food and staring at Oliana. The aroma of the food and the tension in the room made him queasy.

"Atlas. I hope you don't mind; we were in the neighborhood and decided to stop by," Oliana said as she stood. Her white cotton blouse bore the words Ivy Park on them in pale blue lettering. Her long hair was coiled into a bun, and her long nails were as white as her shirt. She looked down at her rose gold watch. "I know it's late, but I figured since it was a Saturday and since we have so much to discuss, I'd just wait for you."

Her brother-in-law nodded, jaw still clenched.

"Did we get enough food for them?" Griffin whispered.

Honore shrugged.

"It's not a problem, Oliana," Atlas lied. "We're heading upstairs to eat. Would you and Faegan care to join us?"

She shook her head.

"No, thank you. I don't eat after eight o'clock. But Mercury and his friends must be famished." She opened her arms wide. "What with spending most of the day in the clink."

The last sentence felt like a punch in the gut. Mercury looked toward his father again, who smiled ruefully.

"I was going to alert you on Monday about this, Councilwoman," his father explained.

"Well, there's no time like the present, *brother*," she replied. She grabbed her purse and strode up the stairs toward their apartment, not bothering to look to see if anyone was following her. Faegan stood and strutted past them, shaking her head at Mercury as she walked by.

"Mr. A—" Ellis started.

Atlas sighed. "Just go."

Mercury took the steps one at a time, his legs still feeling stiff, his knees still hard to bend. Oliana sat at the head of the table, a glass of red wine already in hand, listening for each step.

"That's a bold choice." Sloane nodded toward the wine and Oliana's crisp white shirt. Faegan sat to her right, her bright red nails tapping on the table.

Sloane and Griffin walked toward the kitchen, placing the bags of food on the counter. Ellis moved stiffly into the room. He healed himself while they drove, but like Mercury his body still hadn't caught on to being whole again.

Once he finally stepped into the kitchen, Mercury pulled out the chair across from his aunt and eased into it, stretching his legs stiffly before him as he did so. Ellis and Griffin leaned against the island in the kitchen, while Sloane sat on the banister that led down the stairs. Atlas sat at the chair beside Mercury, and Honore wandered to the mini bar, examining the drinks before pouring gin into a small tumbler. He leaned against the wall behind Oliana.

Mercury bit the inside of his cheek as his aunt took a long draw from her wine glass. She set it down harshly, the foot of the glass clinking against the marble tabletop. She glanced around the room, making eye contact with each of them before her dark brown eyes settled on Mercury.

"So, what was it that you said about these protests being *peaceful?*"

Her right eyebrow raised as she said "peaceful," as though adding more punctuation to the word.

Another punch in the gut. This was his first time seeing his aunt since her threat to him, and she stared at him unblinking. It was as though he was transported right back to the place he'd been after she'd delivered it—he felt as if his insides had been scraped out, as if he were seconds from crying and his cheeks were hot. A stinging lump of bile collected in his throat.

"No one?" she asked, gesturing at the room. "No one wants to tell me just what the fuck keeps happening at these protests that prevents you all from getting from point a to point b without issue?"

"Oliana," Mercury's father began.

"Not you, Atlas." Her voice was razor sharp. She sighed and smoothed down an errant curl. "I don't mean to yell . . . at you at least. No, I want to hear from your son. This movement was your idea, and I can't help but notice that lately everything you touch turns to shit."

"That's fucking rude," Sloane interjected, crossing her arms.

Faegan snapped her head toward her, a bubble forming in her hand. Oliana patted her daughter.

"Faegan, that won't be necessary. You're right, that was rude. It was also the truth. And I do believe I was talking to my nephew, not his loyal pet," Oliana sassed. She snapped her fingers.

Sloane opened her mouth to speak but no words escaped.

"Oliana, you don't need to punish Sloane for sticking up for her best friend," Mercury's father said, his brows lifted. "You remember when we were that age? You, me, and Kessia had the same reaction with each other whenever anyone questioned the other."

She sighed and lifted a brow of her own. "You're not wrong there. We were such firecrackers back then. But at least we had the good sense to be seen and not heard during official business, and we certainly never called the Head of the Witches' Council *rude*."

Mercury could feel his aunt's anger simmering beneath the surface. She slid her chair back and stood, grabbing her wine glass and swilling it as she walked toward Mercury's end of the table. She sat on the table before him, blocking his father's view.

"Now, I'm going to ask you again. What, pray tell, happened at this protest? Hmm? I thought we talked about this."

Griffin cleared his throat. "Uh, Ms. Murtaza?"

He stepped forward. Oliana glared at him as he rounded the table and positioned himself next to Mercury.

"I don't want to interrupt, but you should know that Mercury was hit with a potion at the protest and it paralyzed him. He's barely been able to say anything."

For a brief second, Mercury could see the alarm in his aunt's eyes and he wondered whether it was from worry about him or something else, something more sinister.

Where had the police gotten the potions? Mercury thought. *Does she know?*

"Thank you for letting me know, Griffin," she said quickly. "Don't you have a healer on your team?"

"Yes," Ellis spoke. "I healed him, twice. But he's still a little fucked up. I mean, look at the way he's sitting."

She looked down at Mercury's legs jutting out before him. Mercury blinked twice, convinced he'd noticed a hint of a smile in her eyes.

"Hmm. Well, I still need answers, so who wants to give them?"

Sloane raised a hand.

"Of course." Oliana rolled her eyes yet snapped her fingers.

As the apartment door swung open, everyone turned in its direction.

Joelle sprinted up the stairs and flung her arms around her brother.

"Are you okay? Did you get hurt? What happened?" she questioned.

"It seems I'm not the only one seeking answers," Oliana said.

Joelle looked around the room. When she made eye contact with Mercury, she winced.

"What happened?"

Sloane sighed.

"The cops denied our permit. We were supposed to walk from the Hollywood Walk of Fame to the Council Building, but we were stopped on LaBrea," Sloane began.

"What did they say?"

"They told us we couldn't proceed and we had to turn around."

"So why didn't you?" Oliana asked.

"We tried, but some dickhead decided to shoot his shot and tried to magic his way past the police. Most of the other protestors followed."

"And what happened?"

"The police had potions," Griffin answered. "They had ones that paralyze you, ones that break bones."

"There was another one that took people's breath away," Ellis added.

Oliana took another sip from her drink before setting it back on the table.

"How did it escalate to the police using these potions?"

"We don't know. We were about to leave."

"And abandon your movement?" Oliana rested her dainty hand on her chest, mock concern in her voice.

Sloane sneered.

"We were about to *leave* when we heard someone scream. The guy who'd tried to go toe to toe with the cops was hit by that breath-taking potion and then . . ."

"Then it was chaos," Mercury muttered. His words were slurred, but he couldn't keep sitting silently as his aunt interrogated his friends. "We tried to get people to leave but it was too late."

"Too late?"

"The fight had already begun. Every time we tried to move, the cops were there, beating people or slinging potions. Ellis got hit with the bone breaker. His leg was fucked for hours," Griffin said.

"Your leg was broken?" Joelle said, looking at Ellis.

"That's not really the thing to focus on," Griffin remarked.

He turned back toward Oliana.

"Look, we were attacked. We tried to just march, and the LAPD attacked us. They were ready for a war, and we didn't have a chance."

Oliana looked Griffin up and down before turning back toward Mercury.

"And why didn't you just cast a spell to persuade people to leave?"

The room went silent. He could hear his father sucking in a breath.

"Aww hell," Honore mumbled under his breath.

"Could you have done that?" Sloane asked.

Mercury glanced around the room, at eight sets of eyes staring at him, waiting for an answer.

"It wouldn't have worked for a crowd that big."

"But, a spell like that exists?" Joelle asked.

Mercury nodded.

Joelle gasped, throwing her hands in the air.

"But there's no way to know it would have worked," Mercury explained.

Oliana snorted. "There's no way to know it wouldn't have. You could have done the spell over and over until the crowd dissipated, or you could have recruited your friends here, told them the spell, and within ten minutes the crowd would have gone back to their cars. Over, done. Crisis averted. You and your crew could have spent the rest of the day sneaking booze onto the beach and lounging. The weather was perfect for it."

Mercury sighed, his breath ragged. He tried to make eye contact with the group, hoping that someone, anyone, would take his back. But all of them were silent. Ellis and Griffin looked at the floor. Honore stared into his glass and Sloane looked up at the ceiling.

"We're not supposed to use our magic in public; you know that." Mercury placed his hands on the table and pushed himself up to his feet. "If I would have done that, we would have still gone to jail."

His aunt leaned toward him. "Still would have prevented a lot of violence, huh? It might have even saved your friend from having his leg shattered and you from paralyzation, the effects of which you'll probably be dealing with for a few days even after being healed."

"Why does it matter? The point isn't whether or not I said the spell, the point is—"

"No, Mercury, I think that is the point," Joelle interrupted. "You always take the hard way, the violent way, even when you have the option to stop. Even when stopping could mean saving the people you love."

Mercury gasped, Joelle's words piercing into him like an arrow.

Saving the people you love, he thought. An image of Troian hung and burning over the Iron Bird's sign forced its way into his brain.

Oliana sighed. "I tried to tell you, my dear. I tried to warn you that proceeding with these protests would lead to more violence, especially after the first two resulted in multiple injuries. How many more of your friends need to be hurt before you realize that you're in over your head?"

Sloane blinked repeatedly. "She warned you? You never mentioned that."

Mercury tried to clench his fists. That fire in his belly again. He wanted to scream at his aunt, push her and tell her to stop blaming him for other people's actions. Didn't she know that everything he'd done was for the greater good? Couldn't she see that he was right?

But another part of him, a small part of him, wondered. He'd use the persuasion spell not two hours before to get people to move out of his way at Bath and Body Works. He could've just spelled the witches to leave at the protest, and maybe he would've been arrested, but it would've been a hell of a lot less painful.

You always take the hard way, Joelle had said.

"It wasn't important," Mercury murmured. "We spoke for a second at dad's party."

"But if your aunt warned you—" Joelle started.

"I tried to stop the protest, remember?" Mercury yelled. "We had that awkward-ass Facetime call where each of you tried to talk me out of canceling or not attending."

"Not all of us," Joelle reminded him.

"Yeah, Jo, you're fucking Switzerland," Sloane snapped. "You didn't want to be a part of this from jump."

"That's not true! I was there at the first three protests; I just stopped wanting to go because I was bitten by a goddamn vampire."

"You only got bitten because you refuse to use your magic," Sloane spat.

"I don't want to use my magic because I don't want to be a fucking freak," Joelle cried.

"Wow, tell us how you really feel," Sloane said, folding her arms.

"That's not what I . . . I want to go back to school. I want to be normal. It's not my fault that all you want to do is vape and shit talk people on the internet."

"Bitch, I'm a fucking journalist!" Sloane advanced toward Joelle, but Griffin stepped between them. As Sloane and Joelle yelled at each other, Oliana swilled her wine.

She clicked her tongue. "All of this could have been avoided if you would have just listened to your favorite aunt."

"Oliana, there's nothing Mercury can do to change what happened today. All we can do as a Council is address how to respond to this senseless violence," Mercury's father interjected.

She laughed. "Oh, Atlas. The Council is denouncing, yet again, these protests as what they are: riots. The people who rushed the officers, the ones still alive at least, will be stripped of their powers and exiled. And the others? They'll all be on notice. Anyone who continues these protests will be seen as direct threats to the Council and will be dealt with accordingly. As for your son, well. We already spoke about what the Council would do if he chose not to listen."

Mercury's breath seized and he stumbled back into his chair.

No, he thought. *Not this.*

"Oliana, please—" his father asserted.

"Yeah, Oliana there were mitigating circumstances—" Honore began.

Oliana shook her head. "You were both there when I told Mercury what would happen. Did you think it was a joke?"

"No, however—" Atlas began.

"So you just let him go and continue to wreak havoc?" Oliana replied.

"Oliana, he tried to stop it," Honore said.

"I didn't know he'd left," Mercury's father added.

"What?" she asked.

"We were at brunch and he snuck out the door. He did a transportation spell to get to the protest."

His aunt cocked her head to the side and looked at Mercury, an amused expression on her face. "Well. If he had the juice to do all that and come out whole on the other side, there was no reason he couldn't have stopped the violence that happened earlier today. He chose to put people in danger, just like he did in March. He needs to be off the street."

"Oliana, please," his father hissed.

Oliana threw her wine glass at the wall. Sloane and Joelle stopped arguing, startled at the sound.

"Shut the fuck up, Atlas," Oliana snarled. "I want you to listen to me very carefully. *I* am the Head of Council, not you. Not your son, not Honore, not his Made Witches, me. I make the tough decisions on what happens to this community, whether we keep thriving or succumb to more violence at the hands of vampires. I made the call to make a peace treaty with that leech in the White House so that our people could live freely. Do you think I like seeing these vampires tear our people apart? Do you think I like seeing the violence that happened today? Over 70 people were injured all because your son thinks he knows what's best more than I do. I have sacrificed more than you know for our community, and I'll be damned if I let some fucking child ruin everything."

She grabbed her purse and looked at Faegan, who stood and walked dutifully toward the door.

"You have 72 hours to get your affairs in order before I make that call."

She placed a hand on Mercury's shoulder. "For the record, I am really sad that it came to this."

Mercury narrowed his eyes at her. "I really doubt that."

She smiled, tight-lipped.

His aunt stepped toward the door, her heels clicking on the wooden steps.

"Tell me something, auntie," Mercury said. "If you care so much about our community, why haven't you spoken out about the Identity Act?"

She froze mid-step. "Mercury, I should think that you'd know by now, given the powerful role your father plays in the Council, that we can only lobby for or against laws. It's not within our power to stop such things," she explained. "Besides, like it or not, Kinheld will be established soon and then witches won't have to worry about that."

"Mmm, I get it."

She took another step toward the door.

"Um, just to clarify—how many witches?"

She stiffened then turned around to face Mercury.

"Excuse me?"

"How many witches will be able to reside in Kinheld?"

"Anyone who wants to live there. And who passes our entrance requirements, of course."

"Entrance requirements?" Honore questioned. Mercury looked at him. "You never mentioned entrance requirements."

She sighed. "Why would I?"

"Because I think the Council would have liked to know that there were strings to who was able to become a part of Kinheld and who wasn't before voting on it," Mercury's father said.

Oliana shrugged.

"Don't be dramatic, Atlas. This isn't the *Hunger Games*. Witches will simply need to prove they have power, that they can remain gainfully employed, and that they will pose no threat to the Council."

"Pose no threat? What does that mean?" Griffin asked.

Oliana set her purse down on the banister and took a step into the room. She threaded her fingers together.

"Mercury, this little diversion of yours won't work," she said, her voice sing-songy.

"I don't mean to divert the conversation, auntie," Mercury smirked. "I just wanted to know if the hundreds of thousands of witches in America will all be able to fit into a space smaller than Washington DC, provided they pass the entrance requirements, of course."

"If I were you, Mercury," she drawled. ". . . I'd worry less about the logistics of Kinheld and more about spending what free time you have left with your father and friends."

Oliana rushed down the steps without another word. Faegan cast a sympathetic look at Mercury before she followed her mother down the steps and out of their apartment.

"I'm sorry that it came to this, but I'm glad you're alright," Honore said. He hugged Mercury before descending the steps.

"So . . . is anyone going to tell me what she meant by 'free time?'" Ellis asked.

Mercury turned to his father, but his father looked away.

The Rioter's Blueprint

By Sloane Salvanera

Staff Writer, *Jonquil*

WHAT DOES IT TAKE TO SUCCESSFULLY STAGE A RIOT? PRESIDENT Harvey Vael will tell you all it takes is being a messy derelict who loves ignoring the laws of the land. Councilwoman Oliana Murtaza will tell you it takes a strong appetite for destruction, a willingness to "cannibalize the movement." Vampires and dhampirs will tell you it takes a strong sense of entitlement; witches and harridans will tell you it takes a willingness to cut one's nose to spite their face.

But you know what? They're all wrong.

All it takes to stage a riot is a small militia, bullet and magic proof vests, and an arsenal of potions so juiced with magic that it makes every witchy gathering look like amateur hour. That's right, the "riot" that occurred this past weekend wasn't initiated by witches. It was initiated by the LAPD at the behest of Mayor Tony Rodrick, who no doubt was told to stop the peaceful march through one of America's most populous cities by President Vael himself.

By now, I'm sure you know what happened, but in case you've been following any other news story, the tea is this: the LAPD ordered those of us protesting Kinheld to stop and turn around the second we turned onto LaBrea. They told us we couldn't proceed even though we had a permit. Unfortunately, Matteo Lunez, 37, thought he could force his way past the cops using his magical abilities. He was quickly cut down by Nefastle, a magnolia-scented potion that takes the recipient's breath away. When we tried to pull the rest of the protestors away, the pigs let loose on us, tossing potions to maim, paralyze, and kill our kind. A dozen people were killed, while still more people had bones broken or were temporarily paralyzed. Others were hit with Ivarick and broke out in poison ivy-like sores.

As expected, we're uncertain about hosting another protest. The number of people injured at the last few protests and the potential for even more injuries and more death is far too great. But that won't stop us from being vocal about the treatment of witches in America, nor will it stop the LAPD from doing dirty shit like packing potions and using them on innocent people during a traffic stop or a wellness check.

It's so important for everyone to know how to counteract these potions, and that's why we've compiled this handy guide to help you and yours stay safe.

First, be sure to magic-proof your clothes. I've linked to the <u>spell to repel what's set upon you</u> here, but basically, you'll need the candles of all four elements, plus a white candle, citronella, and to say the spell four times. That covers your clothes (also do your shoes), but what about all those exposed areas? Especially in the summer, it's not feasible to strut your stuff in jeans and sweaters. If you don't have the power of forcefield, you can replicate it in five-minute increments by using this spell. If you've done these things, and you still need extra protection, here's a list of things that can counteract or simply heal a person hit with these potions:

Claudust, the paralyzer - ingredients: pufferfish skin, pulverized jellyfish, foxglove, and camphor. Can be counteracted with mint, sunflower, and salmon skin

Ivarick - the pox - ingredients: poison ivy, caffeine, and peppermint. Can be counteracted with calamine, chamomile, and CBD oil.

Nefastle - the breath taker- ingredients: magnolia, sulfur, capsaicin, and tobacco smoke. Can be counteracted with lavender, spearmint, vervain, and cannabis smoke.

Bergasca - the bone breaker- ingredients: garlic, Star Anais, ground beef bones, and Jimsonweed. Can be counteracted with lidocaine, echinacea, collagen, and bone marrow.

Hellefax - the widowmaker - ingredients: oleander, squid ink, water hemlock, eggplant, and snakeroot. Can be counteracted with blood magic and an experienced necromancer.

In addition to having these remedies ready (or a necromancer on speed dial), it's important that you write the important numbers (like said necromancer or a lawyer) you may need somewhere on your body. That way, if you're arrested and they take your phone, you can make your phone call. Also, be sure to keep a bobby pin with you, which not only will keep your hair out of your face but also may or may not help you unlock Thurguards. As always, stay on the lookout for anti-magic fuckery and make sure you and yours are protected. Stay spelled up, keep your potions with you, and blessed be.

Why the Movement Against Kinheld Is a Dangerous Waste of Time

By Valeria LeFebre
Senior Writer, *Jonquil*

Some say that the road to hell is paved with good intentions. I say it's paved with delusions of grandeur, the inescapable belief in one's own righteousness, and the desire to drag others along for the violent and bloody ride. We've seen leaders of late who exhibit these traits but none more so than Mercury Amell, the originator of the anti-Kinheld movement.

He strolled onto the scene not three months ago, bright-eyed and bushy-tailed, ready to tell the world how it's supposed to be. Ready to tell them that they should denounce the Witches' Council's plans for our own slice of land because "separate isn't equal." Ready to put the kibosh on the plans his own aunt, Head of Council Oliana Murtaza, painstakingly put in place because he believed that witches deserved to fight for "true equality" and that type of equality couldn't come from us having our own space, circulating our own dollars, educating our own children, and removing ourselves from a society that deems us as dangerous freaks that must be put down.

I had the chance to interview Amell several times. I first met him at the second protest, where he spoke at length about their mission, and pontificated on the fact that witches (Black witches specifically) were marching and protesting for reformation rather than restoration (a reference to the slogan "Restore" that Vampire-in-Chief Harvey Vael used in his bid for President). What did he feel was appropriate reform?

"The abolition of the Identity Act, the dissolution of police departments with a proven record of anti-witch sentiment. Repeal of the Lorraine Law so the CDC can study the effects that vampire violence has on witches. The dissolution of the Corvius Accord and of Kinheld especially."

It mystified me that Amell should be so keen to protest the establishment of land we could call our own. He says that true equality is only achieved through integration, but I ask: *cui bono?* Who benefits from witches remaining in this society run by the Devil's left-hand man? Who benefits in a society where one-third of the populace is forced to wear dog tags announcing their magical abilities and emphasizing the very element from which they draw power?

At the same protest, Mercury also spoke about his brother, Troian Amell, who was viciously murdered by a group of vampires who had been looking for Mercury after he started a fight at an Upsilon Gamma Nu (UGN) party on the UCLA campus. Mercury waxed poetically about how his brother would be by his side, in lockstep against their aunt's plan. But would he be so in agreement after seeing the devastation that Mercury has wrought? Would he have been so willing to lay his life on the line for his baby brother if he knew that hundreds of people have been injured, dozens have died, and his brother spent his afternoons vacillating between intense impostor syndrome and a martyr complex?

The second time I interviewed Mercury, we sat at a restaurant in The Grove and the 21-year-old acknowledged the optics of a man reacting so vehemently toward a woman's plan. Though he acknowledged that to the casual observer his vitriol for his aunt—his only living relative that we know of aside from his father, Councilman Atlas Amell, and Councilwoman Murtaza's daughter, interim Councilwoman Faegan Murtaza—bordered on sexist. Mercury's answer was vague: "there are things about my aunt that you don't know."

Of course, that's true because we simply can't know the Head of Council in the same way that Mercury would know his own aunt. But what we do know about Councilwoman Murtaza is this: she spent her youth advocating for witches, specifically Black and Brown witches and those who are members of the LGBTQ+ community. She had her daughter at a young age but still attended classes, where she was actively protesting every chance she got. She graduated college and embarked on a career as a junior Councilmember before rising through the ranks and eventually becoming the first Black woman to Head the Witches' Council. Her tenure includes outreach for home-less witches, education programs for the underserved and underprivi-leged, an internship with the Council to earn college credit at participating colleges, lobbying against anti-abortion bills, against anti-LGBTQ legislation, legislation to permit the relaxation of commercial blood laws, and more.

And what do we know about her nephew, Mercury Amell? This Air Hand was studying music at UCLA before dropping out just after returning from Astera. He attended a UGN party, a fraternity that is widely known to be the preferred house for vampires, and took part in a large altercation where a woman was burned alive. Then, he and his brother tattooed his human friends, giving them magic, and leading (perhaps dragging) them across the country to Astera, where he could "get the support of other, more powerful witches." But he ended up putting more lives at risk, including Councilwoman Effie Hyunh, who lost her life during the scuffle at Astera.

My final encounter with Mercury took place at the LaBrea riot, where protestors were told by police to turn around and discontinue the march toward the Council Building. Though Amell initially tried to reason with the other protestors on the street, he quickly lost control of the situation, in part because he arrived at the protest two hours late, like the protest was his own personal event to which he could be fashionably late. He and his Made Witches tried to "save" the protestors by yelling at them to "fall back" and throwing their hands in the air when they didn't. Potions were thrown, magic was used, and in the end, at least a dozen witches lost their lives, and Amell and 70 other people were taken to jail, many of them while dealing with the effects of the aforementioned potions.

Many of those protestors are still in jail, two days later. And where is Amell? Out on bail, along with his friends, because of the Council and his aunt who he so vehemently opposes yet has no problem taking advantage of their largess. At the time of this article, Amell has yet to address any of the protests and the violence that occurred at them on social media. He has yet to explain what will happen next given that many of the protestors are still in jail. And he has yet to tell the real truth about the anti-Kinheld movement—that participating in it or anything Amell does is nothing more than a dangerous waste of time.

CHAPTER 16

Opening his eyes one by one, Mercury awoke on Sunday afternoon still groggy, his body so stiff that it took him twenty minutes to get out of bed. As his bare feet hit the cold floor, he realized his nightmare was far from a dream.

After Oliana left, he did what he could to push his friends' questions away about what his aunt could have meant about him "getting his affairs in order" and "free time."

"She warned me that if I didn't stop bad mouthing Kinheld, that she'd temporarily bind my powers," Mercury had said then, looking at his father as he did so.

"There's a spell for that?" Joelle asked.

Mercury knitted his brows.

"Yes, but it's not forever. The powers do come back," he said, hoping she wasn't getting any ideas about asking him or his father to bind her powers.

She shook her head. "You ever think about just telling us all of this stuff at once instead of us finding things out after the fact?"

Joelle didn't give him time to respond. She grabbed her brother's arm and started down the stairs, leaving Mercury standing there with his mouth open.

When Mercury finally made it out of his bed, he stood and stretched, the soreness fading from his body. He'd planned to go for another run, grab breakfast on the way home, and try to figure out where to go with the movement against Kinheld. But when he opened his phone and saw himself tagged multiple times in tweets linking to Valeria's article, his heart sank. His chest tightened as he read the article, but reading the comments nearly stopped his breathing. Seeing the things people retweeted along with the article made him want to throw his phone across the room.

"I knew this guy was a clown from jump. He never had any desire to help us, just get famous," read one comment.

"Sometimes it be your own people," wrote another. "The fact that he's trying too hard to exist in a world that clearly doesn't want us says something."

"He claims to be for witches but the people out front leading the movement with him are Made, not Born. They don't experience the same struggles we do, and Mercury should know better."

His phone buzzed repeatedly as he filtered through the tweets. Everyone in the group chat messaged him separately and asked if he'd read the article. At first, he responded to their texts and attempted to respond to some of the retweets. But his friends only had more questions, and the commenters only wanted to fight. Though he'd hoped that the commentary would die down by the evening, there was even more coverage on Monday. Even Cordelia Edwards, the senior writer at *The Vanguard*, wrote a piece in response to Valeria's article. She praised her for her bravery in "standing up" to a "thug" like Mercury and for wanting to honor what's best for the Witch community.

"You don't even care about us!" Mercury shouted at his screen, his hands trembling from the emotions raging inside of him.

His father, who was sitting in the kitchen, wandered over to his room.

"You good, son?" he asked, peeping from the doorway.

Mercury simply clenched his teeth and nodded, grateful that the gesture was enough to dismiss his father. He couldn't talk about what was happening, knowing that if he did, he'd break down. Instead,

Mercury pulled himself together and trudged down the stairs for work. He opened the shop but gasped when he saw the line of protestors pressed against the shop windows, waving their signs and cussing him out.

"Traitor!" someone shouted.

"Asshole!" barked another.

Sloane weaved her way between the crowd, shouting at them to get the fuck out of the way as she strode toward the door. When she finally made it inside the parlor, she heaved a sigh and took a puff off her vape.

"Mercury, what the hell?" she said, exhaling a cloud of smoke.

"I should ask you the same question," he retorted, his anger welling up inside him. "Did you know Valeria was going to publish that piece?"

She lowered her vape pen and gave him an incredulous look. "No! I thought it was going to be something positive about you, about the movement. If I knew she was going to publish this . . ." Her hands clenched and her knives slid out of her wrists. As she took a deep breath and relaxed her hands, the twin silver blades retreated into her wrists.

He dropped his head then glanced upward.

"It looks like more people are coming," he said, gesturing toward the window. Another car full of people pulled up in front of the shop brandishing signs calling Mercury out.

"We can't open the shop like this," his father stated as he stepped into the shop. "I've got to let the Council know."

"Why? Oliana won't do shit. She's already trying to stop me in any way she can. She won't help; she'll say this is what you get for not listening to her," Mercury argued.

His father glowered at him.

"Maybe they'll leave on their own?" Sloane said, trying to diffuse the tension.

Atlas sighed and relaxed his face. "Maybe."

THREE HOURS LATER, THEY SAT IN THE PARLOR, STARING AT THE FLOOR. With their bluetooth speaker blasting a '90s playlist, Mercury kept trying to block out the sound of the protestors outside, the cacophony of their chants against him growing louder.

He glanced at his phone. He'd been keeping a timer, counting down the moments until his aunt put in a call to the LAPD. *Only 36 hours left*, Mercury thought. His heartbeat quickened, and his breath shortened. Still, he received text after text from witches inquiring about his well-being or questioning the things written in the article. Still, his phone trilled with notifications from Twitter, Instagram, and even TikTok. Still, he felt helpless and unsure of what to do.

I can't do this, he thought as his vision blurred. *I can't—*

Someone tossed a slushie at the Iron Bird's glass door, interrupting Mercury's thoughts. The sound reverberated throughout the room, shaking his father and Sloane out of their own thoughts as well.

"Those fuckers, I ought to—" Sloane began. She flinched as Mercury tossed his phone against the wall with a grunt. Glass and electronic pieces shattered and fell to the floor.

"Mercury, why did you—" his father asked.

"I can't fucking do this anymore, man!" he shouted. Tears stung his eyes.

"Hey, shhhh," his father soothed. He stood before him and gripped the sides of Mercury's face in his hands. "It's okay; it's all going to be okay."

Mercury shook his head. "No, it's not. It's never going to be okay. Troian and Delanie are dead because of me. Everything has turned to shit because of me. Oliana was right about me."

"Absolutely not!" his father shouted.

Having rushed over to the father and son, Sloane closed the distance between them and pressed a hand to Mercury's shoulder.

"Yeah, fuck her, Mercury. She was just trying to get under your skin. None of this is your fault," she assured him.

His eyes bounced from his father to his best friend. He looked at two sets of wide, brown eyes staring at him with warmth and fierce love.

And it made him sick. It made him want to crawl out of his skin, to run away and never look back. How could he keep them safe? How could he, when the people he loves, hell, the people he hates, die around him? Mercury tore out of his father's grip.

"I need to be alone," he demanded.

Sloane tried to grab his wrist, but Mercury shrugged out of her grasp, running up the stairs and into his room. He locked the door and leaned against it. Minutes passed and when he didn't hear their footsteps on the landing, he peeled his clothes off and traded them for a pair of sweats and a t-shirt. Then he slid into his bed and stared at the ceiling.

He spent the remainder of the day this way, his gaze alternating between the ceiling and the wall. Every couple of hours, Atlas stood outside his door, trying to sell him on something to eat or drink. Each time, Mercury refused.

By midnight, a headache had set in, along with a persistent cramp in his stomach. He curled into a ball, silently begging the pain to stop.

And then there were the thoughts. Obsessive, looping thoughts about being a failure, not being good enough, being an entitled, privileged brat.

If you weren't a failure, your brother would still be alive, he thought.

If you hadn't had such a fucked-up temper, you wouldn't have killed Delanie, he chided.

If you had been braver, you could have saved your mother.

The last thought broke him. He sobbed, burying his face into his pillows and only sitting up long enough to blow his nose. He didn't know what time it was. It was still dark outside and the street was quiet. He willed himself to sleep, knowing that sleeping would make the thoughts go away. Eyes crusty and head pounding, Mercury slipped further under his blankets.

Minutes later, Mercury found himself back at the UGN party. This time, however, only a few people occupied the room, no one he recognized. He scanned the room in search of the front door and noticed everyone moving in the direction of it. As he followed them, the lights dimmed, causing him to rely solely on sound to find the exit. While in the darkness, he stumbled over what he perceived to be old protest signs and empty glass bottles. Holding his hands out in front of him, he felt the wooden frame of the door then reached for the doorknob. He twisted it once, then twice. He pulled it once, then twice. Then he shook it unmercifully. With the pounding in his chest intensifying by the second, he banged on the door repeatedly, his screams for help muffled. When he placed his ear to the door, he heard someone walking away from the door slowly, a sinister laugh escaping from the woman's throat, one he recognized.

HE WOKE THE NEXT MORNING TO HIS FATHER KNOCKING ON THE DOOR. Mercury ignored him and turned over instead.

"There's a latte and a bagel outside your door. Son, you need to eat," his father advised.

Still, Mercury remained silent as the thoughts returned, as images from the dream returned.

That afternoon, as he lay in bed watching the Food Network, he heard shouting outside and knew that the protestors had returned. He slid out of bed and crossed the room to his window. He peaked out of the blinds to see an even bigger group of people with signs, shouting at the front of the Iron Bird with some of the same signs as yesterday.

"Mercury must pay."

"Stop the performance."

"Down with the anti-Kinheld movement."

Tears flooded his eyes and Mercury stifled a groan as he backed away from the window.

What the fuck do I do? He thought. The chanting grew louder. His head pounded and he felt the weight of all his good, bad, and questionable decisions. He sank to his knees and leaned against the side of his bed.

"Fuck!" he shouted. "Fuck!"

"Mercury, are you okay?" his father knocked on the door.

"Go away," Mercury quavered, tears streaming down his face.

"Mercury—"

"Please, just leave me alone. I'm no good around anyone," he cried.

"Son," his father began.

"Go away! Please!" Mercury begged, sobbing once again, wracking his body.

His father stood outside of his door for several moments before walking away. He took the steps downstairs to the parlor two at a time.

Outside, Mercury could hear Sloane and his father shouting at the protestors. His heavy sobs drowned out their responses.

When the crying stopped, Mercury lay on the floor, staring at his drum kit. He felt like his insides had been scraped out and replaced with poisonous, prickly things. His head ached and his whole being felt exhausted.

He climbed off the floor and drew his black-out curtains closed. Then he slid into bed and pulled his blanket over his head, shaking until he fell asleep.

WITH THE GLOW FROM THE MOON BEING THE ONLY LIGHT, MERCURY awoke sometime in the middle of the night, his stomach aching. Gone were the obsessive, agonizing thoughts. Now, all he could think about was how his stomach felt as if it were gnawing on itself and how he couldn't quite see straight. He quietly opened his door and padded across the living room, headed for the kitchen.

"Mercury?"

He scowled. He felt for the light on the wall and turned it on, keeping the light soft to avoid waking his father. Sloane lay on the pull-out couch, her body covered in blankets despite the summer heat.

"What are you doing here?" Mercury asked. He walked over and eased onto the bed beside her. She sat up and rubbed at her eyes, her messy bun flopping over to the right.

"I couldn't leave, not with how you were yesterday. Plus, those fucking protestors wouldn't let me leave."

"Why didn't you or Dad just use magic?"

Sloane shook her head. "Your dad didn't want to use magic given everything going on. So, I crashed here."

Mercury lowered his head. He hated that this mess had escalated so much that his best friend in the world wasn't safe to go home. He hated that he'd spent all this time thinking about himself that he hadn't even thought to even ask his father how she was when he left food for him.

"I'm sorry," Mercury lamented. "It's all my fault. That fucking article set me off. And then people kept tagging me."

Sloane groaned. "I still have no idea how she got it through our editor. No one on staff knew what she was going to write."

Silence followed her words. It lingered as Mercury searched for words of his own.

"I feel like I can't ever show my face again," he uttered, breaking the silence.

"I know the feeling."

Mercury looked up as Sloane slid out of the bed and padded across the room to the kitchen. She turned the light on above the stove. Mercury followed her into the room and grabbed a bottle of water from the refrigerator. There was a box of pizza in there, and Mercury absentmindedly grabbed a slice of pepperoni pizza. He plopped down at the table across from Sloane, thankful to be sitting there with her.

"The protestors weren't just there for you. I've been getting dragged for my blueprint article, too. Apparently, people feel it's me calling for violence against the police, and by extension *Jonquil*."

"Fuck," he said around a bite of pizza. He groaned, fully realizing how hungry he was.

"So, apart from the article, and the protestors, is the fact that your aunt threatened you why you needed a personal day?" Sloane rested her head in her hand, her bun flopping again.

Mercury nodded. He finished his slice of pizza then clutched the bottle of water in his hands. It was time to tell her the truth.

"It wouldn't be if that was the first time she threatened me."

Sloane knitted her brows.

Mercury gulped. "First at the power stripping ceremony, then at my dad's party. She pulled me into a room with the rest of the Council and threatened me saying that if I didn't stop the protests that she'd call the cops and tell them that I . . . tell them what I did to Delanie."

Sloane gasped. She grabbed her friend's hand and squeezed it.

"So that's why you got so cagey about the protests. Why didn't you say anything?"

"I didn't want to alarm you. She said that she'd not only tell them what I did but say that you all helped me cover it up. I thought I was protecting you by keeping my mouth shut and just trying to cancel the protests. I guess I really fucked that up."

Sloane slid out of her chair and walked over to him. She wrapped her arms around him, and Mercury let out a deep breath. Vocalizing the thing he'd been struggling to deal with on his own for weeks made him feel so relieved. She pulled back from him and sat back in her chair, grabbing his hand to hold.

"Mercury, I can't imagine how much of a struggle it must have been for you to hold all of that inside. I'm so sorry that this happened. I wish Oliana remembered that she was your aunt first and Head of Council second."

Mercury nodded. He drank a sip of water, and though he ate, it still felt as if his head were spinning.

"Are you going to tell the others?"

"Should I?"

Sloane shrugged. "I think it'll make you feel better. And I think it's an opportunity to discuss what we should do next."

"What we should do next," Mercury repeated.

"Fucking right," she yelled.

Mercury chuckled as she looked over her shoulder, praying the outburst didn't wake his father.

They finished the leftover pizza and talked until the sun came up. He told her more about the incident with his aunt, and how he felt like his whole life was coming to an end so many times over the last few days. She told him how Griffin and Ellis had come to check on him that day when they didn't hear from him. Mercury asked if Joelle had joined them; Sloane frowned before shaking her head.

"Maybe she's not the girl for you after all?" Sloane said.

Mercury nodded. "Maybe I just have bad taste in women."

"Or maybe you just fall too hard, too fast."

"I'm not a player, Sloane. I just crush a lot."

They laughed under their breath and whisper-rapped the rest of the Big Pun song.

The two friends fell asleep on the couch together watching spells gone wrong videos. When Mercury awoke, his father was at the table sipping coffee and reading something on his tablet.

"Good morning," Mercury greeted him. He slid off the couch bed and chuckled as Sloane, now alone, tangled herself up in the rest of the blankets.

"Are you feeling better, son?" his father asked.

Mercury took a deep breath then poured himself a cup of coffee.

"For now," he said. "I don't know what time it is, but something tells me that Oliana's hours away from carrying out her threat."

As he leaned against the counter, his father looked over at him.

"I've tried to talk her down, for now. But I don't know what else I can do."

Mercury nodded. "That's okay. I think I have a plan."

"Oh?"

Mercury nodded. "Oliana wanted me to stop the protests and to stop speaking out about things I didn't know about Kinheld."

"But Mercury, you're entitled to your beliefs, even if Oliana doesn't agree," his father said, removing his glasses and setting them down on the table.

"I know. But she's right. There's a lot I don't know about Kinheld, and then I started this movement which, as Valeria addressed in her article—"

His father scoffed. "I can't believe she wrote that. That article has caused a shitstorm that has reverberated throughout our community."

Mercury took a long draw of coffee, the warmth of it bringing his body back to life.

"Well, I can't say she's completely wrong. But I want to address what she said head on. And I want to talk to Oliana and let her know that I was wrong."

"But you weren't, Merc," Sloane interjected.

Mercury shrugged. "But it doesn't matter. Some of the things that she and Valeria have said make sense. And rather than trying to get people to see things my way, I'm just going to tell the truth."

"About what?" Sloane asked as she strode into the kitchen. She pulled a chair back from the table and sat beside Mercury's father.

Mercury took another long draw from his cup, then looked from his father to his friend and said: "Everything."

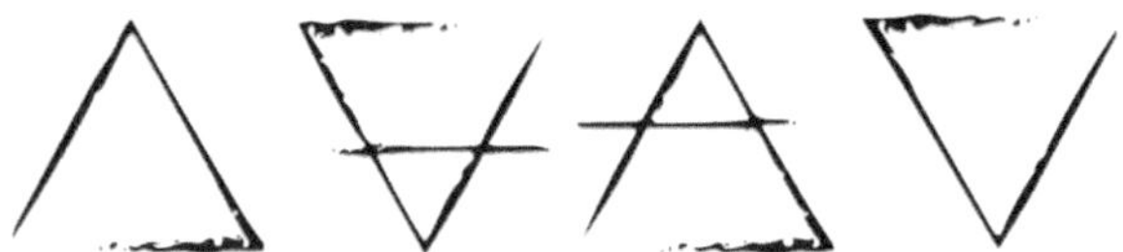

CHAPTER 17

AN HOUR LATER, SLOANE, ATLAS, GRIFFIN, AND ELLIS SAT AROUND THE kitchen table. Mercury told them about the threat from Oliana, how she'd planned to implicate the others in helping Mercury cover up Delanie's murder to quell the movement. Then, he told them his plan.

It was simple, really. First, he'd have his father arrange lunch with Oliana, Faegan, himself, and Mercury. They'd visit the Council House, and Mercury would pretend to be contrite. He'd beg his aunt's forgiveness, and hope she'd decide not to call the police. Before arriving, Mercury would take a potion that would triple his powers, allowing him to see more selectively into a person's memory and stay there for longer, even after he stopped touching them. Then, he'd arrange a sit-down interview with Valeria to discuss her article. During the interview, he'd tell the world about the things he'd learned from Oliana about Kinheld, the Corvius Accord, and more.

He thought back to his dream as he spoke, refusing to be the one caught in his aunt's trap.

"How do you even know the information you find out will be that explosive?" Sloane asked.

"When I hugged Oliana the other day, I got a glimpse into what the truth behind Kinheld really is. But I know there has to be more. And I can't fight this suspicion that I have that she knows something about where those potions came from."

"The potions that the police had?"

Mercury nodded.

"But what if your aunt's already made up her mind?" Griffin asked.

"Yeah. What if she's already called the cops?" Ellis questioned.

Mercury glanced at his father, who tapped his finger against his coffee mug. He stared back at Mercury for what seemed to be an eternity.

"I talked her down a little yesterday, but I won't be able to do it again," he said finally.

Ellis' eyes lit up. "So there's still time."

"Yes. But there is the fact of this potion you mentioned," Atlas stated. "It can have some unsavory side effects."

"I know," Mercury said.

"And I don't have that spell in my new grimoire," his father added. "Is it in your grimoire?"

Mercury shook his head.

"Well then, how do you suppose you'll accomplish this triplication of your power?"

He hesitated then grinned. "I know someone who can help."

⁂

Honore arrived as he always did, in immaculate style. He wore dark jeans, black loafers, and a white button up shirt with yellow daisies on it. His copper hair was finger waved and he wore a small gold hoop in one ear and a gold daisy in the other that dangled from a diamond stud.

"This better be good," he quipped as he stepped into the Iron Bird. He walked over to Griffin and kissed him before settling on the second to last step.

"Honore, we need your help to triple Mercury's power," Mercury's father said.

Honore lifted a brow. "Oh? And why is that?"

"I want to meet with Oliana and get the full truth about Kinheld."

Honore crossed his arms. "You're on one if you think it'll be that easy, pulling information from your aunt about that damn plot of land."

Mercury sighed.

"But, count me in. After hearing her say there'd be some requirements for entry the other night, I'm curious to know what else she's hiding."

"So, what do we need to do?" Mercury asked, the excitement building in his chest.

They gathered all the ingredients they'd need for the spell and walked upstairs to the kitchen while Mercury's father called Oliana to request an audience. The spell required Mercury to drink a tonic of maidenhair leaves, Jade flowers, coffee, and eucalyptus oil. To Mercury, it tasted horrible. He gagged after downing it, praying his stomach would cooperate with the process.

Honore laughed at Mercury and clapped him on the back.

"Don't lose your guts just yet. We don't have enough of this stuff left to make more."

Mercury grimaced.

Still chuckling, Honore opened his grimoire and set the book in front of Mercury.

"You need to say this three times," Honore said.

As Mercury inhaled the aroma of the room, he closed his eyes. His shoulders fell as he released his breath. He opened his eyes and began: "I call upon all the ancestors of the guardians of Air. Grant me your power, lend me your strength and focus."

He repeated the incantation two more times. Afterward, he looked at Honore. He had expected to feel different, but the only thing he was feeling was a sour stomach from the tonic.

"Is something supposed to happen?" he asked.

Honore scoffed. "You asked it to triple your power, not take you to Paris. Test it out."

He held out a hand to Mercury. Mercury grabbed his hand and instantly saw into Honore's mind. While his first stop was Honore's memory of getting a call from Mercury's father earlier that morning, Mercury found himself able to fully immerse himself in the Councilman's memories. He surfed through moments he had with Griffin, meetings with the rest of the Witches' Council, and one at a Beyoncé concert before he landed on a memory that made Mercury gasp.

Honore and Mercury's mother sat at a small marble table in the back of a crowded cafe. It was so clear and perfect in his mind that he would've thought it to be a scene from a movie had he not known the main characters.

"I'm serious, Kessia. You should consider a bid for Head of Council," Honore said before taking a sip from his coffee mug. Mercury marveled at how strong the potion was: he could smell Honore's coffee, could hear drinks being made and the chatter of people in the cafe.

"I don't know, Honore. Sitting at the head was always Oliana's dream, not mine."

"She is just as qualified as you, but she's also power-hungry. I worry that she'll focus more on politicking and less on doing things in the interest of our people."

His mother shook her head. "I can't take her dream from her like that. She's my sister. And I know she's flawed, but I still think she'd make an excellent head of Council even if you don't."

Honore sighed and leaned back in his chair.

"I know there are people that are still planning to vote for you once Pietyr's resignation is official."

Mercury's mother stood. "Well, I can't stop you. But I can also decide not to accept. Anyway, I've got to go pick up the boys. We're going grocery shopping for dinner."

"What's on the menu?"

Mercury pulled back out of Honore's memory.

"Crab cakes," Mercury said. He looked at the Councilman with tears in his eyes. "We were supposed to have crab cakes that night, before she—"

Honore pulled Mercury into a hug.

"I know," he whispered. Mercury didn't know that Honore had been one of the last people to see his mother alive.

"I thought she wanted to be Head of Council."

Honore shook his head. "She knew how important it was for your aunt. But, most of us wanted your mother to sit at the Head, not Oliana. Yet, here we are."

Mercury nodded and looked away. "Well, I can only hope that I do right by her and stand up for what's right."

"And that's exactly what you're doing now. I know your mother would be proud." Honore patted Mercury on the shoulders. "Do you need a minute?"

"I'm fine." He wiped his face with the inside of his shirt then brushed the wrinkles from it.

"Well, let's go join the others."

Mercury and Honore walked back down to the rest of the group. As Mercury glanced around the room, he noticed questions filled each of their eyes.

"Did the spell work?" Ellis asked.

Mercury nodded then looked at his father. "Was Oliana open to getting together?"

"Yes," Mercury's father confirmed. "We can meet her at the Council House at two."

Mercury glanced at the clock. It was noon, and that gave him plenty of time to get ready. He told Sloane, Griffin, and Ellis to meet them back at the shop that evening to discuss their next steps. Honore said he'd join them as well, and after they all left, Mercury prepared for battle. He showered then cut his hair and trimmed his beard. He dressed in his nicest jeans and slipped into a pale-yellow button up shirt.

"Are you sure about this?" his father asked.

"No, but I'm doing it anyway," Mercury said as they locked up their apartment. They snuck out the back way, trying to avoid the protestors still camped outside the shop.

It was a hot but overcast day. Mercury relaxed when he spotted the traffic on the road, which allowed him more time to prepare. Though he knew he had to follow through with his plan, he was in no hurry to get to the Council House. They inched their way down 101 toward Benedict Canyon in perfect timing, the air conditioning on full blast. Mercury was thankful for it; he was nauseous. He took short breaths to stave off puking, and to quiet his thoughts.

They pulled up to the Council House ten minutes late. They parked the car in front of the circular driveway and a Council House staffer slid into Mercury's father's Berlinetta and drove it down the hill to the parking lot. As they walked through the House, Mercury marveled at how much bigger it seemed now that there weren't dozens of people swarming throughout. Again, he heard his mother's voice as they closed in on their destination: "Be careful, son." He paused at the sound.

Oliana and Faegan sat at a table on the patio, sipping fancy, over-priced water from their wine glasses. They looked up as Mercury and his father stepped outside but didn't stand. A smile spread across Oliana's face, but it didn't quite reach her eyes.

"Atlas, Mercury," Oliana said. "Running fashionably late, I see."

Mercury's father offered a tight smile. "Well, you know how important it is for me to make an entrance."

Oliana laughed. Faegan smiled. Mercury tried not to scrunch his nose at the awkward exchange. They took seats at the table, Mercury sitting with his back toward the Council House.

One of the chefs that worked at the House, Mercury believed her name was Monika, walked out and asked if they wanted still or sparkling water.

"Sparkling, please," Mercury said. His father followed suit, and Monika walked back into the house. Seconds later, she returned with their glasses. Another chef followed behind her carrying a charcuterie board.

Once alone, Oliana set her glass down and folded her hands in the lap of her salmon-colored linen dress.

"So, to what do I owe the pleasure?" she said, turning toward Mercury.

Mercury looked at Faegan, who sat with one eyebrow lifted and her lips pursed. Mercury then looked to his father. He carefully sliced into the wheel of brie and spread the cheese on a small piece of French bread. Mercury cleared his throat.

It's now or never, he thought.

"I came here to apologize."

"Oh?" his aunt said.

"Yes. I realize that I went about everything the wrong way. I did disagree with you, but I should have come to you first, just like this," Mercury said, spreading his arms out. ". . . and talked to you. I should never have put things out in public first."

Atlas focused his eyes on the charcuterie board as though considering his next bite. Mercury knew he was listening in on the conversation and trying not to make a face.

Oliana stared at Mercury, her long lashes batting against her cheeks as she considered him.

She's skeptical, Mercury thought.

"I should have trusted your vision," he added.

She waved a hand, and Mercury could tell by the gesture that he'd gotten through to her.

"Yes, you're right. You should have trusted me. Trusted that I would be able to hear out your concerns and that what I ultimately decided was best for the greater good of our people," his aunt replied.

Mercury smiled tightly. He swallowed a sip of water then busied himself with grabbing a piece of French bread and smothering it with brie.

"I know. And I hope that you understand how sorry I am. I told Dad I wanted to meet with you and Faegan because I wanted to try to put this behind us and be family again, like back in the day," Mercury said before biting into the bread.

His aunt smiled wistfully. "Yes, I do miss all those times spent together. But how do I know you really mean this and you're not just trying to save your ass?"

Mercury clenched his free hand at his side, reminding himself not to react to what she said. He couldn't give her any indication that he was there for another reason.

"I'd be lying if I said I wasn't hoping you'd change your mind about calling the cops on me. But I want you to know . . ." he sipped his drink, contemplating what to say to make her believe him. "I want you to know that this time, I'm putting my trust in you."

Oliana placed her hands under her chin and faced her daughter. "What do you think, Faegan?"

Mercury's heart skipped as he looked over at his cousin. She sat, sour-faced, hands working to smear stone ground mustard onto a piece of toasted bread.

"Well, I think it's big of you to humble yourself enough to apologize, after everything. But I also wonder whether it was the protest, my mother's final threat, or that article that read you for filth that finally made you wake up."

Mercury clenched his teeth and smiled. "Everything," he replied.

Faegan responded with a simple "hmm" and slid her piece of bread into her mouth.

"So, what do you say, Auntie?" Mercury said, setting his hand on hers.

Though she was guarded, he saw flashes of his aunt discussing Kinheld on the phone, but he was only able to get bits and pieces.

"Lucky to do so. I don't want witches who can't . . . value. No homeless, no drug users . . . less than $40k a year . . . Witches in Kinheld must be . . . Those who aren't will have to fend . . ."

Mercury squeezed his aunt's hand then let it go.

"Well, I say this is potentially the start of a new chapter, not just for us but for you, Mercury." She patted his arm, and each time her hand connected with his, he got a flash of memories. In one, she was sitting at a bar talking to his father about raising Troian and Mercury alone. In another, she was dancing to the electric slide at the last Ilaris celebration. In the final memory, she asked Faegan if the funds the Council received for Kinheld were in the right account.

Mercury smiled at his aunt.

"I'd really like that," he said. He looked at his father and adjusted his shirt collar, which was the signal they'd worked out to show that he needed more time. "To that end, and Faegan to your point, Valeria's article really pulled no punches."

Faegan laughed. "That girl dragged you to hell and back."

Mercury's father scoffed. "It was very hard to read."

"Yes, it was for me as well. Like it or not, Mercury, I'm still your aunt. I still love you."

"I love you, too, Auntie." Mercury resisted the urge to touch her hand again. Instead, he grabbed a toothpick and stabbed two slices of salami. "Valeria's article sent me spiraling, if I'm being honest. But I want to address the claims she made head-on. I was thinking of setting up an interview with her. What do you think?"

His aunt nodded emphatically. "That's a great idea. Show the world your new attitude."

Mercury nodded, his skin crawling at both having to lie so much to his aunt and cousin and at having to hear her self-righteous approval of his "new attitude."

"I was thinking of doing a simple Instagram Live."

Faegan scoffed. "Oh, no, Mercury. You've gotta come correct with this."

"Yes, my thoughts exactly. Why not have it here? You can still stream it live, but we need to get a professional crew with this. I won't have my nephew looking like an amateur filming on an iPad."

"I like that, having it here. I think it adds more gravitas," his father said, waving his utensil as he spoke.

Oliana looked at Mercury's father and smiled. "I agree! Then it's settled. Faegan and I will handle all the details. All you have to do is show up and look handsome."

"Thank you, Auntie," Mercury said. He sipped his water, stifling a smile as his plan came to fruition.

The rest of their lunch passed by without incident. They spoke about plans for Ilaris, which included catering for food, drinks, and drugs. Last year, he and Troian split a pot brownie at Ilaris and he spent the evening feeling like he was in the clouds, his mind floating. There also would be a talent showcase, where witches from all backgrounds could come and sing and dance.

"Maybe you and your friends could play something," Atlas suggested. "I know you mentioned Joelle is a musician."

"Joelle? That's the girl you're talking to, right?" Faegan asked.

Mercury winced. He wanted to say that he thought that's where they were headed, but after their date and the protests, he wasn't sure where they stood at all.

"It's complicated," Mercury answered instead.

Oliana looked at Faegan. Though she said nothing, he could feel the judgement radiating off her. Rather than play into it, as the old him would have, he simply ate his food and changed the subject.

Three hours later, with only scraps of bread and cheese visible on the charcuterie board, Mercury and his father stood to leave. Mercury embraced his cousin first, and as he did, he could see her memory of finding out about Troian, and how she broke down in the impromptu Council House at Astera. He could see her talking to her mother about how to market Kinheld, the discussion more about using the right buzzwords over anything else. Just before he was about to pull back, he caught a glimpse of her holding onto a box with the name Spalding Wellness on the side of it as she strode to her Porsche.

Mercury tried not to look jarred as he released Faegan.

"It was nice seeing you, cuzzo," he said. He smiled at her, looking into her hazel eyes surrounded by mink lashes.

"You, too, Merc. After all this stuff blows over, maybe we can hit the town and turn up like we used to."

"Oh, I don't know if I can keep up with you. I see those TikToks of you giggin,'" he replied.

She laughed and danced briefly, yelling "ayyyyeeee" as she did so.

He turned toward his aunt and took a deep breath, knowing that this memory mining was the moment he'd been waiting for.

"Auntie," he said.

She smiled at him, her long arms wrapping around him. "I'm so glad you've come around. I'm just sad it almost came to you going to prison."

Mercury tried not to stiffen at her remarks.

Focus, he thought.

Without the power boost, Mercury was able to see flashes of random memories. He was never able to target specific times, and he'd been told by other Air Hands twice his age that the ability to do so took a long time to master and took a great toll on the witch as they mastered it. Now, he was able to pick through his aunt's brain in seconds, his mind like fingers flipping through a rolodex.

More memories of discussing Kinheld—talks about entry fees, discussions on housing, schooling, and law enforcement. She said she was open to adding officers from police departments around the country who were magical. He saw her talking to the Council about her initial plan, saw them vote on the idea, and he saw glimpses of her discussion with President Vael. He tried not to shake at seeing that vampire closer than he had before, the way his fangs glinted and the way his electric blue eyes pierced through his aunt's gaze. Vael looked at her like he wanted to ravage her.

"Spalding Wellness," he heard someone say. Another memory now, this time with the Mayor of Los Angeles and the police commissioner. His aunt sat across from them, discussing the need to bolster their police force's abilities with magic.

"Anything less and your police force will be dominated in less than an hour," she said.

The men looked at each other uncomfortably. Mercury couldn't tell whether it was her magic or her being a woman that made them so uncomfortable.

They agreed to take the potions, and she slid a dossier of information on each potion included in the Spalding Wellness kit. He also saw the price tag: three million.

"Why are you doing this?" the commissioner asked. "Especially with your own nephew leading the effort."

His aunt smiled Chesire-cat like. "Because I know what I want. And he's standing in my way."

Mercury pulled away from her mind, grounding himself to avoid showing how light headed he felt. He inhaled deeply and pretended to smell her perfume.

"You're still wearing your Christian Dior I see," he remarked.

She lifted a brow and shrugged.

"Feve Delicieuse has never let me down," she bragged.

He pulled away from her and glanced at his father.

"Well, best we push back to Venice Beach. We've got a tattoo parlor to run," his father stated.

"We'll be in touch about that interview, Mercury," Faegan reminded him.

Mercury nodded. "Thank you. This was great. Talk to you later."

His aunt waved and took her seat. Faegan copied her mother's actions. As Mercury followed his father out of the house, he was thankful the car had already been parked up front. His father tipped the driver and they slid into the car.

Once they pulled out onto the road, Atlas glanced over at Mercury.

"How'd it go?" he asked.

Mercury's stomach lurched and he gestured for his father to pull over. Once he did, Mercury leaned out of the car and vomited his lunch on the shoulder.

CHAPTER 18

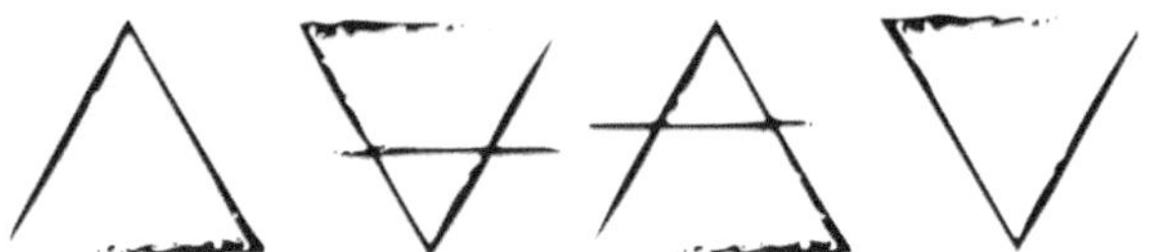

Once they arrived at the shop, a sense of peace surrounded Mercury. He surveyed his surroundings, blinking repeatedly as he noticed not one trace of the mob who'd been practically camped out in front of the parlor for days. Even the air seemed clearer as it filled and emptied from his lungs. When he walked through the door, he looked up to find the group already waiting inside.

"What happened to the protestors?" Mercury asked.

Honore looked at the group conspiratorially.

"Well, I taught your friends how to use the power of persuasion."

Mercury sighed, altogether relieved and anxious.

As curious eyes searched his for answers, Mercury told them about the things he learned from his aunt and cousin. He had spent the car ride reeling both from the knowledge that his aunt was responsible for the potions that hit them at the protest and from the come-down of the power triplication potion slowly dwindling. After several moments of deafening silence and blank stares, Honore was the first to speak.

"Before this new revelation, this would have been a reprimandable offense. Perhaps even something to remove her from the Head of

Council. But this? Atlas . . . if this is true, her powers must be stripped immediately."

Mercury's father pinched the bridge of his nose. "Well, let's focus on getting through this interview and then we can address her actions with the Council."

"I'm sorry, Dad," Mercury said, feeling somewhat responsible for his father's stress. "I know how much Oliana means to you, not just as a sister but as head of Council. She was the one we all wanted to win, and it pains me to know that she was the one who put us in so much danger."

Neither Honore nor his father responded, their bodies stiffening at his remarks.

"So, when's your interview?" Sloane asked. She'd gone to Dunkin Donuts on the corner and grabbed a dozen donuts and several iced coffees. She sat in her reception chair, leaning back and sipping her coffee. Ellis stood beside her, his hand on her shoulder.

"Oliana said she's arranging it. I'm assuming that also means contacting Valeria," he replied.

Sloane's phone buzzed. She glanced at it and lifted a brow.

"Speaking of," she said. "She asked if I knew anything about it. What should I say?"

Mercury shrugged. "Just say that I wanted to address the article and talk about my views on Kinheld in light of the protest. Tell her that I had lunch with my aunt and cousin and we're healing."

He and Griffin stood at the desk, eyeing the donuts still left in the box.

"Are you worried about what Oliana's reaction will be?" Griffin asked. He plucked a blueberry donut from the box and plopped down in the first chair.

Mercury grabbed a cruller as Sloane's fingers tapped furiously over her phone. He bit into his pastry, pondering his friend's question.

"Okay. Texted her. What do we do now? Just wait?" she asked.

Mercury sighed. "That's all we can do."

The bell over the door chimed and Joelle stepped into the shop. Mercury paused mid bite as they made eye contact. She wore a yellow crop top and high-waisted jeans. Her sandals clapped against the floor of the shop as she walked.

"Joelle, how are you, dear?" Mercury's father said. He glided over and hugged her.

"I'm okay; thank you. How are you?" she responded.

"Oh, just plotting to take down the Head of the Witches' Council. You know, just a regular Tuesday," he replied.

She winced then walked over to her brother and sat beside him.

"Are you okay?" she asked.

"Yeah, I'm good," he said.

Mercury hadn't expected to see her, especially after her comments the other night. He tried not to meet her gaze, finding himself drawn back to that moment when she called him selfish and violent. For several minutes, no one else spoke. No one looked at each other, instead busying themselves on their phones or dissecting their donuts before devouring them.

"Mercury, can we talk?" Joelle asked.

His chest ached at her words. His heart pumped furiously and his stomach roiled violently. He nodded but didn't look at her. He gestured for her to follow him upstairs, and all eyes in the room watched them as they disappeared into the apartment. Once there, they sat at the kitchen table.

"Can I get you anything?" Mercury asked.

"No, thank you," she replied.

He hunched over in his chair, staring down at his hands and waiting for her to speak.

"I wanted to apologize," she began. "The things I said the other night, how I've been lately."

"You were only speaking your mind. I can't fault you for that. I can't say it didn't hurt, though."

She sighed and he looked into her large brown eyes.

"Look, I never wanted to be a part of this," she held her hands out. ". . . stuff. I just wanted to go to school, make some friends, and get my degree. I wanted to be a session musician like we talked about."

Mercury nodded then clasped his hands.

"But then the party happened, and Griffin and I were thrown into this thing, and at first it felt so scary and exhilarating and like I was a part of something bigger than myself, but then we got back from Astera and came back to reality. On the road I thought I was falling for you, but when we came back to LA . . ."

"You stopped," he said. It was her turn to sigh.

"I just realized I didn't know you at all. We went from not knowing each other to holding hands to kissing. I mean, I didn't even know your birthday, or your middle name, or even your major."

"October twelfth, I don't have one, and I was double-majoring in communications and music theory. You?" he replied.

Her shoulders relaxed. "July seventeenth, Maria, and I'm majoring in business with a minor in music."

"A music minor?" he asked, an eyebrow raised.

She shrugged. "I know how to play already, and if my teachers suck, I can learn on YouTube. If I'm going to be in the music business, I figured I should know the actual business side of things," she said.

Mercury nodded.

"Makes sense, then again you usually do."

He set his hands in his lap. She pulled the top half of her Senegalese twists up and into a bun then looked back at him, her mouth set in a grim line.

"So, what do you want?" he asked.

"I want to focus on school," she murmured.

Mercury sucked in a breath. There was a part of him that hoped she'd say she also wanted to stay involved with the protests, that her focusing on school didn't mean she wanted to completely walk away. But as the seconds passed and she didn't say anything else, Mercury let out the breath he'd been holding and nodded.

"Can I assume that you don't want to be involved with—"

She shook her head. "I didn't mean to hurt you the other day with what I said. You're not some mindless, violent person. You care deeply about your friends and your family and your people. Your movement is important, but I just don't think I belong in the thick of it. I lived my whole life until three months ago without magic. I never really wondered what having it would be like and now that I've experienced it, I know it's not for me. And this," she said, gesturing from herself to Mercury, "isn't either."

Mercury sat back and wiped his face. Of course, he knew this was inevitable, especially after the things she said the other night. And he knew she was right about them. They didn't know each other, and the time they'd tried to have a normal date had been awkward. As they both looked down at the table, avoiding each other's gazes, he wondered if his affection for her had been a product of the situation or if it had been real.

"I understand," he said. "But maybe we can be friends? I'd still like to get to know you."

For the first time since their conversation began, she smiled. "I'd like that, too."

Mercury stood and Joelle followed suit. As Mercury descended the stairs, she grabbed his arm. "Mercury, I know there's nothing I can say to stop Griffin from being involved."

He lifted a brow.

"Believe me, I tried. I even tried to talk to him about his relationship with Honore, but he seems set on that, too. He seems . . ."

"Happy?" Mercury asked.

"I just wanted to say, please be careful. Not just for yourself but also for my brother."

Mercury nodded. "I'll do my best."

They ambled down the stairs and into the shop. Griffin, Sloane, Ellis, and Honore were playing dominos on the reception desk. Mercury's father sat in his chair, typing on his laptop.

Mercury walked Joelle to the door. They hugged and she waved to the group before leaving.

"Everything okay?" Ellis asked.

Mercury exhaled.

"Yes, everything is fine. Joelle has decided to do what's best for her, and that's leaving the movement."

Sloane paused, her domino hovering in the air. "For real?"

"Yeah."

She looked at Griffin, eyes narrowing. "Why didn't you tell us?"

He scoffed. "It wasn't my news to tell, Slo. Joelle's a grown-ass woman, and I don't want my sister doing something she doesn't really want to do."

"Griffin's right. Whatever it is we're doing here needs to be something that you really want to do. Revolution isn't for the unsure or the faint of heart. She's got her own journey to walk, just like we each have ours," Mercury said.

They each nodded.

"Before I do this, I just want to make sure that none of you feel the same way." Mercury looked from Sloane to Ellis to Griffin, and finally to Honore.

"I've told you several times, Merc, you're stuck with me." Sloane winked.

"Yeah, who else is going to save you or kick your ass on guitar?" Ellis quipped.

Griffin nodded again. "I finally feel like I've got a purpose. I'm not going anywhere."

"Liberation for witches has always been my goal," Honore stated. "If this movement will bring that about, then I'm all in."

"This is so touching," Mercury's father said. He walked over to the group. "I'm glad we're all in. But now's the time to get our head in the game. Your aunt just confirmed your interview for tomorrow at nine in the morning."

Everyone turned to face Mercury.

Though initially wanting to break for the door, he stood there firmly and said: "Let's do this."

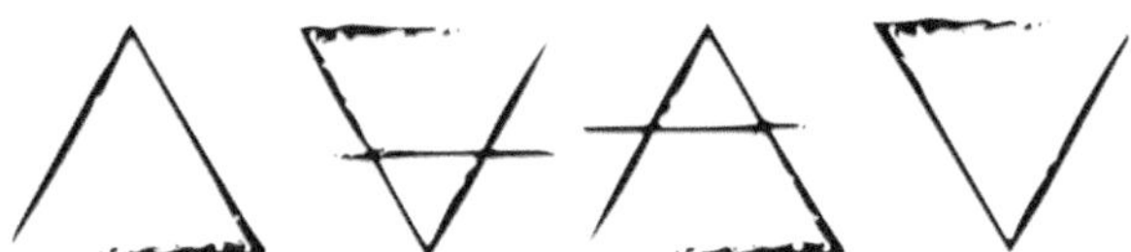

CHAPTER 19

THE NEXT MORNING, MERCURY AND HIS FATHER GRABBED COFFEE TO GO from Pot Head then drove to the Council House. Along the way he looked through several sample menus from restaurants his father was considering for catering Ilaris.

"C'mon, Dad, it's summer. Do you really want to have Italian food? It's so heavy."

"And barbecue isn't?" He scoffed. "Shit. Regardless of what we select, some folk'll end up with food comas."

"Yeah, but the difference is, most barbecues you can eat with your hands or take quick bites. Pasta, you gotta twirl that shit first."

His father laughed.

"Well, if it were up to me, you know we'd keep it traditional with those summertime, Juneteenth classics but you know your aunt. Always wanting things 'elevated.'"

His father shook his head. Mercury chuckled then relaxed the muscles in his face.

"Do you really think this is going to work?"

His father pondered for a moment.

"I do. But you have to go into this confident. No half steppin,'" his father said. "You have the chance to speak the truth, and I think it's important that you take it."

Mercury cleared his throat repeatedly, trying to dissolve the lump that had formed there as he absorbed his father's words. He looked out the window, staring into the other cars on the interstate and wondering what they were doing, whether they didn't have a care in the world, wondering if he was the only person in the world who was nervous.

Much sooner than Mercury expected, they pulled up to the Council House, and like before, a staffer was ready to park their car in the parking lot down the hill.

Mercury's legs felt weaker and weaker with each step he took. He raised his coffee cup to his lips, but his stomach twisted as the lukewarm liquid hit it. He tossed the cup into the trash can just inside the door then followed his father to the sunroom, a long, thin room just off the kitchen with a domed glass ceiling and glass lining the left half of the room.

Hanging plants and planters littered the room, growing everything from fresh herbs to orchids. At the far corner, a small waterfall structure sat. The sound of running water and the heady smell of orchids felt calming somehow, even though he was minutes away from outing his aunt.

A four-man camera crew hustled around the room, one running wiring out of the door of the room, one setting up one camera focused on the center of the table, the other setting one up facing the edge, and the other lighting. Valeria, Oliana, and Faegan sat at a marble table in the middle of the room. They each smiled at Mercury as he approached.

"Good morning, Mercury," his aunt exclaimed. She stood and hugged him. "You look great."

Mercury smiled tightly.

"Thank you," he said. When she pulled back, he smoothed out the sleeves of his silver suit jacket. He'd opted for a suit this time, hoping it would make him feel powerful and help Valeria take him more seriously. His white shirt had small, yellow triangles adorning it. He wore white leather Converse, but he chided himself for it. They were too new, and his feet felt so constricted and achy already.

"It's the shirt for me," Faegan greeted him, pulling him into a side hug.

"Gotta represent," he said. His eyes landed on Valeria.

She wore distressed jeans, heels, and a bright pink blazer. Her braids were now platinum, and she'd twisted the front into victory rolls.

"Hey, Merc," she said. "I'm glad you wanted to do this interview. No hard feelings?"

Mercury tried not to grimace as he sat across from her.

"I wouldn't be doing this if there were," he responded.

She nodded. "Well, like your aunt said, you do look good."

"Thank you," he replied. He looked down at his watch. It was 8:55. *Let's just get this over with*, he thought.

As the camera crew continued their set up, Oliana, Faegan, and Valeria resumed their conversation as though Mercury wasn't there. He looked at his father, who'd stopped at the edge of the room and typed on his phone. *C'mon, I need you*, Mercury thought, wishing he was a telepath.

He took a deep breath and tried to focus on the grounding techniques he'd seen in a post on Instagram. He tapped into his senses. He thought about the things he could feel—the texture of his suit, the slight breeze from the air conditioning, the warmth of the sun shining through. He smelled orchids and an undercurrent of rosemary. He could see the camera crew testing lighting, could see a gardener edging the grass outside. He could hear his aunt, cousin, and the journalist speaking, their conversation sounding too casual for people who didn't really know each other.

At least, that's what Valeria had said when they'd finished the official part of their interview and had moved on to their second round of drinks.

"Your aunt just seems so untouchable," she'd said. "I've always admired her. I was so jealous when Freddie got the chance to interview her exclusively earlier this year. I've only ever seen her at events or gotten email-based responses from her or Faegan."

"Well, maybe after you finish covering this, you'll be able to book a one on one with her and see what she thinks about her nephew's movement."

"Oh, I'm sure she's got a lot to say."

No fucking kidding, Mercury thought.

Now, the timing of Valeria entering his life made sense. He wondered why she'd been put on to cover the protests for *Jonquil* when Sloane was already there. Had his aunt put her on to infiltrate the movement and get the inside details, knowing that Sloane wouldn't ever dare be someone's stooge? The possibility made the fire in Mercury's belly burn. He gripped the edges of his chair, trying hard to bite his tongue and keep up the mask of contrition until it was time to tell the truth.

"Okay, Val, we're all set up," confirmed the camera man.

She glanced at him and nodded. She looked back at Faegan and Oliana, who stood to walk out of the frame.

"Good luck, dear," his aunt said.

"Yeah, you got this," Faegan added.

"Thank you. I really appreciate that." Mercury attempted to hide the edge of his voice.

"Merc, do you need to use the restroom or get something to drink at all before we start?"

He shook his head. "No, I'm good."

"Sure?" Valeria asked.

"Yes. I'm ready," he said. He looked over to the camera, where the crew stood. His aunt and cousin had pulled chairs over and sat next to the camera crew. His father had made his way into the room and was now standing to the left of the camera, coffee in hand.

Valeria nodded. She gestured toward the cameraman.

"Okay, Rich, can you count me in?" She grabbed a set of note cards from the table and held them in her hands, her long black nails tapping the edge of the cards.

"We're live in three, two . . ." the first cameraman pointed to Valeria. The camera's red light blinked on and Valeria turned in her chair to face it. A large, confident smile had replaced her casual demeanor.

"What's good, *Jonquil* fam. It's your girl Valeria coming at you with an interview I know we all were waiting for. I'm sitting down with the infamous Mercury Amell to address the anti-Kinheld movement he started and how it went from a small, peaceful movement into several full-blown riots."

Mercury's lip twitched at the word "riot."

"So, Mercury, let's start with this—what compelled you to reach out for an interview?" she asked.

Mercury nodded slightly. "Well, I wanted to address the recent events and after trying to lay out the facts online and dealing with some opposition . . ."

"Dragging. The people were *dragging* you," she said, nodding.

"Yes, I suppose that is what happened. I figured if writing my piece wasn't enough, I needed to do something else. I thought an interview might work and who better to speak to than the person who covered the movement and wrote about it and myself in such brazen detail?"

She chuckled, covering her mouth briefly. "Yeah, I went in."

"You did. You said I was the most dangerous leader in America right now."

She shifted in her chair and glanced at the camera.

"Well, after seeing the chaos the movement caused, don't you think it's appropriate?"

"I think a vampire president who is all too happy to turn a blind eye to the suffering of our kind as well as humans should probably take that title. After all, what is the Identity Act for if not to make witches easier to clock so they can be disenfranchised, discriminated against, and likely killed?"

"We don't have data on how many witches have been killed since the act passed."

"No, we don't, because Vael allowed the Lorraine Law to pass, forbidding the study of vampire-on-witch violence. Valeria, you wrote an article opposing the Identity Act, why are you so ready to defend it and Vael?"

Valeria lifted her arched brow. "I'm not defending him or the act at all. I spent weeks researching it; I know its implications. I'm simply saying that for a movement that's only existed for less than three months, there sure is a lot of collateral damage around it and *you*."

Mercury nodded, considering her words.

"I grant that a lot of lives have been affected by this movement, beyond those who are on the front lines fighting for it."

"Right, so that brings me to my next question. Why, if you were so concerned about your aunt's decision, did you decide to start this movement? Why not discuss this with her directly?"

Mercury looked over at his aunt and cousin briefly, knowing this was a question they'd fed to Valeria. Were they trying to see if he'd answer differently?

"Looking back, I was reeling from the events leading up to and at Astera. I spent time with my aunt and with Faegan at Astera and to hear the news about this . . . plot of land in the paper instead of from her felt so impersonal."

"Couldn't your father have said something?"

"He tried to tell me, actually. The morning before the party. He told me that I couldn't look to my aunt, who'd been my favorite person at that time, to be the savior."

Valeria tilted her head. Mercury heard his aunt whisper his father's name.

"Well, I'm certain many people think differently. We recently did a survey and found that over 50% of witches liked the idea of Kinheld over," Valeria gestured at him. ". . . whatever it is you're planning."

Faegan giggled. Mercury glanced at her and shifted in his chair. He crossed one leg over the other and leaned on the left side of his chair.

"I'm sure they do. They have no idea what the real truth is," he said.

Valeria's eyes narrowed briefly. "You mean that Kinheld will take longer than what everyone's thinking to construct?"

Mercury was silent.

"I'm quite certain that most logical people know it's going to take at least a year to construct, despite what Twitter would have you think," Valeria added.

Mercury chuckled. "Yes, I saw that hashtag circulating online. I'm talking about the real truth."

He glanced at his father. Honore, Ellis, Griffin, and Sloane had arrived and they now stood beside him. Mercury's heartbeat quickened as he looked over at his aunt and cousin, who sat with their arms crossed.

Valeria sighed. "And what is that, Mercury?"

"The truth is, Valeria," Mercury leaned in. ". . . that the plot of land purchased for Kinheld will only hold a fraction of the witches in America."

He heard someone clear their throat. Valeria looked down at her cards, seemingly uncertain of what to say next. *She hadn't anticipated I would do anything more than apologize*, he thought.

"The Witches' Council gave a press conference about it last month, Mercury. Councilwoman Murtaza—"

"Is lying," he said. He leaned back in his chair and shrugged. "The plot of land she purchased is barely the size of DC. There are over a million witches in America, last I checked. You tell me how all of those people will fit."

"More people have lived in smaller areas, Mercury. Even if what you're saying is true, I'm sure the Council has a plan."

"A plan? Yes, they do. Well, it's not the Council's plan, but with Oliana—I mean Councilwoman Murtaza—as the head, her plans are often implemented regardless of favorability, what with her daughter on the Council and all."

"Mercury, what are you doing?" Faegan whisper-shouted. The cameraman turned toward her and gestured for her to be quiet.

"So, what is it, then? What's the plan?" Valeria set her cards down on the table and intertwined her fingers, resting them on her lap.

"There will be entrance criteria."

Valeria scowled. "Entrance criteria?"

Mercury nodded. "Look, she knew from jump that the plot of land she was getting in the bargain from Vael wasn't going to be enough for every witch. So there will be criteria; some things she might consider are income, education, whether or not a person is a 'druggie,' but, you know, not the rich kind."

"Well, if Kinheld is to be a successful governing body, it makes sense that there would be some vetting," Valeria responded, but Mercury could tell she didn't fully believe the words she spoke. From the corner of his eye, he could see his cousin and aunt scowling at him.

"Does it, though? Does it align with all the things the Council stands for, to uplift all witchkind and fight for our due process, education, and right to life and liberty?"

"Not you quoting the mission statement," Valeria scoffed.

Mercury shrugged. "I'm the child of two Council members. That shit was ingrained in me at birth."

"Okay, okay. Let's say you're right. Let's say that the Council—"

"*Councilwoman Murtaza.*"

"Let's say Councilwoman Murtaza knew that the land would be small, and because of that she's trying to vet those who settle Kinheld. Who's to say there wouldn't be an expansion of the territory once it's shown to work? Who's to say all those that don't get in won't be allowed later, and that some may elect not to go to Kinheld altogether?"

"When has history ever shown that renegotiation of territory is that easy? And if the governing body of witchkind, likely the only organization that the government sometimes listens to when it comes to passing laws that affect witches, moves to Kinheld, what will happen to all the witches who're left here?"

"Mercury," his aunt warned. Mercury and Valeria looked over toward his aunt. The cameraman looked at her, his expression annoyed.

"This is what happens when you shoot live," he whispered to the other cameraman.

Valeria uncrossed her legs and shifted in her seat again. She crossed the left leg over her right and shuffled through her notecards.

"And you knew all of this before you started protesting?" Valeria asked.

Mercury shook his head. "If I did, don't you think I would have spilled all of this sooner?"

"So, you learned all of this from . . ." Valeria tapped her fingers to her temple.

"Memory surfing, as you call it, yes."

"Wow," she said, sitting back in her chair. "You memory surfed your own aunt. Fuckin' ruthless."

"Ruthless?" Mercury questioned. He could see his aunt smile, clearly pleased with Valeria's condemnation.

"Yeah, ruthless. You can't just dig into people's minds without their consent and use that information against them," she argued.

"You'd think the Council would have made a rule about that—but they haven't because this power is too useful, even for them. And you want to talk about ruthless? How about you standing on the sidelines of the LaBrea protest—"

"Riot," Valeria corrected.

"It wasn't a fucking riot and you know it, Valeria. It was an ambush, one that you stood on the sidelines of and videotaped. You didn't do anything to help your fellow witches, and yet you wrote an entire-ass article about me."

"I'm a journalist, Mercury. I can't get involved; it goes against journalistic integrity."

"'Journalistic integrity?' You mean like getting me drunk so you can pump me for information?" Mercury asked.

Valeria's cheeks reddened. She was flustered. Despite his heart pumping in his chest and his head pounding in his temples, Mercury felt ready to drop an even bigger bomb.

"So it seems neither of us can point to the other for being unethical," Valeria said, a smile back on her face. "But what I want to know is why are you spending your energy coming for your aunt when you should be calling out the LAPD for the violence they visited upon our community the other day."

"You're right. And I do call them out. I got in their faces to try to stop them on the ground and got hit with Claudust. I spent over twelve hours paralyzed, literally out of control of my body. A cop could have pulled his gun on me and I couldn't have done anything to stop him. I watched a woman get hit with Bergasca right in her chest, literally crushing her sternum. I saw teens have their breath taken away with Nefastle, saw people's skin break out and slough off from Ivarick. Hell, I got hit with Claudust and spent days dealing with the effects of the paralyzation. I know first-hand the effects those potions had on our people."

The energy in the room changed as he recounted these and other sights he saw on the day of the protests. Valeria sat, stymied. Of course, she saw the damage the potions caused, but it was one thing to see it from a distance and another to hear someone recount the gory details. Valeria leaned forward in her chair.

"Exactly. Direct your energy to those cops and the systemic issues at LAPD that led to them having access to—"

"Why go to the middlemen when I could go straight to the source?" Mercury asked.

Valeria tilted her head and scowled. "What are you saying?"

Mercury stared at the journalist before turning to his aunt and doing the same. Her rage simmered beneath the surface, palpable to Mercury because he knew her deeply. Faegan's anger was less contained. She stood shifting her weight, clenching and unclenching her fists. Ellis, Sloane, Griffin, and Honore stood in rapt attention, each looking between Mercury and his aunt.

"Yes, Mercury. What are you saying?" Oliana said. The edge in her voice sent a pang through Mercury's stomach. He tamped down the voice in his mind that told him he was doing something wrong.

Don't back down, he thought.

"I'm saying I saw the memory of you meeting with the mayor and the police commissioner about a venture called Spalding Wellness. I saw you show them a dossier with the potions you could provide and how much it would cost, and why."

Valeria's jaw dropped. She recovered quickly, remembering the cameras. She flipped her braids.

"Mercury, how can you prove all of this? I mean, anyone could hear this and think that you're trying to frame your aunt to stop the Kinheld project," she countered.

"If that's what I wanted to do, why would I bother sitting down here? Why wouldn't I take that to the *Times* or some shit?"

Valeria lifted her brows. "Oh, it's like that, huh?"

"Don't act brand new. You know your lane, your audience. I'm bringing this to you because our people, who read and support *Jonquil*, are the ones who will be affected by Oliana's deal with the city."

"Mercury."

Another warning, this time from his cousin. Valeria glanced at Faegan and turned back to Mercury. He could see she was unsure of what to say. Gone was the veneer of the snarky journalist. Now, here was someone uncertain of the side they'd chosen.

"I'm only telling the truth. When I looked through my aunt's memories, I saw her meeting with the mayor and the police commissioner. When they asked why she was doing this, she said it was because I was in her way."

One of the camera men gasped. Oliana had risen from her chair and stood, her long arms crossed.

"But—" Valeria began.

"I also saw something about Spalding Wellness in my cousin's memory," Mercury continued. "In it she was carrying a box to her car and the box was labeled Spalding Wellness."

Faegan stepped forward, ready to charge, but Oliana stopped her. Mercury looked back at Valeria, who sat back in her chair, legs uncrossed and arms slack.

"What was she wearing?" she asked.

Mercury scowled. "Huh?"

"In the memory you saw, what was she wearing?"

"A mint green, off the shoulder dress, a long strand of pearls, and gold boots. Her hair was wrapped into a side bun," Mercury recalled.

Valeria leaned forward, resting her elbows on her knees. She pressed her hands to her lips.

"I saw her that day. I saw that box in her car," Valeria said.

It was Mercury's turn to scowl. He looked toward his friends and his father. Each of them wore matching surprised expressions.

"I asked what it was and she said it was a beauty treatment."

Mercury straightened his posture. "I told you I wasn't lying. Councilwoman Murtaza purposefully gave the LAPD potions under the company Spalding Wellness to use against witches."

"Mercury, stop talking," his aunt ordered.

"Who knows how many other departments she's given the same potions."

"Mercury—"

"I mean, think about how many times the police use deadly force on non-magical humans. With magic we at least have the chance to defend ourselves before they slap the Thurguards on. These potions, along with all of the hateful rhetoric from people like Cordelia Edwards and her ilk will no doubt make cops feel more of a need to use them against any witch who so much as even breathes on them incorrectly. And we have none other than the Head of the Witches' Council to thank for all the deaths that will no doubt occur."

Within seconds, Mercury's head hit the floor as his cousin launched at him. She wrapped her hand around his neck, ice seeping from her hand and infiltrating his throat. Mercury gasped for air as he felt his throat being coated with ice.

Someone screamed. Mercury tilted his head to see Sloane gripping Faegan's other arm, pressing her dagger against his cousin's throat. Mercury closed his eyes and concentrated, attempting to throw his force field up. Nothing happened. She was too close and he was losing too much energy. He lifted a hand and tried to push against her face.

"You motherfucker! You're fucking dead! You're gonna lie to me and my mom and jack our memories like you're entitled to our mental space!"

"Faegan!" Oliana yelled.

His cousin stopped, her eyes widening, realizing what she'd just done. As she released Mercury's throat, he gasped, pulling in as much air as he could. Sloane pulled Faegan back by her throat, digging her knife into her throat even more.

"I should murk you right now for that shit," she threatened.

Faegan sneered and touched Sloane's leg, her icy touch causing Sloane to yelp.

"Not if you lose a leg because of hypothermia, bitch," Faegan spat. She turned on Sloane and made the move to grab her arm, but Mercury's father grabbed her wrist.

"Faegan, let her go," he growled. His eyes were narrow and his free hand was clenched tight into a fist.

"I wouldn't try it if I were you," Honore said.

Mercury looked over and spotted Honore standing with a hand on Oliana's shoulder, seconds away from sending poisonous vines rippling through her veins. She stood with her thumb pressed against her middle finger, ready to snap and no doubt cause pain to Mercury's father.

She lowered her hand. Honore kept his arm on her shoulder until Faegan released Sloane's leg. Sloane fell to the floor, tears in her eyes, her leg a deep shade of purple. Ellis rushed to her side and gripped her thigh with one hand and smoothed a strand of hair from her face.

"It's going to be okay. I got you," he said. Minutes later, her skin returned to its normal shade.

Mercury's father released Faegan's arm, and she brushed past him, hitting him with her long ponytail. The cameramen stood, stunned to have captured such a scene live. She stormed over to Oliana, and the two turned to walk out of the room.

"Where do you think you're going?" Mercury's father asked.

Oliana didn't bother to stop. "We're leaving. This whole thing was a shitshow, a hatchet job put together by an unreliable, unscrupulous man and his goons. There's no way you can prove any of this."

"Maybe not right now, but I'm really excited to try," Honore retorted.

Mercury looked to the door to see Paloma and Bati step into the room, twin expressions of disbelief on their faces.

"In the meantime, Oliana Murtaza and Faegan Murtaza, you're both under lockdown until an investigation into these claims commences," Honore stated.

Oliana stood, rigid, staring down at Honore. Mercury's father walked over, standing beside Honore and strengthening the decree.

"Fine," she sneered. "Have fun chasing your tails."

She brushed past Paloma and Bati, her Telfar bag hitting Bati in the arm.

When a witch was put under lockdown, they were confined to a room spelled with anti-magic markings preventing them from leaving. Mercury had only ever heard stories about it, and often that was done to witches who committed egregious crimes, never in a lead up to an investigation.

The Council members followed Oliana and Faegan out of the room, leaving everyone else behind in a state of confusion. As the cameramen began packing their equipment, Mercury turned toward Valeria.

She looked stricken, standing with both hands on the table.

"Are you okay?" Mercury asked.

She took a deep breath.

"I can't believe it," she whispered.

Mercury nodded. "It was hard for me, too. I love my aunt, and I love my cousin. I just couldn't stand by and say nothing."

"So, what happens now?"

Mercury shrugged. "I don't know. The Council will investigate and decide what to do. She might get removed from the Council, maybe even have her powers stripped."

Valeria shuddered.

"What about your movement? Now that there's no Oliana, there's probably going to be no Kinheld. You must be so happy."

"I didn't want it to go this way. I don't delight in taking my family down. I'm still going to fight for our people; that's never gonna stop," Mercury said.

"Let's just hope you're right."

Mercury watched Valeria walk away, her final words repeating in his mind.

CHAPTER 20

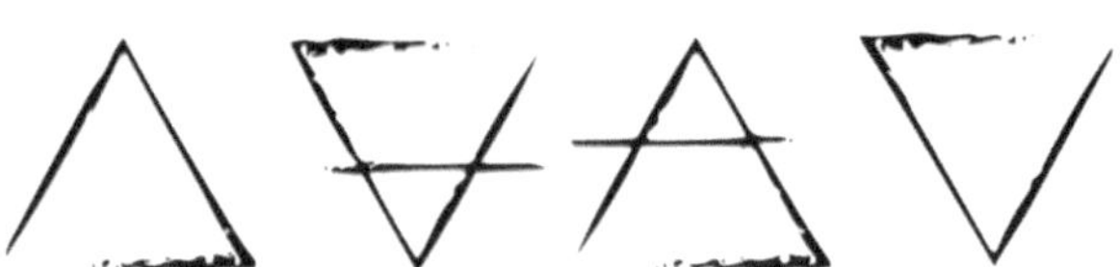

MERCURY WIPED HIS FOREHEAD, BRUSHING IT WITH THE BACK OF HIS hand. He sat on stage behind his drum kit as Ellis stood before the crowd, fingers working over the bass line for "Savoir Faire". Joelle stood beside him, guitar in hand. The crowd at this year's Ilaris celebration was larger than last time. Mercury had been nervous about playing before so many people, but as his father told him, no one really cared whether he played well or not. "Everyone just wants to see the man who took down the Head of Council."

He was still trying to figure out if that was a good thing. In the weeks since the interview with Valeria, much of the hate he'd received had been redirected toward his aunt and cousin. People cut out the clip of Faegan launching herself at Mercury and uploaded it everywhere from TikTok to World Star Hip Hop. The media even feasted on Oliana for being a bougie wolf in sheep's clothing.

Again, Mercury was celebrated by some in the community who either hadn't liked his aunt or who believed what she did was reprehensible. Yet still, his aunt had fans in the witch community, and he had to constantly block messages from those who threatened him with a beating, a power stripping, or death. "Burn in hell, traitor," was a common refrain.

The Council was still investigating his aunt, and every day she spent locked up without her powers, Honore said she only got meaner. With her out of commission, the Council promoted Mercury's father as interim Head of Council because he was the most senior member. If his aunt was officially stripped of her title, his father could run for the position.

"You're a shoe-in," Mercury had told his father as they sipped mimosas the day before Ilaris. His father scoffed.

"Nothing is certain in life but death and taxes. Bati is angling for the position, and there are enough Oliana sympathizers that might give him an edge," his father said, referring to the Icelander who'd been the tie breaker when Oliana had threatened to strip their powers at Astera. Despite his disagreement, Bati had been a loyal devotee of Oliana and was now committed to trying to prove her innocence.

"Well, what's going to happen with Faegan's role?"

Bati had been elected to Faegan's old position, but whoever moved to Head of Council would create a vacant role.

His father shook his head. "We don't know. There's going to be a lot of change happening this summer."

"Like there hasn't been already," Mercury quipped.

With the sweat from the summer heat glistening on their faces, Mercury, Ellis, and Joelle finished their set to massive cheers, high off the euphoria from the crowd. He stood and the trio bowed before walking off the stage.

"That was the shit!" Ellis shouted. He hugged Mercury, and Mercury laughed. Joelle followed suit.

"I've never played before so many people. That was amazing!" she gushed.

"Me neither. We killed it!" Mercury cheered. He'd forgotten how alive playing music made him feel.

Famished, they strolled over to the terrace, where the catered food was set up. Their stomachs growled at the sight of the massive spread. His father had gone with barbecue from a family-owned business in the Valley. Mercury's mouth watered as he piled his plate with chicken, macaroni and cheese, and greens. With their plates full, they walked over to the table where Sloane and Griffin sat, already sharing a joint.

"Planning to share?" Mercury asked.

Sloane rolled her eyes, passing the joint to him as he sat.

"Only if you promise not to bogart it," she said.

Mercury smiled and took it from her, placing the joint between his lips and taking a long puff. He passed it to Ellis beside him, who took a smaller puff. He passed it along to Joelle, who continued the rotation. When it made its way back to Sloane, she frowned.

"See, I should have never let you have any," she said to Mercury.

He laughed. "That's okay. I've got a couple prerolls for the party."

"Well, shit," she said, inhaling. "You should've said that then."

Mercury laughed. Each of them dug into their food, the weed making their movements languid. Mercury sipped his soda, thankful for the caffeine to help him level out.

After eating, they walked over toward the stage area, where another band had taken the stage, hoping to fight off the urge to nap in broad daylight. They sounded like a cross between The Roots and Empire of The Sun, and Mercury found himself dancing along to their beats.

"Damn, this is a vibe," Joelle exclaimed. She danced alongside him. Mercury lifted his head toward the sky, closing his eyes and basking in the warmth of the sun.

"We just want to take this moment," said the singer. Mercury looked at the stage. A petite Black woman with a purple pixie cut stood before the mic, her voice high-pitched. ". . . to honor the witches in our community who we have lost this year."

The singer pulled a slip of paper from her jeans pocket. She began reading the list of names, and with each one the crowd clapped.

"And Freddie muthafuckin' Karr," she shouted last. Mercury joined in the shouting. They chanted the names of their fallen witches three more times before the band left the stage.

As they walked past, Mercury yelled: "Great set."

The singer stopped. Her green eyes were lined in black eyeliner.

Her black jeans and platform black boots looked warm, but she wore a bedazzled bustier.

"Thanks," she replied. "You're Mercury, right?"

Mercury nodded. "Nice to meet you."

"I'm Poppy," she said.

"Poppy, beautiful name," he complimented her.

"Thanks," she smiled. She wore mini diamonds on her canines. "Well, I've got to go. Maybe I'll see you around sometime?"

"Dope," Mercury replied.

She waved before walking away, and he turned back toward his friends. Joelle and Sloane looked at each other and laughed.

He scoffed. "What?"

Griffin shook his head. "You're a whole mess, Mercury."

Mercury slid his arm around Griffin. "Would you want me any other way?"

Griffin groaned. "I'd like you with a little less weed and chicken breath."

Mercury pulled away from his friend, laughing.

"Fine, I'll freshen up," he said. The bands were in between sets, and as "Tell Me When to Go" blasted from the speakers, Mercury danced his way toward the Council House.

He walked past his father chatting with Paloma and Honore, the crisp blue sky offering the perfect backdrop. His father nodded at him as he passed, and Mercury returned the gesture.

Still swaying to the music, he said hello to the witches he recognized, including Bridget.

"Hey, you good?"

"Yeah, I just got some battle wounds," she said, gesturing toward her body. "But I can't believe what's happened just in the last week! Like, holy shit, right? Like, you took down the Head of Council."

He took a step back. "Nah, nothing's official yet."

"Still, everyone is talking about it, even that blonde bobblehead at *The Vanguard*."

Mercury chuckled as he walked away. She was, of course, referring to Cordelia Edwards, who'd written an entire article about the affair.

As always, she used it to support her narrative that witches were bad, that they were so prone to violence they were willing to fight their own family.

"How can witches think we wouldn't see them as inherently violent when the bonds of the family don't even matter?" she had written.

Mercury had plenty of people tagging him in the comments whenever the article surfaced, and he just ignored it. He wasn't about to give *The Vanguard*, or any other publication, more attention.

He ambled down the hall to the bathroom, feeling the need to stop in his tracks before entering the door. He scanned his surroundings, seeing nothing but the fancy décor of the Council house and hearing nothing but the soft hum of the cooling system. Shaking his head, he strolled into the bathroom, where he relieved himself then washed his hands.

Just as he remembered, there was a bowl of mints sitting on a table at the bathroom entrance. He pulled one and walked out of the bathroom, sliding the mint into his mouth. He hummed the song Poppy's group had been playing, running his hand along the wall.

"Be careful, son," he heard one second.

"Mercury?" he heard the next.

He stopped cold as he heard his aunt's voice. He turned toward the door to the room his aunt was locked in. He didn't respond, only looked down to see the shadow of her feet standing on the other side of the door.

My dream, he thought.

"I know you're out there. I can hear you humming," she said.

Still, he remained silent.

"Remaining mum, I see. Well then, I'll keep this brief."

He searched the hall as he took a step back from the door.

"You may have won this battle," she said. There was a thudding sound on the other side of the door that made Mercury scowl. "But I'll win the war."

Mercury closed his eyes and sighed, the weed making him feel as if his heart would burst through his skin. His chest rose and fell as he tried to bring himself down.

"What war, Auntie?" Mercury said. "You're the one who tried to kill me and half the witches in Los Angeles with that potion deal."

"Have you forgotten that I know your secret?"

He paused. "Of course, not."

"Aren't you wondering why I didn't bring it up the other day during your interview?"

A shiver ran up his spine.

"Because I want you to fear each day that it might be the day the cops come to your house and arrest you. Or, to your point, maybe they'll hit you with Hellefax and not bother to ask any questions."

"How would you even notify them? The Council took you and Faegan's phones and laptops."

"What makes you think I don't have other allies that could call for me?"

Is she talking about Bati? He thought.

He breathed in then scowled.

Is that smoke? He sniffed the air and looked down. A slow stream of smoke spilled up from the bottom of the door.

"Auntie, what—"

The door burst open, sending Mercury flying.

"Fuck!" he yelled as his back and head connected with the wall opposite his aunt's room. He looked up to see his aunt standing in the doorway, dressed in jeans, a t-shirt, and tennis shoes. More smoke spilled out from her room and even though Mercury's vision twisted, he saw flames beginning to climb the walls. His aunt sucked in a breath and twisted her hands back and forth. Now that she was no longer trapped in a magic-proof room, she could use the full extent of her power on him. Fear slivered up his spine as she stood over him. She bent down to kneel before him and Mercury shuddered.

"Don't worry, nephew. I'm not going to hurt you. I like knowing that you'll be spending your life now looking over your shoulder, never knowing when you'll get that knock on the door."

"Why do this?" He coughed, his breath labored. "I never wanted to be your enemy."

"Oh, Mercury—don't you get it? You became my enemy the second you decided to oppose me." She patted his cheek then stood.

Mercury watched in horror as his aunt strutted down the hall, the light from the flames reflecting in his eyes. He willed himself to move, but each time he did, pain shot up his spine and into his head.

The fire alarm went off. Then the sprinkler system.

"Help!" he shouted.

But no one came. He reached for his pocket before realizing that his cell phone lay on the ground, just out of reach.

"Help!" Mercury yelled again.

The sound of shouting and screaming reverberated throughout the house in a cacophony of noise. *She's making her way out of the house,* he thought.

Tears streamed down Mercury's face as he lay helpless to stop the violence his aunt had wrought.

"I'm sorry, Mom," he whispered as the horrific scene around him faded to black.

Amanda Ross is an indie author who writes NA fantasy set in modern times. Her Witchkind series—To Astera, With Love and its sequel, To Ilaris, In Desperation— is filled with magic, humor, and social commentary. She also co-published the YA fantasy Girls of Might and Magic. In addition to her books, Amanda is also an Authortuber. She discusses all things fantasy, offers book writing and marketing tips, and more on her channel, Amanda Thee Author.

Currently, Amanda is working on a book featuring a necromancer, a burlesque club, a murder mystery, and several witch houses. She is also outlining the third and final book in the Witchkind series. When she's not writing or YouTubing, she is reading, baking, or eating donuts by the beach.